Mistress of Greyladies

Mistress of Greyladies

ANNA JACOBS

Allison & Busby Limited
12 Fitzroy Mews
London W1T 6DW
www.allisonandbusby.com

First published in Great Britain by Allison & Busby in 2014.

Copyright © 2014 by ANNA JACOBS

A CIP catalogue record for this book is available from
the British Library.

First Edition

ISBN 978-0-7490-1417-9

Typeset in 11/16 pt Sabon by
Allison & Busby Ltd.

The paper used for this Allison & Busby publication
has been produced from trees that have been legally sourced
from well-managed and credibly certified forests.

Printed and bound by

With thanks to Roy Baker, Curator, Leece Museum, for his help with information about the internees sent to the Isle of Man during World War I

Chapter One

Wiltshire

When she heard the sound of a car, Harriet peeped out of the sitting room window and saw two middle-aged men get out of what looked like an official vehicle. They stood staring at the house, muttering to one another.

'They're here, Joseph.'

Her husband joined her. 'They don't look very happy.'

'I'm not happy, either. I wish I didn't have to see them. I told the maids I'd let them in myself.' She waited for the knocker to sound, then walked across the hall and opened the front door.

'Good morning. I'm Mrs Latimer.'

'Good morning, ma'am. We're here to see your husband.'

That annoyed her for a start. 'You've come about the house and I'm the owner, so it's me you need to speak to, not my husband. And perhaps your driver would like to go round to the kitchen for a cup of tea while we have our tour and discussion?'

They stared at her in surprise, then exchanged puzzled glances before one waved to the driver and pointed to the rear.

The other man frowned at Harriet. 'But your husband isn't dead, so the house must be his?'

'It isn't. Greyladies is a trust, which passes down the female line only, and the husbands of its owners change their names to Latimer. Please come in.'

She ignored their surprised expressions and walked back briskly into the sitting room, leaving them to close the front door and follow her. 'This is my husband.'

'Joseph Latimer?'

As they offered him a handshake, they seemed to relax a little.

Ignoring Harriet again, one said, 'I'm Mr Dorrance and my companion is Mr Pashley.' They pressed two cards into his hand. 'We're here about the house.'

Joseph immediately passed the cards to Harriet. 'Greyladies belongs to my wife, as she just told you, so you'll need to discuss the requisition with her.'

Again, a moment of silence, as if they'd been spoken to in a foreign language and weren't sure whether they understood it correctly.

Harriet would have smiled if she hadn't been irritated by the way they'd tried to ignore her. She gestured to some armchairs. 'We'll all be more comfortable sitting down, I'm sure. Can we offer you some refreshments, gentlemen?'

'No, thank you. Um, do you know why we're here, Mrs Latimer?'

She couldn't help answering sharply. 'Of course I do!'

Joseph gave her a warning glance and shook his head slightly, so she tried to speak more calmly. 'The letter explained it quite clearly. You're from the Special Requisitions Section

8

of the War Office. You're here to see if this house will be suitable for your needs.'

And the letter had informed her that she had no choice about whether they requisitioned her home or not. They had the power to turn her and her family out – though she might be entitled to compensation for any damage at some unspecified stage after the war.

'Perhaps I should show you round first, gentlemen? As you will have noticed, my husband walks with a limp and he finds the stairs a bit of a trial.'

'Er, yes. If you don't mind.'

She did mind. Very much.

'I'd better explain that the house is in two parts. The older part at the rear is the original building. We don't use that any longer. The front part is the newer section.'

She led them round the new part of the house, which was just under two hundred years old, then took them into the original house at the rear, which dated from the sixteenth century.

To her surprise, the old house looked run down and felt distinctly damp and chilly. It felt different today and she couldn't understand why until she walked to the other end of the main room, which had been the old Elizabethan hall. Where she was standing felt normal. Where the two men were standing looked even darker and more menacing – as if the house resented their presence as much as she did.

One of the men shivered. 'Such dampness wouldn't be good for convalescent men. Is that why you moved to the front part?'

'Er . . . yes.' She didn't contradict this impression, even

though she knew the old house wasn't at all damp. Well, it wasn't normally.

Once back in the new house, the two men relaxed.

'I wonder if we could be left alone somewhere for half an hour or so to discuss what we call "matters pertaining",' Mr Dorrance said.

'You can stay here,' Harriet said curtly.

'Are you ready for a cup of tea now?' Joseph asked in a politer tone.

'Thank you. That would be much appreciated.'

'I'll have some sent in. My wife and I will wait for you in the library, just across the hall.'

Harriet couldn't settle, so paced up and down. 'They're going to take Greyladies from us, I know they are, Joseph.'

'There's nothing we can do about that, my darling. And if there is a war between Britain and Germany, then we must all do what we can for our country.'

'But the house could be damaged, ruined even.'

'I don't think they'll allow that. And Harriet – please try to be a bit more friendly. It'll do no good to put these men's backs up.'

After what seemed like hours, but was only forty minutes, according to the clock, there was a tap on the door. Mr Dorrance looked in. 'Could we speak to you now, please?'

They followed him across to the sitting room and sat together on the sofa facing the visitors. She resisted the temptation to clutch Joseph's hand.

'We feel that the front part of the house is suitable for our needs, Mr – er, Mrs Latimer. Not perfect, with so many stairs, but it'll do.'

Harriet's heart sank. 'Oh.'

'If there's war, we shall need the house for the duration of the hostilities. We're suggesting it be used as an officers' convalescent home, because it's not large enough for an auxiliary hospital. If peace prevails and there is no war, as we all pray, then the house will be given back to you within a few months.'

She didn't know what to say, felt very close to tears, and now she did reach out for the comfort of her husband's hand.

'We shall not require the older part of the house, however, because of the damp. Also, the rooms there are rather dark and unpleasant.' Mr Dorrance paused, then added, 'Therefore, if you feel you and your family can tolerate those conditions, we would have no objection to you living in the older part of the building.'

Harriet looked at Joseph and he nodded in answer to her unspoken question. 'We would definitely like to live there. And . . . if we can help in any way, we will.'

'That will be up to the commandant and matron, but I'm sure they'll be happy for you to volunteer your services, if only in tasks like reading to the men or writing letters for them.' He looked round. 'In a place of this size, which is not a hospital, the medical officer will probably act as commandant.'

She nodded, feeling relieved that they could stay in the old house, at least. They had nowhere else to go, really. She'd been a maid at Dalton House before marrying Joseph, so relations were always a little awkward. His oldest brother, Selwyn, would inherit the family estate and, of course, Dalton House might be requisitioned too.

Joseph took over from her, gesturing round the room. 'We shall, of course, remove and store any items of value, like the paintings and books, but I wonder whether your department would agree to a requirement that those using the house look after the historical features of the building itself? The doors, windows, panelling and stained glass are all original. I always feel such places are part of our national heritage, rather than the possessions of one family.'

The shorter of the two men nodded vigorously. 'I agree with you entirely. I would definitely be prepared to support that requirement being stated, Mr Latimer. I too believe our country's history is important. It's good to hear you say that. Too many landowners take their possessions for granted.'

Dorrance obviously didn't share his colleague's love of history, and merely shrugged. 'As long as it doesn't interfere with the patients' welfare, I have no objection to such a requirement.'

Mr Pashley smiled at Joseph. 'This panelling is superb.' He gazed up at the ceiling. 'As for the plasterwork, it's magnificent, even though it's later than the period it tries to imitate. I shall make a note of this on the Greyladies file. If you have any trouble about the house, this is my card.'

Harriet watched in annoyance as Joseph easily got his way. She was quite sure she'd not have succeeded. The men had continued to talk to her in a patronising manner, and Pashley had even explained the obvious features of her own home to her. They no doubt considered all women inferior in understanding.

But she'd had many years of biting her tongue and hiding her emotions when younger and working as a housemaid, before she unexpectedly inherited this house, so though she couldn't manage a friendly smile, she did manage to say nothing.

Once the car had driven away, Joseph gave her a quick hug. 'Well done. I know it nearly killed you to keep quiet, but I got more concessions out of them than you could have done.' He frowned. 'I wonder why they thought the older part of the house so unpleasant.'

'It did feel damp and dark today, even to me. I couldn't understand it. Not the whole place, but the part where they were standing.'

'Yes. I noticed. It's as if the house itself had taken a dislike to them. I half expected to see our ghost.'

'Me too. The diaries say Anne Latimer still keeps watch on her house and the legacy she's left behind. And we've both seen her many times.'

'Well, whatever caused the feeling of dampness and unhappiness today, I'm glad of it. It means we won't have to leave Greyladies.'

'But *we* won't be in charge of the main part. They might do anything in here.'

'If we help out, we can keep an eye on things part of the time. And as some of the people from the village will no doubt be employed here, I'm sure they'll let us know if they see anything happening that seems harmful.'

She sighed. 'I suppose so. Joseph, do you think there really will be a war?'

'Yes, my darling, I do. It's as if people have learnt nothing from the Boer Wars.'

She knew he'd lost an uncle during the second Boer War and that he felt very strongly about the shameful tactics used by the British against the enemy women and children, many of whom had died because of their poor treatment as prisoners.

If Britain entered into a war with Germany now, how many others would die? Her heart ached for what the young men of England would have to face.

She turned to the post with a sigh, then a smile. A letter had arrived to say that Joseph's sister had had another daughter, and that Richard's wife was due to give birth.

She wished all news was as pleasant as this.

Things happened quickly after that. Only a month later, on a sunny day towards the end of May, Harriet walked through the central hall of Greyladies with the newly appointed matron, officially handing over her home to the government. The commandant would not be able to start for a few days, apparently.

Harriet felt sad. She and her family had now moved into the old house and it was still in chaos as they tried to squeeze so many precious things into a much smaller space.

She turned to her companion. 'If you need to know anything about the house, don't hesitate to ask me.' She gritted her teeth as Matron Dawkins gave her another of those patronising smiles and deliberately kept her waiting for a reply.

'Oh, I think I can manage to run a convalescent home, Mrs Latimer. I have, after all, been a matron for over twenty years. Various people will be arriving during the coming week to help me: my deputy matron, the quartermaster, a clerk and some orderlies. We'll then be able to reorganise this place and set out the beds and equipment as efficiently as we can, in the circumstances.' She turned a scornful look on the house.

Harriet told herself that it was her country that mattered,

not this uppity woman. 'Nonetheless, I'm always happy to do my bit to help Britain.'

'Some of the patients will probably enjoy a bit of company and others will need help with letters home, those with arms or hands that are injured.'

'I'll be happy to do that, of course I will. But you will need to prepare for your patients and I could—'

'My dear lady, *you* already have a crippled husband, not to mention two small sons to care for, so you must have plenty to occupy your time. You should concentrate on settling into your new home, and leave us to deal with organising the convalescent home.'

In other words, Harriet thought, keep away from Matron's territory. She felt furious at hearing Joseph spoken about like that. He might limp markedly, because of the bad hip he'd been born with, but he was in better health these days than he'd ever been, and seemed to have outgrown his childhood weaknesses. He wasn't crippled in any way that mattered, and since their marriage, he had become skilful at managing the finances of Greyladies.

As for their children, she had plenty of help with Jody and Mal. The head housemaid and the cook acted like aunties to them and let them 'help' in the house and kitchen. No, that might not be possible now, because Livvy and Flora had volunteered to work in the convalescent home, and she couldn't see this woman allowing any children into her territory.

Still, a newly promoted housemaid and their usual washing woman from the village would be helping her family, so no doubt the boys would charm them. They were such happy, lively youngsters. And though the children's governess, Miss Bowers, had moved back to her home in the village, she would be coming in every day to teach them. She might be in her seventies, but she was still hale and hearty, a capable woman who had been headmistress of the village school in her time.

Both children were making such good progress that Harriet and Joseph hadn't sent them to the village school. They were an intelligent pair, too far ahead of the work being done there to settle happily. She and Joseph did, however, encourage their sons to play with the village children outside school hours.

Tim Peacock, the grandson of the owner of the village store, was eight-year-old Jody's best friend. It was Tim who'd shortened young Joseph's name to Jody, to avoid confusing him with his father, and the name had stuck. Malcolm had always been Mal from the time he'd struggled to say his own name in full.

But whatever she and Joseph did, there would be further uncomfortable changes for everyone in the village of Challerton if and when war broke out, she was sure. She could only hope any conflict would be over within a few months, as people were predicting.

Intercepting another frown from her companion, Harriet realised she'd been lost in thought. 'Sorry. I was just thinking about something I need to do.'

She wondered yet again why Matron Dawkins had been so hostile towards her from the very first day. Though, actually, the feeling was mutual now that she'd spent time with the woman. It was so rare for her to dislike someone on sight that this worried her. Was it because Matron would be in charge of her beloved home from now on, or was it because the Dragon, as Joseph referred to her, was simply nasty by nature? She suspected the latter.

As they reached the door between the two parts of the building, Harriet glanced back, feeling sad to see how shabby the bare, panelled walls of the huge hall looked now without the paintings which used to hang there. The library had been stripped of books and the floors of rugs, and now echoing spaces waited for the beds and other equipment to arrive.

'I'll leave you to get on with your work.' Harriet was itching to get away from this woman now.

'Just a moment.' Matron held out her hand. 'You need to give me the key to this door. We can't have outsiders wandering around a convalescent home, can we?'

As Harriet studied the other woman's sour face, something told her the key wouldn't be safe in her hands. There was only one, a huge iron piece several hundred years old, dating from the time when the door between the two parts of the building had been the front door of the small manor house. It would be a tragedy if that key got lost.

She hated lying but did so now. 'I'm afraid we don't have a key. We've never considered it necessary to lock the door.'

'Hmm. I see. Well, in that case, I shall have the door replaced. It's good for nothing but firewood anyway, it's so old-fashioned.'

It was an effort to speak mildly. 'You aren't allowed to do that.'

Matron glared at her. 'I'm allowed to do whatever is necessary for the safety of my patients.'

'Not when it concerns the fabric of the house. You would need permission. It was written into the agreement with the War Ministry that the historic parts of the building would be protected. Mr Pashley, who is in charge of requisitions in

Wiltshire, is very keen to protect our national heritage. That door has been there since the sixteenth century.'

Spots of red burnt suddenly in Matron's cheeks. 'I can and will do anything necessary for the welfare of my patients. I will *not* have strangers wandering through the convalescent home, upsetting the inmates. I shall have some strong bolts put on to the door, then.'

'You aren't allowed to make any changes to the fabric of the building without permission. But I can assure you we won't be wandering around the convalescent home without an invitation.'

'It's not just you, but your servants and visitors.'

Harriet abandoned any attempt at diplomacy. 'If you try to damage the house in any way, I shall summon the local magistrate to deal with you for breach of contract, as well as reporting you to Mr Pashley.'

At that moment war was declared between them and both women knew it.

Harriet didn't intend to back down. She didn't consider herself the owner of the house, but rather its custodian or chatelaine – and for as long as she was mistress here, she would protect her beloved home. Some Latimer ladies stayed here all their lives; others served for a few years, then moved on. No one could tell who would be leaving or when. It just seemed to happen, according to the family diaries.

She might not know how long she'd be here, but she knew that she would understand the correct path to follow if the time ever came to change her role. As her predecessors had done.

And just like them, she would find a successor when one was needed.

* * *

Once inside the old house, Harriet turned to close the heavy door behind her, but for all her care, it slipped from her fingers and slammed shut, almost as if it had a will of its own. That sort of thing happened at Greyladies sometimes.

She strode towards her husband, muttering, 'It'll be a miracle if I don't strangle that stupid woman!'

Joseph smiled at her as he looked up from his desk. The long room had a minstrel's gallery at the far end and its ceiling was two storeys high. It didn't feel at all damp or chilly today, and hadn't since they moved in.

They'd decided to spend most of their time in this room, so the dining table was at the end where she was standing, near the new house, while their sofas and chairs were arranged near the fireplace and leadlight windows at the other end. They'd hung their favourite paintings in the hall, prominent among them the portrait of Anne Latimer, the founder of Greyladies.

People said Harriet resembled her much-loved ancestor in many ways. The Latimer ladies always had red hair, of any shade from the foxy tone of her own to the deepest auburn. She tried to follow her forebear's example and lead a useful life helping others. She might have inherited a trust containing a considerable amount of money, but she would never fritter it away in extravagant living.

Some of their paintings had had to be stored in the attics, for lack of wall space, but the Latimers had been 'required' to leave some of the furniture in the new house for the expected occupants, and anyway, there wasn't room to store everything in the old house. She and Joseph were both praying that the furniture wouldn't get damaged. They treasured these possessions, because she'd grown up poor and he loved beautiful things.

The books from the library were piled along one wall, waiting for Martin from the village to make some temporary shelves for them. Most of their books were too precious to leave in the new house, because they included centuries of the diaries and account books kept by nearly all the previous owners.

Even Harriet, who had never kept a diary in her life, was making a big effort to keep up this tradition. She pitied anyone who read her diary, though, because she didn't have a gift for bringing scenes to life with words.

As she stood there, trying in vain to calm down, Joseph got up and limped across to put an arm round her shoulders. 'Next time you have to talk to the Dragon, I'll come with you. What's she been saying this time?'

Harriet gave him a quick hug. 'She wants a key to the old front door. Only, I pretended we don't have one. I must hide our key somewhere and tell the boys not to mention it. I can't understand why, but I wouldn't trust that woman with it.'

'Not like you to tell lies, my love. Most of the time, you're rather too blunt.'

'You haven't heard the worst. She said if there was no key, she would have the old door removed and burnt for firewood, and a new door and lock put in.'

'*What?* But she isn't allowed to do that.'

'I know. And so I told her. Thank goodness Mr Pashley had it written into the contract that nothing was to be changed without official permission. But she could have the door removed and destroyed before they know anything about it in London. How would we stop her if we don't know what she's doing? I hope the commandant will arrive soon and that he'll be a lot friendlier.'

'He can't be less friendly, can he? I wonder what Anne Latimer thinks about all this.'

'Do you think a ghost can understand such things, Joseph? I always think of Anne as a shadow cast by the past. She won't be able to intervene, I'm sure.'

'I'd not put anything past our beloved founder. Look at the way Pashley and Dorrance thought the old house was too damp to use.'

'We'd better get on. I see the post has come.' Harriet went to sit at her desk and open this morning's letters and Joseph returned to his accounts.

War or no war, she still had her charity work to do. Like all the previous owners of Greyladies, she helped people whenever she could, especially women, who often had less ability to help themselves. This gave her great satisfaction and made her feel more worthy of her inheritance.

That afternoon, a telegram arrived for Joseph. The delivery lad waited in the kitchen in case there was a reply to send.

Joseph tore the telegram open. 'Oh, no! My father's had a seizure and isn't expected to live. Mother wants me to join them at Dalton House. You too, of course.'

'One of us has to stay here. Heaven knows what the Dragon will do if left in charge, and there's been no sign of the new commandant so far.'

'I don't like to leave you to face that woman alone.'

'I'll manage. You must go, if only to say a final goodbye to him. That matters, believe me. And anyway, Selwyn won't be much use to your mother in a crisis, will he?'

'No. But I do have two other brothers.'

'Darling, stop finding excuses. I'll be fine. Now, let's

be practical. You'll need help with your wheelchair while travelling. And there's the luggage to deal with as well.'

He nodded, accepting the inevitable. 'I'll ask young Jack Peddy from the village to come with me. He might be only sixteen but he's a strapping young fellow and very sensible. I'm sure his father will spare him. They have other people to help them on the farm.'

Joseph arrived at Dalton House too late to say farewell to his father. There was a black crêpe bow on the front door and the curtains were drawn, a sign that this was a house of mourning.

His brother Selwyn came to the library door to watch him limp into the house.

'I didn't think you'd make it, given your difficulties moving about.'

Joseph ignored this comment, which was mild compared to some of the things Selwyn had said to him over the years.

'Darling, thank you for coming!' His mother came across from the drawing room to plant one of her soft kisses on his cheek and link her arm in Joseph's.

As they walked to the drawing room, she turned back to her oldest son. 'Do you think we ought to contact your wife, Selwyn? She may wish to come to the funeral. She always got on well with your father.'

He scowled at her. 'No. It's about time you accept how she and I feel about one another. And don't start nagging about children again. There aren't going to be any from me. I'm getting a divorce. I'm providing her with the evidence next week.'

She was so shocked by this, she seemed unable to speak

for a moment or two, then took a deep, calming breath and turned back to Joseph. 'Richard can't be here, because he's volunteered for the army, your uncle's old regiment, and he's in the middle of officer training. He's sure we'll be at war before too long and wants to play his part. I think he was finding the law rather boring. You know how physically active he always was.'

'I'm sure he'll enjoy the army. He enjoyed the cadet corps at school, didn't he? What about Helen and Thomas?'

'Thomas is going to try to get here tomorrow, but if not, he'll be here for the funeral and then stay on to help me sort the paperwork out. His wife can't come at all, because she's due to have the baby soon. They're praying it'll be a son. The poor thing hasn't been well the whole time she's been carrying.'

She glanced at the clock. 'We really ought to go in for dinner now. We have it early these days, for the servants' convenience. It's so hard to get staff these days.'

Selwyn peered into the room, interrupting her flow of conversation to ask loudly, 'Does my idiot brother need his wheelchair? His lad's brought it round.'

She glared at him. 'Don't speak about your brother like that! You only do it to annoy people.'

'I'll speak how I like in my own house. And I'll drink to that any day.' He raised his glass to them in a mocking toast and drained it. 'I'll just get a little refill.' He left the room.

Joseph looked inquiringly at his mother, knowing his parents had been considering breaking with tradition and not leaving the house to the eldest son.

She sagged for a moment, then whispered, 'Your father couldn't bring himself to disinherit Selwyn, no matter what I said.'

'Oh dear. Richard would have made a much better owner. What will *you* do now?'

'I've got some money, though not as much as I'd have liked, thanks to your father paying Selwyn's debts. I'm going to live in a serviced flat in London with just Mrs Stuart as my housekeeper and one maid. Thomas and his wife are going to help me find somewhere in London. I can't bear to live with Selwyn, so after the funeral I'm only staying till I've cleared out my dearest William's things and packed my own.'

'When exactly is the funeral?'

'In two days. I shall be relieved to get it over with.' She looked at him sadly. 'William never recovered consciousness after his seizure and I was glad of that, for his sake. He'd have hated to be helpless and confined to bed. I'd like to have said goodbye properly, though.'

To Joseph, her generation seemed overly fond of deathbed scenes, describing them with relish and wanting to be at the bedside of anyone dying.

'We'd better go and have our meal.' She patted his cheek and became practical again. 'You can stay for the funeral?'

'Of course.'

'Do we need to find you a temporary manservant?'

'I don't need as much help as I used to, but I've brought a young fellow from the village with me. Jack helped with the luggage on the journey. I only use the wheelchair for long distances now or if I need a rest. I know it looks ugly when I walk but I'm much stronger these days. Harriet packed suitable clothes for the funeral, just in case.'

'How is Harriet? And the boys?'

'They're all well. She sends her apologies for not

coming, but we have a problem with the matron in the convalescent home and daren't leave her unobserved. The woman only wanted to pull out and burn the old oak door, a sixteenth-century piece! We're praying the commandant will be friendlier than her, but he's not arrived yet.'

'She sounds dreadful. I don't know what the government is thinking of, taking over people's houses like that when everyone says the war won't last long.'

He didn't respond to that. His mother didn't seem to realise that modern warfare and weapons would cause a far greater number of casualties and there would have to be places where they could recover. 'Selwyn must have started drinking early. His speech was slurred.'

'He's been pouring whisky down non-stop since he arrived, and he's been rude to everyone. I've seen very little of him in the past few years, but Thomas says he's still gambling. I doubt the house will stay in the family for much longer. William was wrong to leave it to Selwyn. Even you would have made a better owner than him.'

She seemed quite unaware how insulting this was, but Joseph didn't protest. He was quite accustomed to the way his family underestimated him. If he told his mother how much money he'd made from his small inheritance during the years since his marriage, or how well he'd managed the annual income from the Greyladies Trust, she'd find it hard to believe.

As he ate his meal, he endured the direct insults of his eldest brother without responding, then went to bed early, pleading tiredness.

He was glad when Thomas arrived the following day. Since his next brother was in banking and knew about

Joseph's improving financial situation, they usually had plenty to talk about. He got on best with Thomas, but it made him sad that he didn't feel truly close to any of his brothers, and his sister was like a complete stranger. None of them had made any attempt to get to know him better, not to mention avoiding contact with Harriet because she'd once been a housemaid.

Joseph doubted he'd come back here again after the funeral, even though he was fond of his old home – well, more than fond, he loved the place and was the only one who knew its history. But the house belonged to Selwyn now, Joseph had a new home and life, and that was that.

He sighed and admitted to himself that sometimes he ached to be back at Dalton House. Perhaps you always had a special feeling for your childhood home. He hadn't let Harriet know how he felt, though, and never would.

Chapter Two

Phoebe

When Phoebe Sinclair was sixteen, she had to grow up quickly because her mother became too ill to work. A failing heart, the doctor told them, and nothing could be done. From then on, Phoebe took charge of their little cottage in the village of Knightsford Bassett and cared for her mother as she grew weaker.

At first she did odd jobs to earn money, cleaning, laundry work or helping on nearby farms at busy times. They scraped together enough to live on, because they had free eggs from their own hens, and bits and pieces of farm produce from her mother's cousin, who lived just outside the village with his second wife Janet.

Horace Reid had no children of his own, even though he'd married a second time soon after the death of his first wife, because a farmer needed a wife. Janet already had a son from her first marriage. Frank Hapton was a surly lad, who refused to take his stepfather's name and made it clear that he hated living in the country and wanted nothing to do with dirty, smelly animals.

He'd moved away from the farm as soon as he turned

fifteen, by which time he looked like a man grown. He hadn't even told his mother he was going and just vanished one day, sending a postcard now and then to say he was all right, but not giving his address.

Phoebe was glad Janet's son didn't live at the farm any longer. She didn't like Frank. He was a big fellow, but very lazy, and seemed to push his way through life, with no regard for others. She was sorry when he started coming back for visits, because now she was older, Frank had begun to look at her in what she thought of as 'that way'. A couple of times, he'd kissed her, laughing when she tried to fight him off. She didn't like to complain to Janet, so avoided going to the farm when she knew he was there.

As her mother's health grew worse, life became difficult. Phoebe couldn't leave her mother on her own all day, so jobs were limited. They'd used up all their savings and she had to start selling or pawning their possessions.

Thank goodness Horace and Janet continued to help them. Without the food from the farm and what she could grow in the garden, she'd have had to get her mother admitted to the workhouse, a place no one went into, except as the very last resort.

It was a relief as well as a deep sadness when her mother died.

The day after the funeral, which had been paid for by Horace, Phoebe begged a lift into Swindon from a nearby carter, determined to find herself a job. She walked round the streets, enjoying being among smiling, bustling people.

At one point, she tripped on the uneven pavement and stumbled against the window of a shop making curtains. A white card said: *Help needed, general duties*. It seemed meant to be and she walked inside to ask about the job. She didn't know anything about making curtains, but she was a good needlewoman. They could only say no, after all.

The Steins, who owned the shop, were foreigners, Austrian, she found out. They asked her some questions, then offered her the job. They seemed so nice, she accepted it without hesitation. 'I'll have to find lodgings first, though, and sell my mother's furniture. She died last week.'

Mrs Stein exchanged glances with her husband, and said in her heavily accented English, 'We hev two little rooms in the attic here. You can live there rent-free, if you clean the shop each evening after it closes.'

Mr Stein nodded vigorously. 'Show her, Trudi.'

Phoebe was shown two tiny bare rooms. She could use the smaller one with the sloping ceiling as her bedroom, and the other as her sitting room. It had enough room for her bookcase, armchair, a table and two upright chairs.

There was an outside lavatory in the yard downstairs and her employers would let her cook in the kitchen behind the shop, which had a modern gas cooker, used to warm up Mr Stein's dinners at lunchtime. That would be wonderfully easy to use after the wood-burning stove Phoebe had in the cottage.

'We won't charge you for the gas,' Mrs Stein said. She waved one hand dismissively. 'One girl, not much cooking.'

As the weeks passed, Phoebe realised how lucky she'd been. She had an interesting job, with a lot to learn, good employers *and* somewhere of her own to live.

She didn't have the time or energy to make many friends. The library had plenty of good books to entertain her in the evenings, and she occasionally went to see a moving picture at the Country Electric cinema with Edith, who also worked for the Steins. The two women marvelled at what they saw, enjoying the pianist who played suitable music while the film was shown.

After the years of nursing her mother, Phoebe wanted only to lead a quiet, restful life. One day she'd look for more, but not yet.

Two years later Phoebe was sent to buy a few groceries for her employers because their housemaid had left them abruptly a day or two ago. She was happy to do this instead of working in the shop, since the errand took her out into the fresh air.

As she walked along the narrow streets of Swindon's Old Town, she lifted her face to the early morning sunshine of what promised to be a glorious summer's day. She'd turned twenty-one a couple of weeks ago, and was now officially an adult, but hadn't told anyone it was her birthday. She smiled wryly. It always felt as if she'd grown up when her mother fell ill.

The Steins were such good employers, she wondered as she walked why the maid who'd been with them for several years would just up and leave without giving proper notice. Perhaps the poor woman had family problems, but she could have explained, surely?

Phoebe enjoyed the bustle and didn't mind queuing in the shops after the quiet of the countryside. She'd recently come back from her annual holiday week, which she'd spent quietly with Horace and Janet on the farm. She'd helped out, because there was always work to be done, and anyway, she'd enjoyed the change of scene and the different tasks.

Janet said Frank had a new job, buying and selling things at the markets, but she didn't know any details, just that her son seemed to be making a better living from it. She wished he'd marry and settle down, was sad to have no grandchildren, and him twenty-five.

Phoebe passed Frank in the street in Swindon sometimes, but did no more than nod to him. He still made her feel uncomfortable because his eyes always lingered where they shouldn't. She'd never seen him at the markets, though, and wondered why he'd told his mother he worked there.

As she went from the brilliance of the sunshine into the dimness of the shop, she sighed. By afternoon, the row of shops was in the shadow of some taller buildings and they had to light the big gasolier that hung from the centre of the ceiling.

Mr Stein was polishing the inside of the shop window. He was very fussy about that sort of thing, insisting everything must look sparkling clean and inviting. He stopped work to smile at her.

'*Guten Tag*, Phoebe.'

'*Guten Tag, Herr Stein. Wie geht es Ihnen?*' She always tried to answer him in his own language, and he was teaching her a few words of German every day.

'*Sehr gut, danke.*'

He always said he was well, but he was past sixty and not in the best of health, and she could see how tired he became by the end of the day. The Steins had fled from Austria to live in England a few years ago, she didn't quite understand why. It must have been difficult for them to change languages as well as countries. They didn't have children or close family, but some good friends had helped them settle into their new country.

Phoebe went through to the rear workroom, where they did the cutting and sewing, to tell Mrs Stein she'd finished the errands. She handed over their house key. 'I've left the things in the kitchen and pantry, as you asked.'

'Thank you, dear. You can make a start in the workroom now. Edith is very late today. I hope she's not ill.'

Phoebe nipped up to the second floor and hung up her coat and beret, then hurried down to the shop. She was surprised not to see her co-worker yet. Edith had been there for years and was always at work long before this time. They had several orders for curtains waiting to be filled and customers didn't like to be kept waiting.

Phoebe put on a clean overall, more to protect the curtains than herself, and continued hemming a set of drops she'd started work on the previous day. She could handle the sewing machine now and do the straight seams and simpler hand finishing, but some of the draping and curtain headings were complicated, and beyond her skill. Mrs Stein and Edith usually did those together.

The materials came in such a lovely range of colours that she often leafed through the sample book, rubbing her fingertips over the rich velvets and heavy silks, loving the feel of them.

Half an hour later, Edith came hurrying in, looking as if she'd been crying. Mr Stein followed her in from the shop, his face crumpled with concern, and Mrs Stein went to put an arm round her employee, which made Edith start sobbing loudly.

'Vat is wrong, Edith, dear?'

'Dad says I have to give notice.'

Everyone stared at her in shock.

'I don't want to, but he says he's not having me working for Germans and if I don't leave here, he'll throw me out of home. I can't give up my family, I just can't.'

'But ve aren't Germans; ve're Austrians,' Mrs Stein protested.

'Dad says it's the same thing. He wanted me to finish today, but I persuaded him to let me stay on till the end of the week. I'm so sorry, Mrs Stein. I really hate letting you down. I've loved working here. I'll work twice as hard to finish the orders before I leave.'

'Thenk you.' Mrs Stein's accent had become more marked, as always when she was upset. 'Ve vill give you an excellent reference, of course.'

Edith hesitated. 'Could you sign it "Stone", do you think? That's what Stein means, isn't it, so you won't be telling a lie, exactly. Only, well, people won't want a reference from someone with a German name, not the way things are looking.'

She took a deep breath and added, 'You should change your name and put Stone on the shop front, too. Do it quickly. This week if you can.'

Phoebe stared at her in astonishment. She'd read about people acting nastily towards Germans living in England, but couldn't see why anyone would attack the Steins. They were well known and liked in Old Town, and their curtains were beautifully made. All their neighbours knew they were Austrian and had had to leave their country to take refuge here.

Only . . . Edith's father hadn't accepted that Austrian was different from German, even though his daughter had been working for the Steins for several years. If he thought like that, others might not realise the difference, either.

Or they might not want to admit there was a difference.

People everywhere were talking about the prospect of Britain going to war with Germany and many were upset, especially those who'd lost family members in the Boer Wars at the turn of the century. Phoebe had heard talk of the possibility of war in the shop, at the market and on the streets.

Wars were terrible things. But what good would it do for people to take their anger out on innocent people like the Steins?

She shivered. She'd seen mobs in action when she was a child. Her family had lived in Northumberland, where her father had been born, and there had been unrest in the mines. She'd been terrified by the crowds of men with dirty, angry faces who'd shouted and broken windows.

Later, her father had been killed in a mine accident. The owner had paid her mother some money in compensation and they'd moved south to Wiltshire, to be near her mother's family, especially Cousin Horace.

But money couldn't compensate you for losing a much-loved husband and father. Phoebe still dreamt about her dad and her mother had turned down two offers of marriage, saying no one could replace her dearest Rick.

And the money hadn't lasted, had it? Not after her mother fell ill.

After Edith left, business slowed down dramatically at the Steins' shop, and Phoebe was terrified it would have to close down. What would she do then?

What would the Steins do?

She heard her employers discussing closing it once or twice, trying to calculate whether they would have enough money to manage on. She couldn't help overhearing them because Mr Stein spoke rather loudly, which she'd noticed sometimes with other older people who were a bit deaf.

She didn't know what to think, only that she didn't want her life to change. If the shop closed, she would not only lose her job but her home, and it wasn't easy to live on women's wages, which were much lower than men's, nor were clean jobs like this one easy to find.

To her surprise, Frank stopped her in the street the next time he saw her.

'You should look for another job and get out of that place you're living in, Phoebe.'

'I like working there and I've still got a lot to learn about making curtains.'

He gave a scornful snort. 'Curtains! There's going to be a war, you fool. Who's going to care about new curtains then? And it'll be a war with Germany. This is *not* the time to be working for Germans.'

'They aren't Germans; they're Austrians.'

'What's the difference? They speak the same language, don't they?'

'The Steins had to leave their country because they were being persecuted, so they're on our side now.'

'No, they're not, and they never will be. They're probably spies. And even if they're not, everyone says people like them should go back to where they came from while they can, or else go and settle in America, out of the way. I'm warning you, Phoebe. You need to get out of that shop while you can, for your own safety.'

'I'm not leaving them. They're good employers. Anyway, I live over the shop. Where would I go?'

He grinned and put an arm round her. 'I could always put you up. I have a nice double bed.'

She shoved him away. 'I don't think that's funny!'

'Oh well, suit yourself. Your loss. But don't say I didn't warn you: you *are* in danger there.' He turned to walk away, then stopped and pulled a piece of paper out of his pocket, scribbling on it with a pencil stub and thrusting it into her hand.

She looked at it in puzzlement.

'It's my address. If you need help suddenly, you'd better come to me. And no, you don't have to share my bed to get help. My mother would go mad if I let anything happen to you.' He grinned. 'What she'd really like, Horace too, would be for me to marry you.'

Phoebe gaped at him.

'I'd like that too. But not yet. I'm too busy making money. I'll definitely start courting you later. Who'd have thought you'd grow up to be so pretty?'

'Will you stop going on like that? I don't like such talk. I'm not interested in lads.'

He gave her a long scrutiny. 'No. And I bet you're still a virgin.'

She felt herself blushing and turned away.

He grabbed her arm, not hurting her, just keeping her beside him. 'Look at that blush. Mind you, that's not a bad thing. Save your assets till you can get a good price for them, I always say. And you can save them for me.'

He let go of her arm and stepped back. 'Anyway, you get out of that shop. You know where I live if you need help moving your things.'

She walked slowly back to work, shivering at the way he'd looked at her. She'd felt as if she had no clothes on. As for marrying him, she'd never do that. She didn't even like him to touch her.

He hadn't meant it . . . had he? No, he was just teasing. But his teasing was usually . . . nasty. Not friendly.

* * *

Frank worried about Phoebe as he walked away. She'd got her head in the sand, like a lot of other folk. They'd wake up with a shock one day soon. He wasn't surprised that she was still a virgin. She was that sort of person.

His mother said he'd be happy with someone like Phoebe. He grinned. He agreed with her. Phoebe was lovely, with that softly rounded body and that wavy, auburn hair which had gold glints sparkling in it when the sun shone.

He was fond of his ma, even if she was another naïve idiot. She was a good cook and he liked going to the farm for the occasional Sunday lunch. It was a run-down place. He was doing so much better than them. Strangely enough, though, he now needed the farm he'd despised for his business.

When the war started, he reckoned all sorts of things were going to be in short supply, especially luxury goods, cigarettes and booze. He had been making preparations for a while now, buying bits and pieces when he saw an opportunity, using up his savings. He'd sell them for a lot more than he'd paid one day.

Very useful having parents with a spare barn. He'd told them his employer needed somewhere to store things and would pay them for the use of the barn. They mustn't touch anything, though, or he'd get in trouble and lose his job.

That same 'employer' was paying them a pound a month for the storage, and they were delighted with that extra income for doing nothing, especially as Frank had repaired the roof of the barn for them and put on new doors with good locks. He had conveniently 'forgotten' to give them a key.

He was going to get rich, and he didn't care how he did it, but he wasn't going to volunteer for the army once the war started. He didn't intend to get himself shot.

If they started conscripting men, he'd have to work out how to avoid that. He didn't want to do anything drastic to prevent passing his medical, like damaging his trigger finger, but he wasn't giving his life for his country. He was keeping it for himself.

He'd find a way. He always did when he wanted something.

A couple of weeks after Phoebe's encounter with Frank, another shop in Swindon owned by Germans had its windows broken. She decided, very reluctantly, that she'd better be prepared to move. Just in case.

She didn't say anything to the Steins, but packed her spare clothes and a few bits and pieces in an old Gladstone bag, in case she had to get out quickly. She couldn't afford to lose everything she owned.

She also memorised Frank's address and found out where the house was. Not in a part of the town where she felt comfortable. Why did he live there? He could surely afford to move somewhere decent. He looked so well fed and his clothes were good sturdy garments, not worn . . . Unless his business was more suited to that sort of run-down area. That wouldn't surprise her.

As the days passed, she didn't say anything to her employers, either about Frank or about her precautions. But she didn't unpack the bag of clothes, either.

Just in case, she told herself. Trouble might never happen, but you had to think ahead.

Chapter Three

Two weeks after his father's funeral, the post brought Joseph a black-edged envelope addressed in his mother's handwriting. He picked it up and stared at it in shock. 'Who's dead now?'

'You won't find out till you open it,' Harriet said.

He read it and gasped. 'It's Richard's wife . . . and the child. Both died in childbirth.' He covered his eyes with one hand for a moment and confessed, 'I was so afraid each time you were expecting a child. I'd have been lost without you and your quiet strength, my darling.'

'I'd be lost without you, too.' She slipped her hand into his for a moment and they stood looking at one another fondly.

Love was wonderful, he thought, and she really did love him. Then he looked back at the black-bordered letter. 'What can I say to my brother? Richard and Diana might not have married for love, but they seemed to grow very fond of one another. I'm not close to him and yet . . . I want to offer him my sympathy, of course I do.'

'There is no comfort when a loved one dies suddenly,

especially when they're so young, but you must write to him.'

He understood instantly what she was thinking. 'Like when your father died.'

She nodded.

'I'll write immediately, to Richard and Mother.'

It wasn't till he was signing the letter to his brother that he said thoughtfully, 'Unless Richard remarries, that leaves Selwyn or Thomas to provide an heir. I hope it's Thomas who does that. Selwyn's rotten to the core. He might have got married, but he didn't father a child, did he?'

Another letter arrived from his mother a few days later saying the same thing and complaining that Selwyn refused to listen to sense and reunite with his wife, for the sake of the family. Richard had, it seemed, vanished into the maws of the army immediately after the funeral, leaving his mother to close down his house.

'You never know what's going to happen to you, do you?' Harriet said that night in bed. 'Look at your family, torn apart in so many ways. Look at us, with the house we love full of strangers and most of it out of our control. You just never know.'

The late summer seemed to pass slowly at Greyladies. They received the occasional letter from Joseph's mother, telling them about her 'bijou apartment' and her new social life in London, which was far less restricted than it would normally have been for a widow.

'She sounds almost cheerful,' Harriet said thoughtfully.

'Mother will be all right,' Joseph told her. 'She's tougher than she looks. It's Selwyn I worry about. I had another letter from Thomas telling me our damned brother's contracted some new gambling debts. He'll throw our old home away before he's through.'

'There's nothing you can do about that. I'm glad you pay such close attention to the Latimer Trust. There are going to be a lot of widows needing help if war really does break out with Germany.'

Like a lot of other people in Britain, the Latimers were disturbed over their morning cup of tea on 5th August by their paperboy banging on the door and yelling at the top of his voice, 'We're at war, Mr Latimer. Britain's at war.'

Joseph hurried to the back door, now their main entrance, and found Jim from the village brandishing their *Guardian* newspaper.

'We're at war,' he repeated, jigging about in excitement. 'Britain's at war, Mr Latimer.'

Joseph took the newspaper from him and shook it open, reading it aloud. 'Great Britain declared war on Germany at eleven o'clock last night.'

He paused to look at Harriet, who had followed him, seeing tears well up in her eyes. 'It's terrible, isn't it?'

'Terrible!' Jim exclaimed. 'It's exciting, that's what it is, Mr Latimer. I hope it doesn't end before I'm old enough to join up. I want to see a bit of the world before I settle down on the farm and going to war is the only way Da will let me do it.' Whistling cheerfully, he cycled off to deliver the other newspapers.

Joseph put an arm round his wife.

'I pray the war ends before Jim's old enough to join the army,' she said quietly. 'It would destroy his mother to lose her only son.'

'He's not eighteen for another year or so, is he?'

'He looks eighteen now. Still, everyone says the war will be over in a few months.'

'But will it? We've discussed that a few times and Thomas has written to me about it. He doesn't think the Germans will be as easy to defeat as people believe. There are a lot of them and they've already invaded Belgium.'

She shivered. 'Where will they go next, do you think?'

'France, I suppose, but they won't capture Britain. I'm certain of that.'

'How can you be certain, Joseph?'

'Because there isn't a man, woman or child in our village, and every other village and town, who wouldn't fight against an invader. Even I would find a way to do something. Only it won't come to that. Thank heavens this is an island. You can't march an invading army across the English Channel, and enemies would be vulnerable when they tried to disembark and unload their ships. No, being an island has saved us before and it'll save us again.'

'But people from the village will die. Young people like Jim will have to fight.' She sighed. 'Let's call the others, then you can read the rest of the article to us.'

So they waited till their two maids and the children had joined them, then Joseph read out the grim announcement from the *Guardian* newspaper.

The Foreign Office issued the following official statement: Owing to the summary rejection by the German Government of the request made by His Majesty's Government for assurances that the neutrality of Belgium will be respected, His Majesty's

Ambassador to Berlin has received his passports, and His Majesty's Government declared to the German Government that a state of war exists between Great Britain and Germany as from 11 p.m. on August 4, 1914.

'So,' Joseph ended, 'I'm afraid we're at war now.'

The maids said very little but both looked upset. Harriet knew that Phyllis's sweetheart was of an age to fight, and that their new cook, a spinster called Mary Cox, had a nephew of twenty, on whom she doted.

The two Latimer children stared from one parent to the other, wide-eyed.

'War's bad, isn't it?' Jody asked as the silence continued.

'Yes, son. It's a terrible thing,' his father told him.

'Miss Bowers has been telling us about it. People kill one another in wars. I don't want to kill anyone. I don't like watching Tim's father kill hens, even.'

'You could fight someone if he was attacking you,' Joseph pointed out. 'Or if he was going to kill Mal or your mother. Only wicked people *want* to kill anyone, but we all defend those we love.'

'I suppose.'

Heaven help her, Harriet thought, she was glad Joseph wouldn't have to fight, and just as glad that her own sons were too young to go to war. You couldn't help being selfish when danger threatened those you loved.

Two hours later, they heard voices arguing in the new house, just outside the connecting door and tiptoed across to listen.

'I can't do it, miss. It wouldn't be right.'

'That's Martin's voice,' Harriet whispered.

Matron's voice came to them loud and clear, so shrill they could imagine her furious expression. 'You've been given a job and you *must* do it. This is for the War Office.'

'Well, I still can't do it, whoever it's for. Mr and Mrs Latimer would throw a fit if you had that old door destroyed, and I wouldn't blame them, neither. Bin there for hundreds of years, that door has, and it'll serve for another few hundred, too. Good wood, that were made from, even if it is a bit rough-looking.'

'We're at war and I *order* you to remove this door and replace it with a wooden barrier.'

'I ent doing it. It won't help the war none to pull that door out.'

Joseph opened the door in question. 'What's going on here?'

'There!' Matron exclaimed dramatically, taking a prudent step backwards and pointing at him. 'This is exactly why we need the door removing, to stop people walking into the convalescent home uninvited.'

As Harriet moved forward, Joseph raised his voice. 'I thought we'd discussed that little matter already, Matron. No one from the old house has come through this door since we last closed it in your presence, not even the children.'

'That was before war was declared. The matter is now urgent. I *will not* have you able to wander in and out of here when the patients start arriving. They'll need peace and quiet and I am not—'

'Sorry about all this, Mr Latimer.' Martin threw Matron a disgusted look. 'I dint know what her wanted when her asked me to do a job, or I'd never have said yes. Everyone

44

in the village knows you have a paper from the War Office saying the house ent to be damaged. Miss Bowers told us 'bout that.'

Matron turned on her heel and stalked off, words puncturing the air behind her. 'Mark my words, I shall find a way to get rid of that door and secure these premises, if I have to chop the thing down myself.'

Martin blew out his breath. 'Proper old tartar, ent she? I don't think I'll do any more jobs here while she's in charge.'

'Don't lose the chance to earn extra money,' Joseph advised. 'You've a growing family to feed.'

He grinned. 'I don't think she'll even ask me after this.'

'Do you want a cup of tea, Martin?' Harriet asked in a low voice.

'Thanks anyway, Mrs Latimer, but I reckon it'll be better if I go back out through the front, the way I come in.'

Joseph closed the door. 'She'll try again to get rid of this.' He patted the dark wood panels affectionately. 'I wouldn't put an axe attack past her. The trouble is, we can't keep an eye on it all the time. Perhaps we should remove it for the duration of the war and board up the opening?'

'What? Give in at her first thrust? Certainly not. If she wins this time, she'll expect to walk all over us afterwards.'

The incident left her on edge, wondering what would happen next, and whether she would be able to protect the old house.

Phoebe woke up on 5th August to hear voices shouting in the streets and a paper seller calling, 'Read all about it. Britain declares war.'

'*War!*'

'We're at war!'

'Come and read this.'

The news was repeated, shouted, cried out by different voices and their words seemed to echo in her brain.

She got dressed quickly and nipped out to buy a newspaper. Passers-by were showing each other the front page, discussing the war. She took her paper into the building through the kitchen door, and grabbed a piece of bread and jam. She didn't even stop to make a pot of tea, but gobbled the food down as she read.

Setting the newspaper aside, she rested her head on her hands, worrying about her possessions. She had to do something. Trouble was coming to this shop. What if people set it on fire?

Going upstairs, she crammed more of her clothes into the big carpet bag and then carried it downstairs. She hesitated for a moment, then decided to hide it in the coalhouse. No one would look for it there, surely.

One thing was certain: Mr and Mrs Stein mustn't open up the shop today. It was still early, so she decided to go and tell them to stay at home.

When she got to their house, however, she was horrified to see a group of people milling about outside it, shouting and gesticulating. She didn't dare push her way through them, so went round to the back alley, and since the gate was locked, climbed over the wall into their garden. She hitched up her skirts as she'd done when much younger, not caring how much leg she showed. To her relief no one seemed to have thought of this way of getting into the house yet and the alley remained empty.

When she heard the sound of breaking glass from the

front of the house, she ran to the kitchen door. It wasn't even locked. They should have locked it. Flinging it open, she went inside, to hear Mrs Stein sobbing.

'Hello!'

They swung round.

'You shouldn't be here,' Mr Stein said at once. 'You're putting yourself in danger, child.'

'I came to warn you not to open the shop today. There are crowds out in the streets.'

'And here too,' he said sadly.

Mrs Stein sobbed and pressed a handkerchief to her mouth as if trying to hold back her tears.

'What are we going to do?' he whispered. 'I don't know what to do. I'm not an enemy of this country, Phoebe.'

'I know that, Mr Stein. I think you need to get away.'

But even as she spoke, someone knocked on the front door and a voice called, 'Police! Open up.'

'Go quickly, Phoebe,' Mr Stein said. 'Stay away from us. Wait.' He looked at his wife. 'Give it to her. It'll be safer.'

She fumbled in her handbag and pulled out a wad of money. 'Take this, dear girl. Keep it safe for us. Or if anything bad happens to us, keep it for yourself.'

Phoebe stared at them in horror at the implications of this.

Mrs Stein thrust the money into her hand. 'Go on now. Run!'

'Come and lock the back door after me.'

But someone was hammering on the front door again and they'd already turned towards it, so after a moment's hesitation, Phoebe stuffed the money down the front of her dress and left the way she'd come.

Desperate to find out what was happening, she went round to the front again and asked a woman why the crowd had gathered. As if she didn't know!

'There are some Germans living there. The police are going to lock them up. Stein, they're called.'

'I've heard of them. They're Austrians not Germans.'

'Same thing, as far as I'm concerned.' She swung round to stare at Phoebe. 'You're not one of 'em, are you? You don't sound as if you come from round here.'

'Me? Course I'm not a German. I'm English, born and bred. I grew up in Northumberland, in the north.'

'You don't sound like a foreigner, I must admit, but you do talk funny.'

'Of course I'm not a foreigner. I'd better get to work now, though. Don't want them docking my pay, do I?'

Phoebe walked away and when she peeped back over her shoulder, the woman seemed to have forgotten her. The two policemen had disappeared inside the house.

She stopped again at the corner, watching from a distance, not speaking to anyone. She wouldn't dare try to defend the poor Steins again. You couldn't reason with hysterical people.

After a while, she saw the policemen come out of the house again, escorting her poor employers, who looked pale, terrified and suddenly much older.

A few stones whizzed in their direction and the crowd pressed in on them. One policeman roared at the bystanders to get back. 'This is England. We don't tolerate mobs causing trouble here. We leave that to foreigners.'

For a moment all hung in the balance, then a woman said calmly, but in an equally carrying voice, 'He's right. We're English and should act like it. Let the law take them away.'

The Steins tottered off with their two blue-clad protectors. Phoebe could only hope the poor dears would be safe.

They weren't her employers now, were they? They wouldn't dare open the shop again, even if they were released. She'd better find another job and somewhere else to live.

With nothing more to see, the crowd started dispersing. She realised she was wasting valuable time. Another mob was bound to turn on the Steins' shop at some stage, if they hadn't done so already. She hurried away to pick up her bag of clothes and as much else as she could carry.

At the shop she found that the violence had started. A policeman was guarding the premises, but the big shop window was broken. Stones and shards of glass littered the pavement. She stared at the damage in dismay, then went up to him.

'Stay back, miss, h'if you please.'

'Can I go inside and get my things?' She gestured to the shop. 'I work there. Or I used to. I've been living above the shop, so I need to get my clothes out.'

'How do I know you're not a looter?'

'I'm not! I've come here openly, haven't I?'

'I suppose so. What's your name? Right. Wait there.' He went to the next shop and yelled inside. 'Police! Can someone come out here, please?'

Mrs Harby peeped out of the door.

'Do you know this young lady?'

'Yes, Constable. She's called Phoebe Sinclair and she works – I mean *used to work* for them.' She jerked one thumb in the direction of the Steins' shop.

'I'm definitely not working there any more, Mrs Harby, but I need to get my clothes and my other bits and pieces.' Thinking of the Steins and how afraid they must be made tears come into her eyes and she let them fall, squeezing out others on purpose. 'All I have in the world is in there.'

'I can't let you go inside on your own,' the policeman said, 'and I can't leave my post. If I do, people will break in.'

'How about I go in with her?' Mrs Harby offered. 'I can check she's not taking anything that's not hers – not that I think she would anyway. She's a nice lass and I've always found her very helpful and willing, I must say.'

He frowned, seeming uncertain still.

'Oh, go on, Constable. You can't let that poor lass lose all she owns as well as her job. It's not her fault they're foreigners. She's as English as you and me.'

'All right. Get your things, miss. But nothing else. And hurry.'

Inside the shop, Mrs Harby stared round, clearly enjoying the drama. 'What a waste! Look at how the broken glass has torn that lovely material.'

Phoebe couldn't bear to look at the destruction and led the way quickly to the rear. 'I packed some things this morning and put a bag in the coalhouse. I wonder if it's still there.'

'Let's go and look.'

They retrieved the bag, then Phoebe said, 'The furniture upstairs is mine, and there are all sorts of bits and pieces I don't want to lose.'

'Well, you can't carry everything. You can leave some of your stuff with us, if you like, though, just till you find somewhere else to live.'

'Can I? That's very kind of you. I know I can trust you.'

'You definitely can. I haven't forgotten you getting my washing off the line when it came on to rain, and more than once, too.'

'We should all help neighbours.'

When they'd finished gathering together Phoebe's bits and pieces of crockery from the kitchen downstairs, Mrs Harby asked, 'Do they – um, keep money on the premises?'

'No. Well, only the petty cash for buying milk and tea.'

'You should take that with you. It'll just get stolen otherwise.'

'I can't do that. It'd feel like stealing. Anyway the tin's locked and it's quite big.'

'Leave it with us, then. Me and Mr Harby will look after it for them.'

Phoebe had a feeling that the Steins would never see the money again, but she didn't say so. And better the neighbours had it than a mob. She packed the rest of her things rapidly, bundling her bedding into a sheet.

'I suppose these were your mother's,' Mrs Harby commented. 'It's sad you lost her so young. Do you have any relatives to go to now?'

'Yes. A cousin of my mother. He has a farm. I'll go to them till I can get another job, but I'll have to find someone to take all my stuff there.'

When Phoebe had finished packing, Mrs Harby brought her husband and son to help carry the boxes of smaller things next door.

The policeman checked everything. 'You're sure she's not stealing these?'

'Of course she isn't!'

A police sergeant came up just then, and the bundles

had to be explained to him. He nodded. 'Take your things, Miss Sinclair, and don't work for foreigners again, if you can help it. We're keeping order here, and it's only property that's been damaged, but there are other towns where people have been harmed and buildings set on fire. Foreigners bring trouble with them.'

She answered with a slight nod because she wanted to get her things away. She didn't agree with him about foreigners, though, not when they were as nice as the Steins.

When they'd got Phoebe's bags inside her house, Mrs Harby filled the kettle. 'We'll have a cup of tea, then you'd better go and look for someone to take you and your things out to your cousin's. We haven't got a spare bedroom, though if you're desperate, you can sleep on the sofa tonight.'

'I think I'd better go and see my cousin's son. He works in Swindon. He might know someone.' She didn't like asking Frank, but there was no one else.

'Good idea.'

'Thank you for your help. I'm very grateful.'

Mrs Harby had said nothing about the petty cash, either to the police or her family. Phoebe didn't mention it, either. She thought it a small price to pay for the neighbour's help.

Chapter Four

Phoebe walked to the address Frank had given her, not liking the mood of the people she met in the streets. She passed quite a few small groups talking and gesticulating, and felt there was a hard, angry edge to them. She didn't feel comfortable near them, was sure the slightest thing would set them off like roasting chestnuts exploding near a fire.

Frank's home was in a very seedy street, and people there stared at her strangely, as if assessing what she had in her pockets.

She didn't expect to find him home at this hour of the day, but hoped someone would know where he was. To her relief, the woman who answered the door yelled over her shoulder, 'Frank! It's for you.'

He came to the door, not wearing a shirt, pulling his braces up over his vest as if he'd been getting dressed. He studied Phoebe. 'I was just having a lie-down. Trouble?'

'Yes. I need help. Would you mind?'

'I'll finish getting dressed and take you for a cup of tea at the corner cafe. Keep an eye on things here, Flo.'

'Is this the new girl?'

'No. She's a relative of mine.'

'Pity. She's quite pretty.'

The predatory look in the woman's eyes made Phoebe shiver.

He gripped Flo's shoulder so tightly she winced. 'Remember: this one's a relative of mine. Not to be touched.'

'Yes, Frank. Frank, don't! You're hurting me.'

'Remember.' He shoved her away so hard she nearly fell, then said to Phoebe, 'Wait for me outside. I don't want you in here.'

She wondered why he was undressed so late in the day and why he didn't want her here. What was this place?

As they set off down the street, she told him what had happened.

'You're all right, though?'

'Yes.'

'Lost your things, have you?'

'No. Mrs Harby next door helped me get the smaller things out and she's looking after them for me till I can find some lodgings.'

Another of those stares, then, 'Better go out to stay with my mother.'

'Yes. That's what I thought. For the time being, anyway. But I've got quite a bit of furniture still in the house and I don't want to lose it. Do you know anyone with a cart?'

'Might do. We'll see what you've got, but first we'll have something to eat and drink.'

She didn't feel hungry, but forced some food down. She had to keep her energy up. Frank didn't talk much, but he ate a lot and finished off what she'd left on her plate as well.

'You don't eat much, Phoebe. No wonder you're so slender. It suits you, though.'

She didn't want him talking about her appearance. He looked fatter and puffy. 'I'm not hungry today. Too upset.'

'About them Germans?'

'They're *not* Germans.'

'Whatever they are, they're foreigners and I bet the police will lock 'em away till the war's over.'

'Where will they send them? Will I be able to visit them?'

'How should I know where they'll be going? Don't you go near them. You've got to start looking after your own interests.'

'They've been kind to me.'

'You're too soft for your own good, you are. People take advantage.'

She'd rather be soft than hard like him, but she didn't say so. She was watching what she said today.

She would not, she decided, tell any of them about the money. Especially Frank. She had to find some way of hiding it. On her person would be best. She'd need to make some sort of money belt.

She'd sew one tonight after everyone else had gone to bed.

When they got to the shop, the policeman called out, 'There she is! Hoy, miss! Come here.'

Another policeman standing there, called, 'Are you sure she's the one?'

'Yes. It's definitely her.'

Frank took hold of her arm and edged her forward. 'No use running away,' he said in a low voice. 'Smile at them.'

But Phoebe couldn't summon up a smile, just couldn't.

'You're Miss Phoebe Sinclair?' the policeman asked.

'Yes.'

'I have this letter for you. It's been opened to check it's got nothing dangerous in. It's from your former employers.'

'Are they all right?'

'Mr Stein isn't well, but he dictated this letter to his wife, and since it's to your benefit, and you're British, the inspector decided to pass it on to you.'

She opened the letter, gasping as she read it.

To whom this may concern

Everything in the shop is to go to our former employee, Phoebe Sinclair, all stock and equipment. She's English through and through. She's been a hard worker and better she has it than the looters.

   Hubert Stein

   Trudi Stein

She read it again, amazed and touched that in all their troubles, they'd thought of her.

Frank twitched the letter out of her hand and read it, letting out a low whistle. 'You fell lucky there.'

'I don't understand. Aren't they coming back? Or selling the business?'

The policeman gave her a condescending smile. 'They'll be kept in custody for the duration of the war, together with other enemy aliens. And who'd pay good money to take over a ruined shop, especially if they had to give the money to foreigners?'

The poor Steins. What had they done to deserve this?

'I should clear the contents of the shop quickly, if I was you,' the policeman said. 'The mobs will get in and loot it if you don't. We're only keeping a man on duty here till the end of the day.'

'I'll see to that for my fiancée, Officer,' Frank said. 'Thank you very much for helping us. I'll buy you a drink one day . . . when times are easier.'

Phoebe was puzzled by the nods they gave one another, then it suddenly sank in what Frank had called her. 'I'm not your fiancée!' she whispered.

'Shh. It'll make things easier for me to help you. And you could be, if you wanted.'

'No, thank you. I don't want to get married, not to anyone.'

He laughed. 'We'll talk about that another time. You go inside now and start sorting out the shop stuff that isn't damaged. I'll fetch some fellows and a couple of carts.'

She didn't like the idea of pretending to be engaged to a man like him. Something inside her shrank from the mere thought of it. But she did as he told her, consoling herself with the thought that she'd give everything back to the Steins once all this stupidity was sorted out. She didn't want to benefit from their troubles.

Even if there was a war, everyone was saying it wouldn't last long. She didn't know if they were right. What did she know about wars? She felt very ignorant of everything after her years in a small village, focusing on caring for her mother, then her years in this shop.

She should have read more newspapers to keep up with what was going on, instead of novels from the library, but she'd felt so tired after her mother died, so very weary. She'd needed time to recover.

And now . . . well, she didn't know what she felt. Or what she'd do to earn her living.

When the two carts laden with furniture and goods got to the farm, Frank explained to his parents what had happened, then took charge.

'We'll put the things from the shop into my boss's barn. They'll be safer there because it has a good strong door and proper locks.' He saw Phoebe's puzzled look. 'He's paying my parents to store some things for him.'

'Oh.' It was the first time she'd heard about him having a boss to answer to. She was beginning to feel very suspicious about how he earned a living.

'There's another shed where we can put your furniture and household stuff,' Cousin Horace told Phoebe. 'It's a bit ramshackle, but it's waterproof and I'll put some rat poison and mousetraps down.'

She could only say, 'Thank you.' She was so tired now that everything was starting to feel unreal.

'You come inside and leave the men to put things away,' Cousin Janet said. 'You're white with exhaustion, you poor thing. Must have been a terrible day for you.'

Her son overheard and grinned. 'It was a very *good* day for her. She got given the stock of the shop. Nice lot of money that'll bring in after the war. Do you know how to make curtains, Phoebe?'

'Straightforward ones, not the fancy sort. Mrs Stein and Edith did those.'

'Bring in good money, does it, a curtain shop?'

'Not bad. Enough for the Steins to buy their own house with a few years' profits.'

He nodded slowly, looking at her thoughtfully.

He'd better not start calling her his fiancée again. The mere thought of being kissed and mauled about by him made her shudder.

She sat in front of the kitchen fire, her eyes closed, feeling relaxed after a nice cup of cocoa and a currant bun. Frank came in and stopped in the doorway. 'Got a minute, Mum?'

Cousin Janet went out into the hall.

Phoebe could hear them talking, even though they kept their voices low, because Cousin Horace had gone to bed and the house was quiet. They thought she was asleep and she didn't bother to tell them she was only resting her eyes.

'Phoebe's got a lot of stuff, hasn't she?' Cousin Janet said. 'Worth a nice bit of money, that is. And she's a good-looking girl. You could do worse than marry her, Frank, love.'

'I was thinking that myself today. She's very ladylike, too. I wonder where she gets that from?'

'Takes after her mother, Horace says. Not that *she* had money or anything but she was a Latimer.'

'That name doesn't mean anything to me.'

'It didn't mean anything to me till I married Horace. The Latimers have land in Wiltshire somewhere. I don't know where exactly, but that's probably where Phoebe gets that refined air she has. She carries herself like a duchess, Horace always says, just as her mother did before she got ill. Why she fell in love with a rough miner like Rick was a mystery.'

There was silence, then he said slowly, 'I think you could be right, Mum. I pretended we were engaged to make it easier for me to get the stuff from the shop. But Phoebe's a good girl, if you know what I mean. Hasn't been with any other fellows.'

'How can you tell that?'

'Shh. Keep your voice down. It was the way she blushed when I said something. Pink as a peony, she went. I'm beginning to think I'd better get married before this war gets much older. It stands to reason they'll be taking the single fellows first.'

'You come over on Sunday and have dinner with us. You can start courting her then. Talk to her nicely, mind. No bullying. Women don't go for bullies and you do push your way around.'

'It's them as push who get the money, I've found. And I intend to make a lot of money out of this war.'

'Profiteering? Frank, is that wise? People won't like it.'

'People can lump it. But I will come over on Sunday and spend some time with her. Let's hope it'll be fine so I can take her for a walk and kiss her a bit.'

'Tell her she's pretty, too. Women like compliments. And it's true enough.'

'All right. Words don't cost anything. Hey, look at the time! I'd better get going now. My friends with the carts are waiting for me at the village pub.'

He called a goodbye to Phoebe and Horace. His stepfather replied from upstairs, but Phoebe didn't say a word. She was too indignant. Marry her for her possessions and to stay out of the army, would he? Well, he'd get a slap if he tried to force a kiss on her. She couldn't stand him and nothing he did would ever change that.

She wished she'd not gone to him for help with the

furniture and stuff from the shop. She should have tried to find someone else to help her.

When he realised she wasn't going to let him court her, he'd probably not give her the curtains and other stuff back. Might was right, as far as he was concerned. Better lose them than give herself into his power, though.

At least he didn't know about the money the Steins had given her. She had to make a hiding place for that.

When Cousin Janet came in, Phoebe pretended to wake up. 'Oh, sorry. I must have fallen asleep. I'll go straight up to bed, if that's all right.' She kept yawning and muttering about being tired as she climbed the steep, narrow stairs. She didn't want Cousin Janet to suspect that she'd overheard them talking about her.

Frank hadn't made the slightest pretence that he was fond of her, or cared whether she was fond of him. All he wanted was a presentable wife and the money Phoebe would bring him.

Lying in bed, with the curtains of the cramped little room open to show the clear, starry sky, she gradually grew less angry and her thoughts turned to the Steins. Where were her poor employers sleeping tonight? Were they being treated decently? She was particularly worried about Mr Stein, who had looked so ill and afraid as he was marched away.

Once she was sure Horace and Janet were asleep, she lit her bedroom candle and sewed a money belt out of a tea towel. It was rough, and her stitches were more like tacking, but the belt would hold the banknotes safe under her clothes.

As the next two days passed, she could only wonder how the war was going. Things were so cut off here at the farm. Horace and Janet didn't even go into the village unless they had to, and would have stared if she'd said she felt like a walk. They had plenty of jobs for her to do, kept her busy from dawn till dusk.

They didn't even take a daily newspaper. Janet said there was only bad news these days and Horace didn't seem to read anything, just sat gazing into the fire after he'd had his tea, then went to bed early.

Phoebe would have to get hold of a newspaper and see if there were any jobs on offer as soon as she left here.

Only how was she going to get away?

On the Friday, Cousin Janet said, 'Frank said he would be coming to dinner on Sunday. You know, I think he's sweet on you, dear.'

Phoebe didn't like to say anything rude about Frank to his mother. 'I may not be here on Sunday,' she said. 'I have to find myself a job.'

'Oh, there's no hurry for that. We like having you, don't we, Horace?'

'Mmm. Nice to have a pretty young face about the place.'

'It'd make us very happy if you and Frank got together,' Janet said when Horace had gone back outside to work.

Phoebe forced a smile and decided not to protest about these hints. Instead she bent her mind to finding a way to escape before Sunday. They were a long way out of the village here, especially if you were carrying a heavy suitcase. And she suspected they'd try to stop her, maybe take her things away from her, to force her to wait till Frank arrived.

She was determined to be away before then.

Yet it was Cousin Janet herself who offered her visitor a possible way of getting back to Swindon.

'You were saying you felt like going out for a stroll. Do you think you could fetch the milk money from the stone near the gate tomorrow morning, Phoebe, love? Bob always leaves the payments for us on Thursdays, but we never know quite what time he'll arrive, later than usual, anyway. If you go, it'll save Horace hanging about after he puts out the milk for collection.'

'Yes, of course. What time should I get to the gate?'

'You could ride down with Horace and walk back once you get the money. It's going to be another sunny day, so you could take one of your books and sit reading. I never saw anyone who reads as much as you do. You'll addle your brain with all them books. Still, you won't have time for reading once you're wed and the children start coming, so you might as well enjoy it now.'

Phoebe breathed deeply and didn't respond to this, waiting for the gentle flow of words to continue. She didn't have to say much, just make the occasional noise or brief remark to show she was listening. Janet seemed starved of female companionship. Apart from her dislike of Frank, Phoebe didn't want to live here in the middle of nowhere like Janet did.

'I go into Swindon with Bob sometimes in the morning when I need to buy clothes and things you can't find in the village. I get the bus back to the village afterwards and Horace picks me up when he takes the evening milk down to the gate. Bob's a lovely fellow. Help anyone, he would. So . . . you'll wait for the money tomorrow?'

'Yes, of course. I'm happy to help in any way I can. It'll be good to stretch my legs a bit.'

'My legs have been stretched too much,' Janet joked,

waggling one leg with its swollen ankle at her. 'At my age, I get tired out by the end of the day. If Frank doesn't take over this farm, we'll have to think of selling in a year or two. Me and Horace are getting a bit old for all the hard work.'

She looked round and sighed. 'I'd miss the place, though. I've lived in this house since we got married, though we had Horace's father living with us at first. Perhaps when you marry Frank, you can persuade him to take over and let us live here. He could bring everything up to date and it'd pay better. It's a lovely peaceful life and he'd be his own master. The lad's had his fling, should be ready to settle down now, as I keep telling him.'

She shot a quick glance at Phoebe, as if to assess her reaction.

Frank wasn't a *lad* in any sense that Phoebe knew. He was a bully and a lout, had been since he got his man's growth. And he was lazy with it, never stirring himself unless he had to. 'It's early days for me to talk of marrying anyone, Janet. The country's at war and I want to do my bit. I'm sure Frank does too.'

'He doesn't want to go into the army. He won't put up with being ordered around, never has done, not even when he was a little boy. The times that schoolmaster gave him the cane! It upset me to see the weals. It never did any good, neither. Frank wouldn't do as he was told if he set his mind against it, not if they killed him, he wouldn't.'

She shook her head, her eyes blind with memories, and continued to reminisce. 'That last year he didn't even go to school half the time. The rascal used to forge my signature on notes saying he'd been ill. Well, he was ill sometimes. No one complained to me, though, so I didn't say anything. I think that schoolmaster was a bit afraid of him, he'd grown so big.'

Phoebe could imagine that. She'd be afraid of Frank, too, if she was stupid enough to marry him. Which she wasn't.

She let Janet drone on till bedtime, then escaped to her room. As they had to go outside to the privy, no one would worry if they heard her go downstairs during the night.

She packed her clothes as quickly as she could, thankful that it was a moonlit night, then lay down fully dressed till Cousin Horace began snoring and Janet stopped talking.

As she crept across the farmyard, the dog started up, making soft huffing noises, but settled down quietly when she spoke to him.

The bag was heavy and as she walked down the lane, she had to swap it from side to side. Her fingers were hurting and she couldn't walk quickly. She didn't like being out on her own in the night and stopped a couple of times, thinking she'd heard something, her heart beating faster. But it must just have been her imagination.

She sighed in relief when she got to the milkstone, a big, flat slab of rock laid across two low drystone pillars. It was designed to hold the full milk churns ready to be collected and taken to the dairy. She looked round for somewhere to hide her case nearby, settling in the end for behind a big clump of nettles.

That cost her a few blisters, but she picked some dock leaves and rubbed them on the itchy bits. She didn't think Cousin Horace would go fumbling amid the nettles. Even the dogs took care not to poke their noses too near the stinging plants. Luckily the ground was dry and she scuffed the dust around to hide her footprints.

Then she walked back to the farm and upstairs to her room.

'That you, Phoebe?' a sleepy voice called.

'Yes.'

'You were gone a long time.'

'I've got a bit of an upset stomach. I think I'm all right now, though.'

'Let me know if it starts again and I'll give you some of my special mixture.'

'I will. Goodnight, Janet.'

Phoebe thought she'd have difficulty getting back to sleep but she was so tired, she fell asleep almost immediately.

Chapter Five

When Phoebe woke up, it was time to go with Horace to set out the big milk churns for collection, which he did before breakfast.

She needed to put something into her stomach. 'I'm hungry today, Cousin Janet. All right if I have a piece of bread and butter before I go?'

'I'll cut one for you. And some of my strawberry jam, too, eh?'

Which made Phoebe feel guilty. She kissed Janet's cheek, but the older woman wasn't satisfied with that and pulled her back for a hug, exclaiming, 'It's grand to have you here, lass. Grand.'

How did such a kind woman get a son like Frank? Phoebe wondered. The nastiness must come from his father's side.

When they got to the big stone slab, Horace paused before he lifted the first milk churn out of the cart, staring at the patch of greenery nearby. 'Something's been in them nettles.'

Phoebe stiffened, terrified he'd investigate. 'Perhaps it was a fox.'

'Animals usually has more sense than to get themselves stung. But the dog would be barking if anything was there now, so you'll be all right. Keep your eyes open, though. Here.' He reached under the cart seat for a walking stick with a thick handle and gave it to her.

'You watch out for yourself, girl. There are some odd types tramping the roads. Use this if you have to. It's nice and heavy. And come straight back when you get the milk money.'

'Um . . . thank you.' She took the stick, feeling worse than ever to be running away when they were so kind to her.

She watched Horace drive the empty cart back to the farm, then dragged her bag out of the nettles, earning a few more blisters in the process. Again she rubbed dock leaves on her skin, but the blisters were still itchy.

After that, she had nothing to do but wait for Bob to come and collect the milk.

Time seemed to pass very slowly and half an hour had gone by, according to her mother's little fob watch, by the time she heard the sound of a big motor vehicle chugging along the narrow country lane.

When Bob stopped, he called, 'Hello, lass. What are you doing here? Come to collect the money for Horace?'

'No, he's coming down for it later. I wanted to ask you for a lift into Swindon. I need to find a job.'

'Horace was saying you might be staying with them for a while, you being friendly with their Frank, like.'

She decided to stick as close to the truth as she could. 'They hope so, but I'm not courting Frank. He's not my type.'

Bob nodded. 'Sensible of you. I know Janet thinks the world of him, but he's a bit of a rough sort, that one is. He knocks around with people I'd not like my son to call friends.' He tapped the side of his nose. 'I don't say anything to Horace and Janet, but you stay away from him, girl. His

68

type will thump a wife as soon as look at her. What sort of life is that for a woman?'

She was surprised Bob would say this to her. 'I agree.'

'Ah. I thought you was a sensible lass.'

When they got to the outskirts of Swindon, Bob dropped her off at a bus stop, then rumbled away down the road.

She felt very alone as she stood there, and nervous of running into Frank. In fact, she was starting to wonder if she'd be better moving to another town. Only, she knew Swindon and didn't really want to leave it. And after all, Frank could hardly attack her in the street, could he? She'd just have to be a bit careful till he accepted that she wasn't going to marry him.

And if that lost her the curtain-making things stored in the shed at the farm, well, better lose money than lose your freedom by marrying a brutal man.

She deposited her big squashy bag in the left-luggage office at the station, and trudged the streets looking for work. She went into shops where she was known to ask if they'd heard about any jobs. Some insisted on making her a cup of tea which took time, but she didn't want to upset them.

Just as she'd given up hope, she saw a job sign outside one of the big pubs that did meals for working men. It wasn't a very good job: in the kitchens clearing up, washing dishes, peeling vegetables as needed. But beggars couldn't be choosers and it might see her through for a while.

'The kitchen hand has gone and volunteered for the army. The dratted fool might have waited till the war got going,' the manager grumbled. 'He just up and left without giving notice. Still, it'll be cheaper hiring a woman. Ten shillings a week.'

Phoebe didn't like the looks of the man and these words annoyed her. 'I'm going to need more than that, because I'll have to pay for lodgings. You pay a man more, after all.'

'You can live in. A couple of the other women do. There's space in the attics, plenty of beds and bedding up there, as much food as you can eat, what with kitchen leftovers . . . and ways of earning a bit extra.'

The way his eyes flickered over her breasts made her take a quick step backwards and shake her head. 'No, thanks. I don't think it'd suit me to live in. I'll look elsewhere.'

'Sure?'

'Very sure.' She thought he was going to touch her and jerked back again.

'Please yourself. But jobs don't grow on trees, you know, not jobs with accommodation provided.'

She shuddered as she walked outside. Men like him seemed to be popping up everywhere lately, she couldn't understand why. She didn't encourage them, nor did she dress in a way that would make people think she was free and easy.

Of course she had to bump into Frank when she hurried outside without checking first, didn't she? The last person she wanted to see till she'd found a job and lodgings.

He barred her way when she would have nodded and walked on. 'What the hell are you doing in Swindon?'

'Looking for work.'

'You don't need to find work. You can stay at the farm.'

'I do need to work. I like to earn my own way in the world.'

'Then I'll find you something to do.'

'I'd rather find my own job.' A clock outside a jeweller's shop caught her eye. 'I have to get on now, before the shops close.'

'Where are you staying?'

She hesitated, but didn't want him finding her somewhere to sleep. He was too big, too . . . overpowering. 'Next door to the shop, with my old neighbours. I left some of my things there.'

He followed her gaze to the clock. 'Dammit. I have to meet someone. Look, I'll collect you from your neighbours and take you out to tea somewhere nice. We'll talk about a job then.'

She nodded and hoped her smile was convincing, but the look he gave her made her shiver. *That sort of look*. She didn't want his help, didn't want to be in his power. But where was she going to sleep if she didn't go to Mrs Harby?

She walked round the rest of Regent Street, but there were no other jobs advertised in shop windows. She hesitated about where to go next. Should she go to the Harbys' and sleep on their sofa? No, Frank would be coming there to look for her.

Perhaps she should find some lodgings and carry on searching the next day? Yes, that would be safer. She was careful with her money and had a savings bank account, as well as the banknotes from the Steins, which she was going to stitch into the lining of her handbag as soon as she could buy some stronger needles and thread of the right colour. She'd only use them in an emergency, though, and if she did, she'd pay her former employers back after the war was over.

Yes, that was what she'd do next, find a room. It was getting late.

She stopped walking for a moment, still not sure she was doing the right thing. If she got a job in Swindon, she was bound to bump into Frank regularly. Surely he'd get tired of pestering her if she didn't give him any encouragement?

She shivered. Would he, though? He'd made her feel nervous today, as if he was intending to take over her life by force if necessary. But she didn't want to go anywhere else. It was daunting to think of being on your own in a strange town where you didn't know a single person and couldn't even find your way around.

And what was she doing standing in a shop doorway like an idiot? She'd noticed a small hotel near the station which advertised itself as a 'family hotel' and had a vacancies sign in the window. She'd try there. It wasn't too far from the station.

Even that wasn't easy. The lady behind the counter studied her, eyes narrowed. 'On your own, are you?'

'Yes. I lost my job when my employers moved away. I'm looking for work.'

'Where's your luggage?'

'At the station, in the left-luggage office.'

'Shouldn't a young woman of your age be staying with family?'

'I don't have any family, only some cousins who live out on a farm. There are no jobs there, so I've come back into Swindon.'

'Who were you working for?'

She hesitated and saw suspicion grow on the woman's face, so told the truth. 'I was working for Mr and Mrs Stein. They're Austrians not Germans, but they were taken into custody because they're foreigners, so I'm out of work.'

Expecting to be told there were no rooms, she was given a smile instead. 'Ah. I thought your face looked familiar, but I couldn't place you. The Steins made the new curtains for the hotel sitting room last year. They did a lovely job of it, too. I agree the government has to be careful with foreigners, but

I can't imagine *them* harming anyone. All right. I'll give you a room. I'm Mrs Falshaw, by the way.'

Phoebe let out her breath in a whoosh. 'Oh, thank goodness! It's getting a bit late to be wandering the streets looking for a room.'

Mrs Falshaw reached for a key. 'No men allowed in the bedrooms, mind.'

'I don't have a boyfriend. Do you do meals?'

'No. But I'll provide you with a pot of tea and two biscuits for sixpence and there's a shop on the corner which stays open till nine. They'll do you a sandwich and they usually have some little cakes.'

'Thanks. I'm very grateful to you.'

'That's all right. I don't like to think of a decent young woman walking the streets. I'll have to ask you for payment in advance, though.'

Phoebe paid the money and was taken up to a small but clean room and provided with a ewer of cold water to wash in.

'Hot water is twopence extra.'

'I'd rather save my pennies and use cold, thank you. What time does the left-luggage office close, do you know?'

'It's open till midnight. Come to the desk when you want your pot of tea, but make it before half past nine. We close the hotel at ten.'

It was lovely to have a quiet room and some time to simply sit without having to chat. After a while, Phoebe realised the shadows were lengthening and the sun had started to go down. She'd better go and buy something to eat before the corner shop closed.

The shop owner was very obliging and made her a ham sandwich.

'We get quite a few people coming in at this time for something to eat,' the woman said, obviously in a chatty mood. 'Off the trains, usually. We don't often have much bread left over by the end of the evening.'

'It must give you a long working day, though.'

'I don't mind. I put my feet up for an hour in the afternoon and leave things to my husband. There you are. A shilling with the bun.'

Outside Phoebe was tempted to sit in a small public garden nearby for a few moments, enjoying the cool evening air. She saw a man come into the garden and tensed, ready to get up and run, but he chose another bench to sit on and didn't even glance in her direction once he'd sat down. He was a bit older than her, quite good-looking, though rather thin. She liked his face, which had an intelligent look to it.

After a while, she decided she'd better get back to the hotel and stood up.

Someone called from the street. 'Phoebe? Is that you?'

Oh, no! It was Frank. Why did she keep bumping into him?' She watched him amble across, not hurrying, but still making her feel like prey being hunted.

'Mrs Falshaw said you'd gone to the corner shop.'

'Why would she tell you anything about me?'

'Because I went round asking at places where you might have found a room. I was worried about you. Your old neighbours haven't seen you. Why did you lie to me?'

'Because I want to find my own job, make my own life.'

'Sit down. I need to talk to you.'

'I don't want to talk to you, Frank. I'm tired and I'm going to bed.'

In spite of her protests and struggles, he took hold of her

arm and dragged her to the nearest bench, sitting her down on it forcibly. 'I'm *not* having you wandering around this part of town on your own at night.'

'It has nothing to do with you whether I *wander* or not.'

'Oh, yes, it does. I promised Horace and Mum I'd keep an eye on you. They're worried about you, what with the war and everything. Anyway, I've found you a job and you can start tomorrow.'

'Doing what?'

'Working in a laundry.'

'I don't want to work in a laundry.'

'It's just temporary till we get married.'

She gaped at him. 'Who said we're getting married?'

'I told you before. I know I should have asked you properly but I realised when I took you and those curtain materials out to the farm how well we'd suit. You're a clever woman and pretty with it, and you haven't been going with anyone else. I'm going to need a wife like you after the war, and it makes sense for us to get married straight away, because the married men won't be called up yet. By the time they are, I'll have worked out how to avoid going into the army.'

Was this his idea of a marriage proposal? Well, it wasn't hers. She was so astonished by his arrogance that she couldn't speak for a moment, then she bounced to her feet. 'We are *not* getting married, Frank – not now, not ever. You aren't my type, and anyway, I don't want to marry anyone.'

He gave her a sneering smile. 'Of course you want to get married. All women do. They need a breadwinner.'

So she said it bluntly. 'I've been trying to be polite, but the truth is, I don't want to marry *you*, Frank. I don't think we'd suit at all.'

He scowled at her. 'You'll get used to the idea.'

'I won't! I don't even like you to touch me.'

His expression grew ugly. 'You'll get used to that, too. Women do, once they're broken in.'

'No, I won't. I'm *not* marrying you.'

'You'd better, because if you *don't* agree to marry me, you won't be able to find a job in Swindon at all. I've worked hard to make useful connections in the town, and that includes the police. I shan't hesitate to make things uncomfortable for you.'

She could only gape at him.

He gave her a nasty smirk of a smile. 'When I want something, Phoebe, I find a way to get it. Always.'

He was so confident of himself, she began to get seriously worried. He didn't really have the power to stop her getting a job, did he? Then she looked at his face and shivered at how confident he looked. 'If I can't get a job in Swindon, I'll go elsewhere. I am *not* going to marry you, Frank.'

He was on his feet now, facing her. 'You will, you know. I'll be a good provider, you won't find better. But you'll have to learn to obey me, Phoebe. A man is master in his own home.'

'You can be as masterful as you like, but it's not going to be with me. Now, leave me alone.' She turned to walk away, but he grabbed her and dragged her back.

'I reckon I'd better make you mine now, then you'll *have* to marry me.' He pulled her into the shadows and began grinding his face against hers in a rough kiss, running his hands over her body, pinching and nipping.

She began to fight back in earnest, trying all the tricks she'd heard of for dealing with cheeky fellows and yelling for help. But Frank was so big and much stronger than her, she felt like a butterfly caught by a big cat. He put one big meaty hand over her mouth to stop her calling for help.

Suddenly the grip on her eased and Frank cried out in shock.

It took her a minute to realise what was going on. The man who'd been sitting on a nearby bench had grabbed Frank and pulled him off her.

Frank swung his fist, but the man dodged the blow and clipped Frank on the side of the head.

Phoebe was afraid someone was going to get hurt and shouted, 'Stop it! Stop it now!'

But Frank had an ugly look on his face and he punched the fellow in the chest. Only, once again, his opponent dodged the full force of the blow.

Running footsteps made her turn round to see a policeman coming across the garden to join them. 'Oh, thank goodness!'

'What's going on here?'

'This fellow attacked me for no reason,' Frank said at once.

Phoebe gasped at this lie. 'He did not. It was you who attacked me and this man came to my aid.'

'Don't tell lies, Phoebe, just because we quarrelled. We're walking out, Officer, and she got upset with me.'

'How are you—'

The policeman held up one hand and said, 'Quiet, please. Now, miss. Do you know this man?' He indicated Frank.

'Yes. He's my cousin's stepson. But I'm *not* walking out with him. He wants to but I won't. He grabbed hold of me and started pawing me. I was trying to get away and calling for help, and this man kindly came to my rescue.' She turned to the stranger. 'I can't thank you enough.'

'I don't like to see men forcing themselves on women.'

Frank glared at him. 'I wasn't forcing her. It was just a lovers' quarrel. Mind your own bloody business or you'll regret it.'

The policeman got in between them. 'Now, sir. Calm down, if you please. She'll come round.'

'*I will not come round!*' Phoebe shouted at the top of her voice. 'Leave me alone, Frank Hapton. I'm going back to my lodgings to get a good night's sleep and I don't ever want to see you or speak to you again.'

Into the silence, the stranger said quietly, in an educated voice, 'Shall I walk you back, miss? Perhaps you can calm this fellow down, Officer.'

Frank jerked forward, but the policeman was almost as big and much more muscular. 'I think you've done enough for tonight, sir. Leave her to calm down and talk to her more gently tomorrow. You won't get anywhere by forcing a woman.'

The look Frank gave her, the way he bunched his hands into fists, made her feel afraid of what he'd do next, but he breathed deeply and let his hands fall. 'You're right, Officer.'

The policeman looked at Phoebe. 'You go straight to your lodgings, miss. We don't want any more trouble.'

As if she'd started this, she thought indignantly. She turned and walked away. The stranger fell in beside her.

'My name's Corin McMinty. I've been visiting relatives and I'm catching the last train to London. I'll walk back with you, but I promise you that you'll be quite safe with me.'

She believed him, liked his quiet voice with its educated tone. Though he had an Irish name, there was no sign of an Irish accent. 'I'm Phoebe Sinclair and I'm *not* walking out with Frank.'

'He seems pretty determined to marry you.'

She sighed. 'Yes. I don't know what to do about it. He won't take no for an answer and he knows a lot of people in Swindon, so he says he can stop me finding a job. He only decided to marry me recently.'

'Is there a particular reason for that, apart from the fact that you're very pretty?'

She glanced sideways, but he wasn't looking at her in that way, hadn't even spoken as if he was offering her a compliment, only stating a fact. 'I inherited some things he wants to get hold of. And he thinks I'll be useful to him as a wife because I speak nicely and look presentable.'

'Some people do marry for those reasons.'

'Not if they dislike the other person.'

'No. Definitely not.' After a few more steps, he asked quietly, 'Have you thought of leaving Swindon and going to live somewhere else? If that fellow can't find you, you can get on with your life in peace.'

They'd reached a corner and instead of crossing the road she stopped, her thoughts in a tangle and only one thing clear. 'I didn't want to leave Swindon. Even though I don't have any close family now, everyone I know is here. But I think you're right. I'll have to go.'

'How are you going to get away? A man as determined as that might try to stop you.'

Mr McMinty was very perceptive. They said an outsider could sometimes see more than the person in the thick of things. 'Yes. He will definitely try to stop me leaving. What on earth am I going to do?'

'Why don't you leave tonight? I doubt he'll be expecting that.'

The words seemed to echo around her, making so much sense. 'That might do it. But where would I go?'

'There's a train to London leaving just after midnight. I'm catching it, actually. Why don't you take that?'

'I've never even been to London. I wouldn't know where to go. And is it easy to get work there?'

'Actually, there's a hostel for young women quite near the station. My aunt and some of her friends run it specially for girls new from the country. They'll take you in, whatever the time of day, and they're very respectable, I promise. You'd be quite safe with them.'

She studied his face. She believed him, trusted him, was surprised that fate was suddenly helping her, instead of seeming against her.

'Do you need to get your luggage from the hotel first?' He glanced up at a clock outside a shop. 'We'll have to hurry, though.'

'I don't need to go back to the hotel at all. I left my bag at the station. I was going to pick it up after I'd eaten my sandwich.'

'We'd better keep our eyes open for that fellow as we walk to the station.'

'I know a back way through some alleys.'

Even so, when they came out of the alley, she saw Frank standing down the road, watching her hotel.

'Let me put my arm round you.'

Mr McMinty did so and as they hurried into the station, she nestled against him, praying she was hidden from view.

She moved to one side as soon as they were out of sight of the street. 'Can you buy my ticket for me, Mr McMinty? I've got the money but I don't want to be seen.'

'Yes. And give me your left-luggage ticket. I'll get that for you, too. Wait for me over there, behind that trolley full of boxes.'

She didn't relax till they were on the train, then realised they were sitting in first class. 'How much was my fare?'

'Let me pay for you. I'm not short of money. I have a sister about your age. I'd not like to think of her on her own in the world. You keep what money you have.'

She hesitated, then nodded. 'Thank you. I'll accept it as a loan. But you must tell me where you live and I'll pay you back once I'm settled in a job.'

'It's my pleasure to help you.' He laughed. 'And I don't know where I'll be living. I'm in the army and I've been summoned back to join my regiment tomorrow.'

'I'd still rather pay you back.'

'You can write to me care of my aunt. Let her know where you'll be. Perhaps I'll catch up with you again when I come back to London. I have a feeling that helping you will bring me luck, keep me safe.'

What a strange thing to say! But if he wanted to believe that, she'd not stop him. It must be hard for men, having to face battles and death, or having to kill others. If the war went on for too long, so many young men would be killed.

She couldn't believe nations like Britain and Germany, with all their well-educated statesmen, wouldn't find a way to compromise once they'd had a few months of war. This was the twentieth century, not the Dark Ages.

Chapter Six

Phoebe woke with a start as someone shook her gently. She sat up, her heart pounding in panic when she didn't recognise her surroundings. For a moment or two, the person she had been cuddled against seemed a complete stranger, then everything that had happened slipped into place.

'You fell asleep,' he said. 'I didn't like to disturb you.' He eased his arm from behind her, moving it about as if it was stiff.

She was horrified. 'I'm so sorry. You should have woken me, Mr McMinty.'

'Why? I fell asleep too. And I thought we'd agreed to call each other by our first names.'

She could feel herself blushing. They were the only occupants of the compartment, cocooned in the intimacy of a poorly lit railway carriage rattling along through the tunnels of darkness. She'd felt so comfortable with him, they'd chatted like old friends, exchanging information about their families and sharing their thoughts about the world.

She'd been surprised to find that Corin was a career

soldier, stationed in London, an officer, of course. His name meant 'spear', which seemed appropriate, because for all his gentleness, he had an air of command. They hadn't spoken of the war, however, because he'd guided the conversation away from that subject every time, as if he didn't want to focus on it.

Well, she didn't want to think about it, either.

Now, in the grey light of morning, she felt confused, worried that she might have revealed too much about herself. But Corin was smiling so warmly at her, she couldn't have offended him, so she settled back against the seat and relaxed again.

'I woke a few times in the night,' he said, 'and each time it was because we were stopping at places not on the usual schedule. I suppose that's because of the war. The train will get into London much later than usual, which will be more convenient for you. I woke you because I recognised the last station we passed through. We're nearly there now, about ten minutes away from Paddington, unless we stop again. Do you want to go and tidy yourself up?'

She nodded and made her way along the corridor of the train to the lavatory, which was much nicer than the ones in third class. She stared at herself in the mirror, horrified to see how tumbled her hair was, how her cheeks were still flushed with sleep.

She worked quickly, knowing he would need to use the facilities, too, and by the time she got back to the compartment, she was tidy again.

He greeted her with, 'You looked prettier with your hair down.' Then he chuckled. 'You do blush easily. Aren't you used to compliments?'

'No.'

'You will be. I'm sure you'll have young men queuing up to squire you around London.'

She didn't know what to say to that. She'd never had the time or opportunity to flirt and joke. At first she'd been too busy looking after her mother to fuss about her own appearance, then she'd been too busy learning about curtain making and cleaning the shop every evening.

'My turn.' He got up and strode off down the corridor.

He had a long, lean body and walked easily, as if he was fit and comfortable with himself. She liked to watch him move. She'd never met a man like him. But kind as he was, she didn't like owing anyone money, so she would pay him back once she was settled. At the moment, with the unknown problems of London to face, she didn't like to spend a halfpenny more than she had to. She wanted to keep something to fall back on, just in case she couldn't find a job for a while.

It seemed a long time before Corin came back, but it was only a few minutes. He smelt of soap and had combed his hair neatly into place, but he needed a shave. He sat opposite her this time and she missed having him by her side.

How silly she was getting! She'd probably never see him again after today.

'Soon be there. You'll like my aunt Beaty. She's a jolly old stick.'

'I hope she can help me find a job.'

'If anyone can, it's her. Look, we're just coming into Paddington station. It looks strange with hardly anyone around, when it's usually so busy. Like a ghost station. My aunt won't be awake yet. Let's have something to eat at a cafe I know. We'll take a taxi because it's about half a mile away from the station and we've both got heavy bags.'

They threaded their way through the milk churns that the porters were unloading from the train. Most of the other passengers were men and Phoebe seemed to be the only woman from the first-class carriages. People looked tired and no one was chatting. There was only the sound of footsteps and the metallic clank of milk churns banging against one another as they were hauled off the train and rolled to one side.

Corin let a porter take their luggage, though he could have carried it easily. He saw Phoebe's surprise at this and whispered, 'He looks as if he needs the tip.'

The porter found them a motor taxi and when Corin slipped him a coin, beamed and said, 'Thank you *very* much, sir.'

She thought that was very kind. It must be nice to be able to help people. Then she realised she was one of the people Corin was helping. She usually managed on her own, but this time she'd needed it.

The taxi took them to an elegant cafe with a sign saying *Lamb's*, the sort of place she'd never have dared go into on her own. 'Are cafes usually open at this hour in London?'

'This one is. It prides itself that it never closes, night or day.'

An older man approached them. 'Good morning, Captain McMinty.'

'Hello, Gus. This is Miss Sinclair, a friend of mine. Phoebe, this is Gus Lamb, who owns the cafe. Table for two, please, then a nice big breakfast. We're going to visit my aunt Beaty but she won't be awake yet and I'm ravenous.'

'How is Her Ladyship?'

Phoebe blinked in shock. *Her Ladyship?*

When the waiter had taken their coats and shown them to a table, Corin turned to her with a rueful smile. 'Don't look at me like that. I can't help it if my aunt married a lord. *I* wasn't born into the nobility. Nor was she, come to that.'

No, but he was obviously from a family with money. He had that air, and tossed tips to people as if they meant nothing to him. 'I've never even spoken to a member of the nobility.'

'Well, don't start bowing and scraping to my aunt. She hates that.' He grinned. 'Look, Beaty was an actress, which our family didn't approve of. She was doing quite well, destined for fame and fortune, then she met Podge and that was it. Love at first sight. She was his second wife and he was much older than her, but they were very happy together.'

'My mother said it was the same with my father. Love at first sight. But *she* married beneath her and her parents were furious, wouldn't have anything to do with her after that.'

'You didn't think of asking their help?'

'No. They never replied to her letters, not even after I was born, though she wrote to them every year. They're dead now. Dad was a miner, you see. He hated it, but it was the only work available when he was growing up. He was killed in an accident underground.'

'I'm sorry you lost your father so horribly. At least your parents had some happy years together. I like to hear about people falling in love. So many married people I've met seem indifferent to one another, or worse, like that fellow in Swindon who wanted you even though you didn't like him.'

The food arrived, so much of it that Phoebe was sure half of it would be wasted, but seeing Corin eat like a starving man made her feel suddenly hungry too.

As a waiter cleared the table, Corin looked at his watch. 'We could make a move now. It's six o'clock. Someone will be up at the hostel.'

'Does your aunt live there?'

'She does at the moment. When Podge died last year, he left her well provided for, with a life tenancy of his family's dower house in the country. But she doesn't get on with Lester, the son from Podge's first marriage who inherited the estate, so she lives in London most of the time. She keeps a maid at the dower house, though, and most of her possessions. Sometimes she sends sickly young women there for a holiday. Lester hates that. He's a dreadful snob.'

Corin paid for the meal before she could stop him and she didn't like to make a fuss. Picking up Phoebe's bag as well as his own, he led the way out of the cafe, letting the waiter hail another taxi for them.

She envied him the ease of accepting help from people and the way he didn't need to count his pennies. But when he wasn't chatting to her, he sometimes looked faintly unhappy, as if he had troubles of his own.

Something to do with the war, perhaps, if he was a career soldier.

What else could it be?

The hostel was a tall house in a quiet street near Paddington station, close enough for them to catch a glimpse as they drove to it of the work being done to build what Corin told her would be a fourth train shed for the station, which already seemed huge to her.

'The London stations are getting busier every year, so they're expanding,' he explained.

She nodded but felt too nervous to chat as they stood waiting for someone to open the front door. She was glad when he didn't seem to expect an answer.

What if Corin's aunt turned her away? Where would she go then? How would she survive in this huge city which made her feel such a timid country mouse?

The door was opened by an older woman with iron-grey hair, drawn back into a severe bun. She was wearing no-nonsense modern clothes with the more practical shorter skirts.

'Master Corin!' she exclaimed. 'Captain McMinty, I should say.'

'Hello, Ruth. I prefer you calling me Master Corin. Makes me feel young again.' He gestured towards Phoebe. 'I've brought you a young woman who's in need of help. She's homeless, escaping from a bully and knows no one in London. Phoebe, this is my aunt's housekeeper and, dare I say it, her dearest friend.'

'It isn't right to call me Her Ladyship's friend.'

'Even if it's the truth?'

Ruth gave him a tight smile and stopped arguing, turning her attention back to the stranger.

He didn't speak again until Ruth had studied Phoebe carefully and nodded. It was as if she'd passed some sort of test, though of what, she wasn't sure.

'Come inside properly, miss. No need to hover by the door as if you're going to run away.'

Corin grinned at this. 'Is my aunt up yet, Ruth?'

'Of course I am,' a low, musical voice called from the first landing. 'Dear boy! How lovely to see you.'

He ran up the stairs and gave her a big hug.

Phoebe watched them enviously.

Then he looked down and gestured towards her. 'I've found you another young woman in need of help. Come and meet Phoebe.'

His aunt seemed to drift down the stairs, looking elegant, even at this early hour. Her hair was silver, though her face was youthful. Phoebe's mother had gone white at a young age, due to her red hair, she'd always said. Though she hadn't been a real redhead, just 'foxy-coloured' as they'd joked, unlike her daughter's rich auburn colour.

Phoebe had a sudden stab of desperate longing for her mother. Just one more chat, one more piece of advice . . . one more hug. She realised his aunt had said something. 'Oh, sorry. I missed that. I'm a bit tired.'

'I said, we'll have a cup of tea and you can tell me all about what brought you to London, Miss Sinclair.'

'Call her Phoebe. I do,' Corin said.

Her Ladyship raised one eyebrow as if to ask her visitor whether that was all right and Phoebe nodded, appreciating the courtesy.

He pulled out his pocket watch and checked the time. 'I'm afraid I have to report to the War Office at nine o'clock, so I can't stay long.'

A shadow of sadness passed across his aunt's face. 'This horrible war. It's got its claws into you already. Promise you'll stay safe, my lovely boy.'

He raised her hand to his lips, a theatrical gesture that seemed natural with his elegant aunt. 'I'll do my best.'

They stared at one another for a few moments, then Her Ladyship said, 'This way, dear.'

Phoebe followed them into a small, cluttered sitting room

at the rear of the hall. Tea was brought in by Ruth within minutes, by which time Corin had explained to his aunt how he and Phoebe had met.

'I'd be very grateful if you could help me, Your Ladyship,' Phoebe said when he'd finished. 'I'll try to find a job quickly and not be a nuisance.'

'Oh, I'll help you find a job, but we won't rush into any old job. I like to place all my girls carefully in jobs where they'll be happy, so I need to get to know them first. People can get lost in a big city. I've never forgotten how scared I was when I first started in a London show. I had to fight for my virtue more than once.'

Phoebe stared to hear her say that so frankly.

Her Ladyship's voice softened. 'I do understand what it's like. But please don't "ladyship" me. Call me Beaty. It's my name, after all.'

'I can't call you by your first name!'

Beaty grinned. 'I won't answer unless you do. I don't use Lady Potherington, either, now. I only put up with it for my husband's sake. Well, who would want to be called such a stupid-sounding surname? Look at the nickname my darling got from it. Podge! Of all the ridiculous names. He wasn't at all podgy. *I* always called him Reggie. So . . . I'm Beaty now, eh?'

'Well, all right . . . Beaty.'

'Good. Now, you must both be hungry.'

Corin shook his head. 'I took her to Lamb's.'

'What a treat! They do the fluffiest omelettes in town.'

He drained his cup of tea and stood up. 'I've got to go, I'm afraid. I need to shave and change before I report in. Phoebe, don't forget your promise to keep in touch. Aunt Beaty, don't lose sight of her.'

'I'll see you out, dear.'

He and his aunt disappeared into the hall, and their voices were too low to make out what they were saying. Not that Phoebe would have tried to eavesdrop.

She leant back in her chair, feeling tired, but as Corin had said, she did feel safe here. And welcome, too. She had been very lucky to meet him.

In the hall, Corin said abruptly, 'Look. I have to tell you, Phoebe interests me. I want to get to know her better. There's something about her that I—' He broke off and shrugged.

His aunt looked at him in surprise. 'I never thought I'd hear you say that again.'

'I didn't think I'd say it, either.'

'She's not of our class.'

'No, but she's intelligent. I feel really comfortable with her, as if I've known her all my life.'

'It happens. If the feeling persists, don't let anything stop you pursuing the attraction.'

He squeezed her hand, knowing she was thinking of herself and Podge. 'There's something else. I feel as if Phoebe's lucky for me. I'm going to war. A lot of men will be killed. She seems like a guiding star who'll see me through it all safely. Does that sound foolish?'

'No more foolish than a lot of other things in a world idiotic enough to go to war instead of talking things out. Besides, we both know our family has these feelings – intuition, some call it. I've known my mother foretell things no one could possibly have guessed, and about complete strangers, too. They call it being psychic these days. It's as good a word for the gift as any. So if you feel there's something special about Phoebe, well, go for it.'

'I shall. But, given the war, it may be hard to keep in touch with her. Will you help me there? It'll be easier for her to stay in touch with you. I'm being transferred and I don't know where I'm being posted or what exactly I'll be doing.'

She kissed his cheek. 'Of course I will help, darling boy. Unless your young lady doesn't improve on acquaintance.'

'I'm not afraid of that. We spent time chatting last night, talking about real life, real feelings.' He chuckled. 'She doesn't know how to flirt and turns scarlet at the slightest compliment. And yet she's so pretty, you'd think she'd have grown used to men's attentions.'

'What about the chap you rescued her from? Who was he?'

'Her mother's cousin's stepson, someone she doesn't like. Frank Hapton, he's called. He won't have the faintest idea what's happened to her now, will he? And if she's got any sense, she'll not go back to Swindon again.'

The clock in the hall chimed half past seven and Corin sighed. 'I really have to go. I mustn't be late for the war, must I?'

When Beaty came back to join her, Phoebe jerked upright. She'd nearly fallen asleep, felt utterly exhausted.

Her hostess sat down beside her on the sofa and patted her hand. 'My nephew's left now and I shall worry about him.'

'I shall too,' Phoebe admitted. 'He's a lovely person. He's been so kind to me.'

'He likes you too.'

She could feel herself going red.

Beaty smiled. 'He said you blushed at compliments.'

'I can't help it, Your Ladyship.'

'Don't try to. It's charming. And we agreed that you'd call me Beaty. Now, you need a rest, but I must tell you a little about this hostel first. I started it to help girls on their own in London, and to give myself something worthwhile to do after I lost dear old Podge. We'll provide you with accommodation and meals, and help you to find a job. I'm afraid we're a bit crowded. We've had to fit four beds to most rooms, because there are so many girls needing this sort of help. Luckily for you, I have a vacancy.'

'That's wonderful. I can pay for my keep.'

'Not till you find a job – though you can help around the house. Those not working usually do.' She stood up. 'Now, let's get you to bed before you fall asleep sitting upright.'

They stopped in the hall for Phoebe to collect her bag and Beaty led the way up the stairs.

She tapped on a door and called, 'Are you decent?'

A young woman with wildly curly black hair opened it. 'We're just starting to get up.'

'I have a newcomer needing a bed. Phoebe, meet Alice, Eleanor and Maude. Girls, Phoebe's exhausted. She travelled up to London overnight. You can question her about her background later.'

She pointed to the only unoccupied bed, which was piled with clothes and said with mock severity, 'Remove those at once. She needs somewhere to sleep. Anyway, if Ruth sees a mess like that, she'll read you a lecture.'

They scrambled to reclaim their garments. One pile included some very pretty lingerie, of a sort that Phoebe had never seen before. Knickers were edged in broderie anglaise to match a waist petticoat and camisole top.

One of the young women blushed and snatched up a small pile from the end. 'Sorry. I was so tired last night I forgot to put my knicker liner in my laundry bag.'

'That's all right.' That set of clothing was like her own, dull and old-fashioned, which was a relief.

Within five minutes, Phoebe had undressed behind a screen and was snuggling down in bed. She tried to listen to their conversation, wanting to find out about her new roommates, but couldn't keep her eyes open.

She was woken at two o'clock that afternoon by Ruth.

'Best you get up now, Phoebe, or you'll never sleep tonight.'

'Oh. Yes. Sorry.'

'Nothing to apologise for. You needed a sleep, so we kept out of your way. Now, there's a bathroom at each end of the corridor. No taking baths in the mornings, people are in too much of a hurry to get off to work, but you can book a bath for the evening any time. You can have a bath now, if you like. There's no one else needing a bathroom. Here's your towel. You'll get a clean one every week. Don't forget to wipe the bath out afterwards.'

'I won't.'

'When you're ready, Beaty would like to chat to you and I'll bring you something to eat, to put you on till dinner. This is your chest of drawers, and you can hang up anything that needs it in the wardrobe by the window. You'll be sharing it with Maude. Don't go back to sleep, now.'

She whisked out and Phoebe stretched, enjoying the comfort of the bed and the fine cotton sheets. Then she got up and took Ruth's advice by having a quick bath in a lovely modern bathroom which had an indoor toilet and a big mirror over the washbasin. Such luxury!

She unpacked quickly. Well, there wasn't much to unpack, was there? She'd had to leave some of her clothes and other possessions behind.

Beaty called out to come in when someone knocked at the sitting room door. She was sitting near the window at a desk strewn with papers and neatly slit envelopes, and she was glad of the interruption, being tired of office work, necessary as it was.

'Shall I come back later, Lady – I mean, Beaty?'

'No, dear. I'd welcome a break. Sit down and tell me what jobs you've had.'

'I did any old job while I was looking after Mum: scrubbing, laundry, ironing, picking for farmers. I've worked in a curtain shop for the past two years and I was learning curtain making.'

As she explained about her mother and the Steins, Beaty saw tears well in her eyes. 'Give me the full names of your Austrian friends and I'll see if I can locate them. I may be able to get them sent somewhere a little less spartan, though it'll probably take time. Do you want to find more shop work?'

'I hadn't really thought. I don't mind what I do, actually. Things are bound to change with the war, aren't they? Some of the men's jobs will be vacant.'

'Unfortunately, yes. People who say it'll be over in a few months don't know their history.' Beaty sighed. 'I shall worry about Corin and I have other young relatives who'll be caught up in it, as well. But I must admit he's my favourite nephew.'

Phoebe opened her mouth as if to comment, then shut it again, looking down at her skirt instead.

Daren't talk about him, Beaty thought. Is she interested in him as a man or not? Perhaps she doesn't think there can be anything between them. Or perhaps I'm getting ahead of myself. After all, they only met yesterday. Though that's all it took with me and Podge.

'Well, let's get back to your needs, dear,' she said aloud. 'I think you need a few days to get used to London. I can show you round a few places, if you like.' She cocked her head, waiting for an answer.

'I can't ask you to do that.'

'Why not? I'll be out and about, and you can simply come with me. If there's some function or meeting I can't take you to, I'll send you home again or show you somewhere to wait for me. We'll have fun.' And she'd get to know Phoebe properly, see if she was worthy of Corin.

'Oh. Well, if you're sure, your l–um, Beaty, I mean. I'd love to do that.'

'I'm very sure. And one other thing. If you've ever wanted to do some other type of job, one you'll enjoy, now is the time to say. I know a lot of people, so I may be able to help you realise your ambition.'

'I've never even thought of finding a job because I enjoy it, only because I need to earn a living.' Phoebe hesitated. 'You're being very kind to a stranger.'

'I try to be kind to all the young women who come to this hostel. I think of them as my girls. I never had children, though I'd have liked to. Now I've lost Podge, having a lot of young people around me helps keep my spirits up. I still miss my husband very much.' She could see the understanding in

Phoebe's eyes and wasn't surprised by the next confidence.

'I still miss my mother, though it's over two years since she died.'

'Well, then. We can provide some company for one another as you get to know London. Now, go and have a look round the other rooms on this floor. There are two sitting rooms, a quiet room and a library. You can choose a book if you enjoy reading. Just write down what you've borrowed on the list. The evening meal is at seven o'clock.'

When Phoebe had left, Beaty stared thoughtfully at the door. Corin was right. The young woman was easy to talk to. You found yourself telling her things you didn't normally share with strangers.

There had to be a better job for someone like her than serving in a shop.

Especially if Corin continued to take an interest in her.

Beaty turned back to the desk, sighed at the sight of the papers, then paused, one hand stretched out to pick up an envelope, as an idea struck her.

Chapter Seven

Phoebe enjoyed getting to know London, and one week stretched into two. She helped in the house and went out and about with Beaty. It felt as if the country was hovering, as if the war hadn't really started, then one day her pleasure was marred by the sight of men in uniforms, marching or driving around, looking serious and busy.

One morning she was walking past Waterloo Station, on an errand for Beaty, when she saw a line of horse-drawn ambulances lined up outside. Like other passers-by, she slowed down to see what was happening.

'It's some poor wounded soldiers sent back from the war,' a plump, motherly woman told her. 'They'll bring out those who can walk first, then the men on stretchers. I saw another group arriving yesterday. They'll be taking them to hospitals in London first, but one of the orderlies told me they'll send most of them out to country hospitals tomorrow. Except for those who're badly wounded and need operations.'

'I hadn't expected this to happen so quickly,' Phoebe said. But of course, she should have. If the fighting had started, there would inevitably be casualties, even on the first day.

'They haven't wasted time hurting one another,' another woman said bitterly. 'I've a son in the army. He's just gone out there. I can't bear to see this.' Her voice broke and she hurried away.

'It's only the beginning,' an older man said gloomily. 'It'll be far worse than those damned Boer Wars, this one will, because the weapons have got nastier.'

Phoebe couldn't move on till she'd seen what was happening, and she soon found that the woman next to her was right. The walking wounded came out first, escorted by orderlies and a few young women.

'Those nurses look so young,' she exclaimed involuntarily.

'Bless you, they aren't nurses.'

'What are they, then? Those look like nurses' uniforms.'

'That's the uniform of the VADs, voluntary aid detachments, that stands for. They're nursing aides or they do other jobs as well, driving, cleaning, whatever's needed. This group are Red Cross VADs and they arrived not long ago to help out. They wear blue dresses with a red cross on the apron bib. See it?'

'Oh, yes. They look very smart, don't they?'

'Yes, they do. My cousin's youngest volunteered to be a VAD, but she's with St John. They wear grey dresses with a St John VAD armband. They're not as pretty.'

'Them lasses won't care whether they look pretty or not when they're dealing with blood and worse,' the gloomy man said, determined to look on the black side. 'I was an orderly. I'll never forget the things I saw.'

'Don't be so grumpy. That won't help us win the war,'

the plump woman scolded. 'The soldiers will care once they start getting better. Nothing like a pretty face to cheer a man up, whether he's young or old.'

Phoebe took her time walking back to the hostel, needing to think about what she'd seen. She couldn't get the sight of the injured men out of her mind and envied those helping them.

By the time she arrived, she was certain what she wanted to do, so went to see Beaty immediately. 'You asked me to consider what to do with my life. Well, while this war is on, I'd like to become a VAD. If they'll have me, that is.'

'You're sure about this? Are you any good at dealing with blood and gore, or scrubbing floors?'

'I've been scrubbing floors ever since I was big enough to do it because Mum was always sickly. I've also worked on farms, killing chickens, helping when they killed pigs. And I looked after my mother, who was helpless at the end.'

Beaty studied her face intently, then nodded. 'Well, volunteering to become a VAD is a very worthwhile thing. I'll take you to see my friend Rosemary. She'll advise you.'

'Thank you.' Phoebe hesitated, then gestured towards the desk. 'In the meantime, is there any way I can help you with the letters and deskwork? I can't help noticing that the papers are piling up and you're always so busy.'

'I think the papers on my desk breed overnight. There always seem to be twice as many in the morning.' She sighed. 'I've never been good at keeping up with letters, let alone doing accounts. I was thinking of asking you if you'd like to stay here and help me permanently, act as my secretary. You seem an intelligent sort of girl.' She cocked her head on one side, as if asking her young companion to consider this alternative.

Phoebe didn't have to think about that for long. 'I think I'm a more active person, Beaty. I like *doing* things better than dealing with paperwork. But if there's anything I can do, I'll be glad to help you till I find a job. You might like to consider asking Maude, though. She's not strong and she's finding her job in the shop very tiring physically.'

'That droopy little creature in the old-fashioned clothes?' Beaty grimaced.

'You could take her in hand. She's shy but she's not stupid. You'd be just the person to bring her appearance up to scratch.'

'Hmm. You may be right. It's worth a try.'

Phoebe went upstairs, feeling better than she had for a while. She wanted to serve her country, didn't see why men should be the only ones to do that. And she especially wanted to help the soldiers who were risking their lives.

Like Corin.

Ruth came to find her half an hour later. 'Captain McMinty's here to see you.'

'To see me? Not his aunt?'

'Beaty's gone out, so he asked for you. Men aren't allowed to come up here to the bedrooms, so I've put him in the sitting room. No one else is there at this time of day.'

'I wonder what he wants.'

'I asked. He wants to take you out for luncheon.'

'Oh.' Phoebe could feel herself blushing. 'Do you think I should go?'

'Oh, yes. He can be trusted to toe the line. I wouldn't advise it with some fellows, who're only after one thing.' She shook her head, smiling slightly. 'You aren't used to dealing with young men of any sort, are you?'

'No. I've never had time, let alone I never met anyone I was interested in.'

'Well, you'd better get used to fellows if you're going to help look after them as a VAD. They'll pester a pretty one like you.'

'Even if they're ill?'

'*Because* they're ill. They'll have nothing to think about except what's going on around them.'

'Oh.'

'It can be fun, you know, flirting. I may not look much now, but I had my share of followers and fun when I was younger. But I never wanted to get married.'

'Can I ask why not?'

'I was the oldest in my family. I'd helped raise six brothers and sisters, and I didn't want to raise any more children.'

Phoebe wanted children. One day. After the war. Oh, she did!

Corin looked up as Phoebe came into the sitting room to join him. He'd come to ask his aunt out to lunch, and when he found that Beaty was out, it had been an impulse to ask for Phoebe and invite her instead.

For a few moments he could only stare at her. She seemed far prettier than he remembered. 'I wondered if you'd like to go out to lunch with me? I'd enjoy some company.'

She hesitated, then gave in to temptation. 'Yes. I'd like that very much. You're looking awfully smart today, Captain.'

He stared down at his uniform. 'For what that's worth. They're sticklers on the officers presenting well. But things are changing rapidly at the moment. There are youngsters of eighteen coming out of school cadet units, who are starting off as second lieutenants and going straight into commanding men. That's not always a good thing.'

She gave him one of her long, level looks. 'You sound rather discouraged about it all.'

'To tell you the truth, I was thinking of leaving the army. I can't do that now, of course. Have to wait till the war's over.'

'You mentioned on the train that you don't always like the way things are done in the army.'

'Did I? Well, keep that to yourself now. It'd sound like treason to some of the high-ups.' He gestured towards the door. 'If you'd like to get your coat and hat, we could stroll to the restaurant. It's not far and I think the rain will hold off till later.'

When she rejoined him, wearing a very dowdy coat and a hat that wasn't much better, he smiled at her, feeling better merely for seeing her serious expression, clear grey eyes and that lovely russet hair. He'd met a lot of beautifully turned out, but insincere women, to his cost.

When they went out into the hall, Ruth called down from the landing, 'Wait a minute! I've got something for you.'

She ran down the stairs and took Phoebe's hat off before she could protest. 'Never wear that ugly thing again. You can keep this one. Beaty never wears it, because it doesn't flatter her, but it'll suit you.'

'I can't do that!'

Ruth held the old hat out of reach. 'If I didn't think you'd need this horrible thing when you're trudging around the countryside in all weathers, I'd stamp on it.'

Corin couldn't hold back any longer. He burst out laughing. 'I thought the old Ruth had been tamed.'

She winked at him. 'Not completely. Am I right about the hat?'

'Yes, definitely. Do keep it, Phoebe. Ruth used to be my aunt's dresser and she's really good at choosing clothes that flatter. You deserve better than that thing.' He offered his arm to her and they left the house.

As they began to walk along the street, she asked, 'Was the old hat really that bad?'

'I'm afraid so.'

'It wasn't my best hat. I had to leave some of my clothes behind when I ran away from the farm.'

'It wouldn't have mattered too much to me. The hat, I mean. Not as long as you continue to give me your lovely smiles.'

And of course that made her blush again.

Once they were seated in a quiet restaurant, he asked what she'd been doing with herself, desperate to talk about something other than the army.

'Learning to get around in London, with your aunt's help. It made me nervous at first, but I'm getting more used to it now. I've been thinking what I want to do with myself and I decided this morning that I'd like to join the VADs – if they'll have me, that is. Beaty says she'll help me get an interview.'

'A nursing aide? Are you sure?'

'It's not exactly nursing, because I'm not a trained nurse. It's helping nurses and patients with whatever they're trying to do, and even driving motor vehicles. I'd really like to learn to drive a car.'

'It'll be a bloody business, this war, and if you're attached to hospitals, you'll see some terrible things. There are other ways you could help, ways that wouldn't be as upsetting.'

She shook her head stubbornly, so he added, 'Modern weapons carve up soft human bodies in dreadful ways, Phoebe. How will you feel dealing with men who have no legs, because they've been blown off, or men whose faces are mangled?'

He heard her suck in her breath and wondered if he'd gone too far.

She answered quietly but firmly, 'I grew up near farms. I'm used to killing and dismembering animals. I'll cope. Someone has to do it, after all. Such men deserve the best we can offer them, don't you think?'

'You're an amazing woman.'

'*Me?* No, I'm not.' She fiddled with the food on her plate.

He changed the subject, though it was fun making her blush.

As they were finishing their dessert, he dared to ask her to write. 'They'll probably post me somewhere outside London before I go to the front. Will you write to me?'

'If you like.'

'I'd like it very much. And whatever happens to you or to me, you'll stay in touch? You can do that through my aunt.'

She nodded.

'I shall look forward to getting to know you better.' Beyond that, he wasn't prepared to go, as yet. There were hard times ahead. She shouldn't tie herself to a man whose future was so precarious.

Not only was she still finding her way in life, but the world was changing quickly around them. 'Don't cut off your lovely hair,' he said suddenly.

'Why not?'

'It's beautiful.'

'Red hair? I used to get called "Foxy" when I was little.'

'Your hair is auburn. Titian hair. Artists love it.'

'What a lovely compliment!' She fingered a strand of hair that had drifted free to caress her cheek.

A few years ago he'd believed he'd lost everything that mattered to him on a personal level. He hadn't coped well.

Perhaps he had been shown the way towards a new start. It felt like it, anyway.

When she got back, Phoebe decided to tackle her clothes. The other girls at the hostel had been urging her to bring her clothing up to date. She needed a few new garments, but would wait until she found out what she'd be doing before she bought anything. No use buying fashionable clothes if she was going to be working in the country.

The way the other girls talked about the world and men as they sewed together in the evenings was very enlightening. Some of them were very modern young women and others, like her, were fumbling into the new ways. Some were from comfortable backgrounds; others, like her, came from poorer families. But they all got on well together. Ruth and Beaty wouldn't have allowed any quarrels or spiteful behaviour, she was sure.

Phoebe had been wondering about having her hair bobbed. It'd be much easier to manage and wash. But remembering what Corin had said, she decided to leave it long. She shouldn't be thinking of pleasing him, but she consoled herself with the thought that it'd cost less to keep her hair long, because she wouldn't need to spend money on having it trimmed regularly.

She couldn't stop thinking about Corin, going over their conversations in her mind. He was above her in status, with a background so different, he couldn't be thinking of courting her seriously . . . could he? Only some of the things he said seemed like hints.

She waited for Beaty to say something disapproving about their outing, but her kind hostess only asked how it had gone.

'I hope you cheered him up.'

'Does he need cheering up?'

'Yes. He has done for a while.'

But Beaty didn't explain what she meant by that and Phoebe didn't like to ask too many questions about him.

She went back to her sewing after tea. She was shortening all her skirts. That would give her greater freedom when she was out walking, make her look more modern.

She wouldn't touch the Steins' money, of course, but she still felt a need to guard her own money, just in case she ever needed to get away, so hadn't bought any new clothes.

Oh, face it, you fool! she told herself. You're still afraid Frank will find you again. He knew a lot of people and she'd met some of them over the years, especially a couple of his closest friends, who'd visited the farm. If one of them came up to London and saw her, recognised her, she might be in trouble.

No, that would be stretching coincidence too far, and why should mere acquaintances recognise her now? She'd change her appearance and though you couldn't change your face, Frank didn't have a photo of her to show anyone to remind them.

Then she remembered that Cousin Janet did have a recent

photo of her. She loved collecting photos. But surely Frank wouldn't go to the length of getting hold of one from his mother and showing it around?

She tried to banish Frank from her mind, but even in the safety of the hostel, his shadow still lingered.

It only seemed to go away completely when she was with Corin.

The next day Beaty took her protégée to meet the lady in charge of the selection of VADs for the Red Cross in this part of London. Phoebe had the satisfaction of looking like a modern young woman now in her first shortened skirt, a woman capable of becoming a nursing aide or driving a car – or scrubbing a floor, if that was what they needed most.

Beaty touched the hat as they got out of their taxi. 'Ruth said she'd given that to you. I hope you've thrown that old felt pudding basin away. I don't think I've seen a more unflattering hat.'

'It was my mother's. I was saving money.'

Her hostess shuddered. 'Ugh. A young woman has a duty to make the best of herself.'

As they went into the building, she said, 'You'll have to wear a uniform if you're accepted. It's rather dull, all the young women dressing alike. Still, the white pinafores and caps brighten the blue dresses up, and look quite smart and professional, considering.'

Phoebe wondered what white pinafores would look like when they were worn to help nurse men with bad wounds. They didn't sound very practical.

The secretary stood up to greet them. 'Good morning,

Lady Potherington. How nice to see you again! Miss Rufford is expecting you. I'll show you in.'

'I do wish you'd at least call me Lady P,' Beaty grumbled. 'You know how I hate that name.'

'It wouldn't be right. This way.'

Phoebe hid a smile.

Rosemary Rufford was almost as beautiful as Beaty, and just as elegantly dressed. But she spoke far more crisply and her gaze was shrewd.

After introducing them, Beaty left Phoebe to speak for herself.

After only ten minutes of searching questions, Miss Rufford leant back and smiled at her. 'You're clearly a very suitable candidate, and we'll be happy to give you a trial, Miss Sinclair.'

'Thank you so much. I'll try not to let you down.'

'Of course we'll pay you wages. No one can manage without money and you won't have a rich family to subsidise you, as some girls do.'

'Oh. I didn't realise. Thank you.' Phoebe hadn't thought of this, had just assumed she would receive a wage. Would she be working alongside daughters of the gentry, then? They might manage without being paid wages, but how would they cope with menial chores?

'Don't buy the uniform until we're all sure you're suited to this job. We spend a few days training our VADs before we let them loose on the men. You'll probably know by next week how you're fitting in.'

'Yes, Miss Rufford.'

'And please remember at all times that you will be working for the Red Cross. You'll have to perform unpleasant tasks and menial, sometimes disgusting duties. You'll deal with men out of their minds with pain, men whose physical injuries are not nice to deal with. You'll need to be patient and courteous at all times. However unpleasant the duties you're asked to undertake, you must do them to the best of your ability and obey instructions at all times, especially from the doctors and nurses.'

She paused as if to make sure her words had sunk in, so Phoebe nodded and took the piece of paper Miss Rufford was holding out.

'Very well. Report to this address on Friday. Perhaps you could wait outside for Beaty now? There's something else I need to talk to her about.'

When Phoebe had left, Rosemary raised one eyebrow. 'Not like your usual protégées, Beaty, my love. Where did you find this one?'

'Corin found her in Swindon. She'd just lost her job and a man was attacking her. Naturally my dear nephew stepped in to rescue her.'

'Well, she looks and talks as if she already knows how to work hard, which is what we need most of all from a VAD.'

'She does. And . . . Corin's very taken with her.'

'Is he now?'

'Yes. He hasn't looked at a woman since Norah and the baby died. I was beginning to despair about him, he was in low spirits for so long.'

'He's always been a sensitive fellow. I remember him as a lad crying over that puppy of his that died suddenly.' She gave her old friend a very direct look. 'Would you welcome a young woman like Phoebe into the family?'

'I don't know yet. Oh, not because of her background. You know I'm not a snob, for heaven's sake. It's whether she'd make Corin happy. Norah didn't, not really. I'd hate him to make another bad choice.'

'Well, this lass seems very nice.'

'Yes. I'm getting to know her better and waiting to see how things play out. Corin took her out to lunch yesterday and Ruth said he looked happier than he had done for a while when he brought her back, was laughing and chatting, just like in the old days. Anyway, if this goes as far as marriage, he's only following my example, isn't he? I married way out of my class.'

'Yes, and you managed brilliantly. I don't know how you put up with some of the snobbery you encountered.'

'I had Podge. He used to mimic the old dowagers and make me laugh about them. You're never as afraid of people you've laughed at. He'd have made a good actor, my Podge would. And he was all that really mattered to me. I didn't need their approval.'

Rosemary's voice softened. 'Not many people find even a shadow of such a great love.'

Beaty blinked her eyes furiously. 'We were talking about Phoebe, not me. She gets on well with the other girls, and has an eye for someone in trouble. I offered her a job as my secretary, but she said she preferred to do something more active. Then she suggested a girl who might be able to help me, someone who was struggling with hard physical work. I should have noticed that myself, but I didn't.'

'It'll be interesting to see how Phoebe fits into the VADs, how she mingles with our eager debs. There are more positions to fill than bodies to fill them, so we have to rush them through training. I must say, some of the VADs have coped remarkably well with the menial work they're expected to do. Others have crumbled at the first serious problem or mangled body, and have found a reason to leave the organisation.'

'Are they allowed to do that?'

'We don't want shirkers and sulkers dealing with men who've lost limbs or been badly hurt.'

'I predict that our Phoebe will fit in well.'

'Good. We need some stalwarts. Send her along on Friday and be prepared to take her shopping for a uniform later next week.'

Chapter Eight

Greyladies, September 1914

The front part of the house seemed to slumber quietly in the autumn sunshine, as if waiting for something, or someone, to wake it. Harriet looked at it with a sigh. She hadn't so much as been invited inside since her confrontation with Matron over the old door.

She continued on through the side gardens and out of the gate leading to the crypt, pausing there, as she always did, to admire the intricate metal grille that kept strangers out. The grille had been put there to prevent strangers from damaging the beautiful stonework inside. The crypt was all that was left intact of the original chapel used by the nuns. Not a big chapel, but if it had been as beautiful as the crypt, she wished she could have seen it.

Pulling out another of the large old keys which had served Greyladies for so many centuries, she slipped it into the lock of the grille door. Even the lock was surrounded by a pretty semicircle of smaller metal pieces in a sunburst pattern, which was completed by a matching semicircle on the grille next to the door. There were three sunbursts across the metal barrier in all. The blacksmith who had fashioned this ironwork had been as much an artist as any famous painter, she always thought.

'You do like to keep your secrets locked away, don't you?'

She swung round to see Matron Dawkins standing a few paces away, looking as if her whole body was as starched as her apron.

'I like to keep my family's inheritance safe, if that's what you mean.'

'One has to wonder what you're hiding in there, Mrs Latimer.'

On a sudden impulse, Harriet flung open the wrought iron door. 'Come and see for yourself. I'm hiding nothing, simply protecting an ancient building.'

Matron stiffened still further. 'You're inviting me to come inside?'

'Yes. We often show visitors round, because we're proud of the crypt. There's nothing secret in here.' She led the way inside, but it was a moment before the other woman followed her into the shadowy interior.

Opening the lantern which stood on a stone shelf near the door, Harriet pulled out her vesta case, lighting and adjusting the flame. She really must buy some of the new electric torches, which were so much less messy than oil lamps.

Holding the lantern high to illuminate the front part of the crypt, she started her usual talk. 'There are only two graves here, each marked by a woman's name, age and the words *Sister in God*. The church was knocked down and much of the stone used elsewhere only a few years after its founding, but for some reason they stopped short of demolishing the crypt. No one knows why. We're just grateful something was saved during the destruction of the religious houses in England.'

'Mmm.'

'Look at the arches and carvings, how beautifully executed they are. We've had archaeologists and architects visiting our ruins, and some have come back with their students.' But even that got no more than another grunt out of the woman.

Harriet shortened her talk, walking across to shine the lantern on the delicate rows of small figures carved into a little shrine about a yard and a half wide, set back a couple of feet into one wall. 'Apparently the nuns prayed here for the souls of those who'd died, or came to ask special help for those in trouble. I have the journal kept by the first abbess, Anne Latimer.'

'Latimer. The same family as yourself?'

'Yes. The house passes down the female line and it's our tradition that the men change their names.'

'Unusual.'

'It was a small community and the nuns wore grey habits, hence the name of the house. As abbess, Anne Latimer wore a silver cross on a chain, and the others wore wooden crosses. They lived modestly, because they weren't a rich order, but also so that they could use what money they had to help the poor. Sadly, that didn't protect them from the King's desire to destroy the power of the Pope by closing down all the religious foundations.'

'I think Henry VIII was right to do that. Even modern papism is full of idolatry. But I suppose if you're a descendant of these,' she flicked a scornful hand towards the graves, 'you're a papist too.'

Harriet bit back a sharp response. It seemed impossible to reach out a hand of friendship to such a sour woman, whatever she said or did, so she wasn't going to try any more.

'You've seen me attending the parish church every Sunday, so I don't know why you would think I'm a Roman Catholic.'

She waited, but there was no apology. She moved on, letting the lantern show stone shelves, at present loaded with items they'd removed from the new part of the house.

'What are the shelves for?'

'I think the builders intended them for future burials, but we're using them for storage now that our home is serving as a convalescent hospital.'

'Hmm. This space would be better used by *us*. The soldiers' welfare is far more important than your bric-a-brac.' Matron turned round to study the crypt walls nearest to the house. 'Why wasn't I told about this place? Presumably there's a corridor connecting it to the cellars in the main house? I don't want people coming into the house that way.'

Harriet breathed deeply and took a moment to calm herself.

Matron walked to and fro. 'I can't see a door.'

'Unfortunately there isn't a connecting corridor, which is why the officials from the War Office decided not to use the crypt.'

'Are you sure about the lack of a passage? That seems very strange.'

'I've never seen one.' There was a rumour in the family about a secret passage, only no one knew where it was, or even if it really existed.

As they turned to leave, a light seemed to glow in one corner. Harriet paused, knowing what this meant, but saying nothing.

'What's causing that light?' Matron asked sharply.

'What light?'

'The one over there.' She pointed, then gasped and took a step backwards. A moment later she let out a cry. As she backed away, the glowing figure drifted forward towards her. 'No, no! Keep it away from me.'

The ghost of Anne Latimer pointed towards the exit and edged forward again, as if urging the intruder to leave.

Matron shrieked and ran out of the crypt.

Harriet followed her. 'Are you all right? Did you see something?'

'You arranged for someone to pretend to be a ghost. You only invited me into the crypt to frighten me.'

'I'd never do anything like that. Why would I want to frighten anyone?'

Matron eyed her searchingly and Harriet looked steadily back. She'd seen the ghost of the founder of Greyladies many times, but was surprised that such an unpleasant woman had seen it. So few people could.

'Swear you didn't do anything to frighten me.'

'I swear that I didn't do anything whatsoever to frighten you. And I'm quite sure that no one else did, either. Since I have the only key and keep it in a safe place, I can be certain no one has gone inside the crypt since well before your arrival. There are sightings of the ghost of the founding abbess, though.'

Matron frowned at her, then glanced uneasily towards the shadowed entrance behind them, muttering something under her breath.

'I check the crypt every now and then,' Harriet went on. 'But I'm far too busy to spend much time here, let alone play tricks. However, as there is no way to get to the crypt from the house, its use is rather limited for us all.'

'I don't believe in ghosts, so it must have been a trick of the light. I'm rather tired today and reacted hastily. Such a nasty, damp place, that crypt of yours. And if there is no passage leading to the house, you're right about one thing: this place wouldn't be any use to us for storage.'

She edged back a few steps, still watching the entrance. 'And then there are the graves. The patients wouldn't like those. Anyway, we can manage with the attics and cellars for our storage.'

She swung round and walked off towards the gardens without a further word, back ramrod straight, feet thumping down hard on the path.

Harriet wondered why Anne Latimer's ghost had appeared to such an unpleasant woman. To frighten her away? She couldn't imagine the first owner of Greyladies wanting to frighten anyone. Her journal showed her to be a kindly woman.

But then, who knew what lengths a family member would go to, in order to protect this place? Some of the former ladies of the house had had to tread carefully at times.

She locked the door carefully. Light was still glowing faintly from inside the crypt as she turned back towards the house, but when she looked back again from the gate into the garden, she saw that everything was dark again behind the grille.

She looked up at her former home. Strange items of hospital furniture showed at the windows of it now, while outside two flower beds had been cleared away completely and gravel laid down to allow more access for ambulances. The garden paths near the house had been widened to accommodate wheelchairs.

There were no officers convalescing here as yet, but a great deal of equipment had been delivered, not just beds and a miscellany of comfortable armchairs, but medical equipment and supplies.

She'd read in the newspaper about the first casualties returning to England. It was only a matter of time before this place would come into use. She hoped the peace and beauty she'd always found in both house and gardens would help the men regain their health.

The following week, Joseph and Harriet were strolling round the side garden when the first patients arrived at Greyladies. A motor ambulance drew up and four officers were helped out. One was on crutches, two had their arms in slings, and the last one to get out looked chalky pale and walked as if it hurt him to move.

Matron surged out to meet them, giving orders in her loud voice even before she had ushered the men inside.

'Being under her control wouldn't help me get better more quickly,' Joseph murmured into his wife's ear.

'No. She'll keep them away from us, I'm sure.'

'If she tries to do that, they'll only be more eager to meet us. They're young men – well, youngish – not used to being incapacitated. They must be fretting at their enforced inactivity.'

She gave his hand a quick squeeze. She knew how he fretted at his own physical limitations.

He frowned. 'Actually, I think I recognised one of them. If I'm right, he's a friend of Selwyn's. I must find out whether it is Lucian Averill. If it is, he's changed and looks a lot older.'

He sighed as he began to walk awkwardly back to their part of the house, stopping for a moment to mutter, 'Men like that won't think a cripple like me is of much use, will they?'

'They'll know perfectly well that you can't join up and no

one will think the worse of you for something you can't help.'

'I suppose not. Well, at least these men are alive. Lists of those killed are being published already.'

The following afternoon, the postman brought a letter from Joseph's mother, giving them all the latest news.

He opened it at once. 'Goodness! My brother Thomas has volunteered and gone into the army.'

Harriet had met Thomas and found him very stiff and patronising towards her, but hadn't said anything about that to Joseph.

Joseph's mother was a lot more pleasant to Harriet these days. She'd changed since her husband's death, shortened her skirts, had her hair cut to shoulder length and grown more modern in all sorts of minor ways. And she really did care about her youngest son's welfare, as well as doting on Joseph's sons, the only living grandsons in the family so far.

He finished perusing the letter and handed it to his wife. 'Here. Read it yourself.'

She took the piece of fine, cream-laid paper from him and skimmed through it quickly.

'I'm sorry Mrs Stuart hasn't been well.'

'Yes. So am I. Mother would be lost without her.'

'She'd cope. She's a strong woman.' Harriet handed him back the letter. 'I don't mind helping your mother find another housekeeper, but she's not coming to live here, whatever happens. It wouldn't work. She and I would soon be at odds.'

'No. I suppose she'd try to undermine your authority.'

'Not only that, but she'd try to change Greyladies. We live at peace with the people in the village. Can you imagine her treating them as equals? I'm sorry. I didn't mean to insult your mother, but better I make myself plain now.'

'I'm not upset. You're telling the simple truth. Mother is used to ruling the roost and she'd expect to be waited on in a grander style than we do. Let's hope Mrs Stuart gets better more quickly than the doctors predict.'

They exchanged warm, loving glances, but Joseph fell silent, lost in thought for a few moments.

She waited until he looked up again and said, 'Let's stroll round the garden again while we can. Autumn is upon us already.'

In more ways than one, she thought. She'd been having some puzzling dreams since they moved to the old house and needed to share them with him. 'Joseph . . . do you think we can ever go back to how things were at Greyladies? Once the war's over, that is.'

He looked at her in surprise. 'What do you mean?'

'I have the strangest feeling, as if I'm starting to say goodbye to the house. Some owners do move away after a while, you know.'

'I can't imagine you ever doing that willingly.'

She couldn't, either. But one thing still worried her. 'We don't have a daughter. Who will I pass the house to? I'm supposed to know that instinctively, only how?'

'This house seems to have ways of guiding its owners. It's the strangest place. I love it, but I never quite know what to expect. Things just . . . happen.'

'We haven't seen Anne Latimer around the house for a while, have we, though it was definitely her in the Crypt?'

'Perhaps our resident ghost doesn't like the Dragon and is sulking.'

Harriet gave him a half smile, as if her attention was only

partly on what he had been saying. 'If anything happens to me, what will become of you and the boys? Your home will be taken away by a new lady owner. I'm not allowed to leave it to you or to them.'

Joseph put an arm round her. 'Don't borrow trouble, my love. You seem in fine health to me and we'll have worked out the succession by the time we grow old. We'll make sure the boys are in good professions, able to earn their own living. They already understand that only female Latimers can inherit. Besides, I've done quite well with my investments. Who'd have expected that? So we wouldn't be penniless, even if we walked away from here with nothing belonging to the Latimer Trust.'

'Yes, of course. I don't know what came over me to worry like that.'

But it wasn't the first time she'd wondered about who would follow her at Greyladies. Or how she would know who ought to inherit. Oh, well, the house would no doubt continue to give up its secrets gradually and then she'd find out.

A few days later, it was sunny enough for the two officers with arms in slings to stroll round the gardens. Inevitably, they found their way to the rear of the old house.

Joseph was returning from visiting a former gardener in the village. Peter was too old and infirm to work, but had spent his life at Greyladies, so they supplemented the government's old age pension with produce and extra money.

The pension of five shillings at age seventy had been introduced in 1909, and even this small amount made sons and daughters much more willing to house and look after their old folk, because they were no longer a burden. He could remember the excitement among the older people when they received their first payments. They still found it a matter of wonder that they kept receiving the money without working for it, because they could all remember the much harsher treatment of the old before the pension was introduced. The greatest fear of their parents had been to be sent to the workhouse.

Joseph had been enjoying the fresh air and the fact that no one who lived in the village stared at the way he walked. But the two officers walking round the garden did stop to stare, so he moved forward to introduce himself and offer them a belated welcome to Greyladies.

'Are we intruding if we walk round this side of the house?' one of the men asked. 'The Dragon Lady told us we'd not be welcome anywhere in your part of the house and grounds.'

'We call her that, too,' Joseph said with a smile. He tried not to show his annoyance as he added, 'I don't know why she'd tell you that, though. Men who're serving our country will always be welcome in our house.'

The taller officer was still staring at him, but trying not to show it. 'You're the owner?'

'Yes. Or rather, my wife is.' He held out one hand. 'Joseph Latimer.'

'Charles Humphreys. And this is Lucian Averill.'

As they shook hands, Joseph said, 'I thought I recognised you when you arrived.'

'Ought I to know you? I don't know any families of that name, I must admit.'

'I was born Joseph Dalton, but changed my name when my wife inherited Greyladies.'

'Ah. You're Selwyn Dalton's youngest brother?'

'Yes.'

'But I thought—'

'That I couldn't walk? That I was not only a cripple, but a halfwit?' He was well aware what his oldest brother thought of him. At the other man's shamefaced nod, he added, 'My brother doesn't like the fact that my limp is rather ugly. But my bad hip doesn't stop me getting around, and it certainly doesn't affect my brain. Fortunately, as I grew up my health improved greatly. Enough for me to marry and father two sons. Would you care for a cup of tea?'

'I'd love one.'

A shrill voice called, 'Major Humphreys? Captain Averill? Where have you got to?'

The two men winced.

'Can you hide us?' the major asked. 'We need an hour's peace and quiet. That young woman has a voice like a siren.'

Joseph grinned and gestured to the back door. 'You'd better get out of sight quickly.'

By the time the nurse who'd been calling came round the corner, he was on his own, limping with deliberate slowness towards the door.

'Excuse me, Mr Latimer.'

He turned.

'I'm looking for two men with their arms in slings.'

The woman spoke slowly and clearly, as if he might find it hard to understand. Why did so many people assume that if you couldn't walk properly, you didn't have all your wits, either? He didn't allow his anger to show, however. He was used to this sort of treatment by now.

'Were you speaking to me?' he drawled, using his most upper-class accent.

'Um.' She looked at him as if trying to assess his mental capacity.

'You must want something if you're here in the private part of our gardens,' he continued. 'How may I help you?'

She began to look a bit embarrassed. 'I was looking for two of our patients, actually. They have their arms in slings.'

He gestured around. 'And do you see them?'

'Er . . . no.'

'If you feel they're hiding in the outhouses, please feel free to search for them.' He turned and moved quickly into the house, not wanting to lie to her.

After he'd closed the door, he leant against it for a moment, trying not to laugh as he heard her start calling the officers' names again. Then he walked across the room to where the two visitors were standing in the corridor outside the kitchen. 'Could we please have a pot of tea and some scones, Phyllis?'

'Yes, sir. And I'd suggest you draw the curtains in the window opposite the bookshelves. You don't want anyone peeping in at you if you're hiding these gentlemen from the Dragon Lady.'

'Good idea.' He winked at her and turned to the two men.

'This part of the house is very old,' Averill said. 'I hadn't realised.'

'There have been Latimers here since the sixteenth century. Come and meet my wife.' He threaded his way through the large pieces of furniture, too much of it, but they had to put it somewhere. He pulled the curtains closed as he passed the window.

'Ah, there you are, my dear. We have visitors, who're hiding from dragons.'

Harriet came forward, smiling. 'There's only one dragon round here.'

'Sorry to contradict a lady,' one officer said, 'but there are other dragons in training even as we speak. The nurses are following her example.'

'Oh dear. Poor you.'

Soon they had the men sitting comfortably. Within five minutes, Phyllis had brought in a tea tray and some of Cook's freshly made scones, but it was the company the men seemed to enjoy most.

They chatted pleasantly for half an hour, then the door to the kitchen opened and Phyllis came hurrying in. 'Excuse me, madam, but them two orderlies are searching the gardens and calling out for your visitors. Everyone seems very anxious. I thought perhaps the gentlemen might want to leave now.'

'Very intelligent of you, Phyllis.' Harriet turned to her guests. 'I could show you an arbour which is hidden from the front of the house. I doubt they'll have found it, and you can pretend you've been there the whole time.'

'Good idea.' Captain Averill stood up.

'You're welcome to come back at any time,' Joseph said quietly. 'If you don't want to chat, or we're busy, you can simply sit in the library area and read. Tell the others that.'

The major followed his companion's example. 'Thank you. It's been an oasis of peace already. That woman never stops chivvying people round from dawn to dusk. And she's forcing the nurses to do the same. Unfortunately, a medical officer is arriving tomorrow and if he's in cahoots with the Dragon, we might not be able to get away again to see you.

We'll be here for another couple of weeks or so, apparently.'

'We can try to get the MO on our side, though,' the captain said. 'Is it all right if we tell him you're opening your library to anyone who likes to read quietly?'

'Yes,' Harriet told him.

'And I also intend to explain that I'm an old family friend of yours, Mr Latimer, if that's all right with you?'

'Of course it is.'

'I'll show you the arbour.' Harriet led the way to the back door, and checked that no one was in sight, then showed them the way.

'That woman is so annoying!' she said to Joseph when she returned.

'We can only do our best, darling.'

'I know. But I can't help getting angry. This hostility is so unnecessary.'

A letter was delivered to the old house by one of the orderlies an hour later. Noting the man's wooden expression, Joseph guessed he wasn't happy about delivering it.

'From Matron, sir.'

'I see.'

'Um, she'd like a reply straight away, if you don't mind.'

'You'd better come in, then.'

Joseph took him into the long room, opened the envelope and found a brief note inside.

Matron Dawkins would be obliged if Mr and Mrs Latimer would refrain from interrupting the treatment of patients by inviting them into the dampness of the old house.

He stared at it in disgust. What a fool the woman was!

Harriet came across to join him, and he passed the note to her without comment, moving away from the orderly so that they could speak privately.

'Why does she do this?'

'She wishes to be Queen of her little world, I suppose. But this isn't a hospital; it's a convalescent home, and surely the best thing would be to keep the men happy so that they complete their recovery?'

From near the door, the orderly glanced at the clock and cleared his throat.

'I will not be bullied,' Joseph said to Harriet, speaking loudly enough to be heard.

'Nor will I.' She spoke equally loudly.

The orderly shuffled his feet and stared at the floor, his expression wooden.

Joseph went across to him. 'Tell Matron I'll reply when I have time.'

The man hesitated, so Joseph walked to the kitchen door with him.

Their governess, Miss Bowers, who was as much a friend as an employee, came down from the schoolroom just as the door closed behind the unwelcome visitor. She was followed by their two sons.

Joseph held out his arms and they came running to hug him. Ah, they were two lads to be proud of.

At eight, Jody seemed to get taller every day, while little Mal, at six, followed his brother everywhere, trying to imitate him.

They went on to hug their mother, then asked if they could go to the kitchen and get something to eat.

As they left, Joseph raised one eyebrow at his wife. Harriet understood what he was asking and nodded, so he shared the letter with their friend, who was also disgusted by the mean-spirited approach of Matron Dawkins.

'You could have provided a quiet reading room for the men who are nearly ready to leave, or taken books round to the other men,' she said. 'There are all sorts of small tasks you could have undertaken to help cheer them up. It's iniquitous for her to behave like that.'

'What are we going to say to her, Joseph?' Harriet asked.

'I'm going to ignore her note till I'm calmer. I'll just say something rude if I reply now.'

'Why reply at all?' Miss Bowers said.

'Why indeed?'

'May I borrow the note?'

They looked at her in puzzlement.

'I won't say why, so that you know nothing about what I intend to do. I've lived in the village nearly all my life and I have friends in London as well. You get to know a lot of people in seventy years. If I can see a way to help you curb that female, I will.'

With a shrug, he handed over the note. He trusted Margie Bowers absolutely. Everyone in the village did.

The following day, Joseph was walking back from the village when a motor car stopped beside him.

'We can give you a lift back to the convalescent hospital,' the officer in the back said. 'You look as though walking is still difficult and you don't want to overdo things. I'm the new medical oficer, by the way – Benedict Somers at your service. I'm commandant at the hospital as well, obviously.'

'Ah. It's a kind offer, but I'm not one of your patients. I've had a bad hip since birth. I'm the owner and live in the rear part of Greyladies now. Joseph Latimer at *your* service. Any time I can help you or your patients, just ask me.'

'Oh, sorry. You must come and share a cup of tea with me once I've settled in, tell me about the district and the village.'

'I'd love to, but I don't think Matron would approve of that.'

'I beg your pardon?' He looked puzzled.

Joseph didn't intend to tittle-tattle about this foolish quarrel, so continued hastily, 'But you're welcome to visit us any time, Doctor.'

The newcomer was still frowning but took the hint not to pursue this. 'I'll visit you as soon as I've settled in, then. I'm still happy to offer you a ride back.'

'It does my hip good to walk and exercise it, though I know it looks rather ungainly.'

That won him a shrewd look. 'Good attitude. It must hurt quite a lot sometimes, but at least you're retaining some muscle tone. So many people stop trying to walk and then, after a while, they can't. One day, we'll be able to do more for children born with this deformity. Goodbye for now. Drive on!'

Joseph stepped back to let the car continue on its way. He had taken an instant liking to the MO, and wondered how the man would get on with Matron Dawkins.

That would be an interesting thing to watch.

Chapter Nine

Phoebe managed a final outing for tea with Corin, walking up and down outside the cafe as she waited for him to arrive, because she was nervous of going into such an elegant place on her own.

'Sorry to be late!' he called as soon as he was close enough to speak. 'I got called to a sudden meeting.'

'Is everything all right?'

'I'm under orders, so I can't tell you where I'm going or what I'll be doing, I'm afraid. But you can write to me care of this address.' He held out a piece of paper. 'You will write, won't you?'

She saw him watching with a near smile as she put it in her handbag, a large practical affair made of leather, not the fashionable smaller ones used by most young ladies of his acquaintance.

'I like your handbags,' he said unexpectedly. 'They're as practical as you are. Most of the young ladies I know carry silly little velvet pouches, pretty but useless – like them.'

She was surprised at the bitterness in his voice, but when he didn't continue or explain anything else, she didn't push for an explanation, just said quietly, 'Yes, of course I'll write, Corin. I promised I would, didn't I?'

'Not everyone keeps a promise.'

He sounded sad as he said that, then he looked at his wristwatch as if time was pressing. He tapped it with one finger. 'This thing is practical too. I only bought it yesterday. It's much better than my father's old pocket watch.'

He put his hand over hers as it lay on the table, and she didn't even think of pulling away, but twisted her hand round to clasp his properly. That brought a smile to his face.

'I'm glad I made it today, Phoebe, but I hope they bring our food soon. Half an hour is all I dare take. I would have hated to miss saying au revoir to you in person.'

Thanks to a sympathetic waitress their tea was brought out ahead of other customers' orders. They didn't say much as they ate. It was enough to be together. She mentioned a couple of incidents from her training. He replied with an approving comment about her becoming a VAD.

And then it was time to separate.

Outside, he bent his head to kiss her on the cheek, then put his hands on her shoulders and stared into her eyes. For a precious few moments, he held her at arm's length. 'I'll remember this day, with the sun shining on your glorious hair.'

'There will be other days, Corin.'

'So I pray. Damn this war! I want to get to know you better. Dear Phoebe, don't fall in love with anyone else while I'm away.'

As she stared at him in surprise, he kissed her other cheek, then stepped back, giving her a smart salute before striding away down the street. He didn't turn till he reached the corner, where he gave her a final wave, then vanished from sight.

Which made her feel bereft, made her want to run after him. How foolish was that?

She didn't move for a few moments. *Dear Phoebe*, he'd said. And *Don't fall in love with anyone else*. Was it possible he was starting to care for her?

She hoped so, because she was definitely starting to care for him, even though they'd known one another for such a short time. She didn't know why she felt comfortable with him, why she trusted him completely. It was as if she'd known him for ever.

It was a few minutes before she managed to pull herself together and walk back to the hostel to finish her packing.

She too had a duty to her country. Hers might be voluntary, but it was no less important to her to play her part.

A week later Phoebe stared at herself in the mirror. Her hair was pulled back into a neat bun and she thought she looked both smart and efficient, which pleased her. She turned from side to side. The uniform fitted her well, flattered her even. Beaty had seen to that.

She felt proud that she'd passed the VAD training. Two young women hadn't. One couldn't face the menial duties and collapsed in tears when faced with filth of any description. The other had fainted at the sight of blood, upsetting the patient, which had made the sister nursing him furious. The poor girl had fainted on three more occasions, then vanished from the group.

Most of the young women, whether born of rich or ordinary folk, had done what was needed without complaint. They all believed in contributing to the war effort and that was starting to draw them together, for all their differences.

Phoebe had been told she'd be working in auxiliary or convalescent hospitals anywhere in England, doing whatever chores were necessary, except for the nursing itself, of course. They didn't send VADs to the front. Only men were sent into such immediate danger.

She'd be assisting the trained nurses as asked, and must obey them in all matters, medical or otherwise, or assisting in housekeeping duties, or even learning to drive. That was fine by her. *She* didn't faint at the sight of blood! Or at her first sight of a man who'd lost his right leg. Or at the thought of scrubbing a filthy floor.

After smoothing down her starched white apron with its red cross on the bib, she turned to close her suitcase. It contained overalls for dirty work, further aprons, several white caps, and plenty of spare white collars and cuffs. There were also six pairs of white sleeves with elasticated ends that reached from wrist to past the elbow, designed to keep her dresses clean.

The 'ward shoes' had rubber soles and heels, so that she could move more quietly, and were very comfortable. Beaty had insisted on buying them from a better shoe shop, and had supplied her with extra underwear too, more than she'd ever owned in her life before.

'You won't forget to write to Corin,' she said as she walked with Phoebe to the front door.

'Of course I won't forget.'

Beaty smiled. 'If things change and you have to write to him care of me, I won't open your letters.'

'I know.'

The older woman gave her a sudden hug. 'You're a good girl, Phoebe. I wish you well and I'll always have a bed for you any time you come to London, if it's only on my sofa.'

So Phoebe had to give her an extra hug. 'Thank you. For everything.'

Today the VAD 'girls' were to assemble at the building where they'd attended classes during their training to find out where they'd been assigned. After that, they'd be taken to their new postings straight away.

Phoebe was driven to the meeting place by Beaty's elderly chauffeur. She felt very grand sitting there as he drove her through the streets of London.

She wasn't the only one to arrive in a chauffeur-driven vehicle, but she was sure she was the only one for whom this was the first time she'd been driven around on her own in such utter luxury.

Her luggage was unloaded and collected by two orderlies with a trolley, then piled up with some other suitcases.

After thanking the chauffeur, she walked up the stairs into her new life, feeling excited and happy . . . and just a little apprehensive. Well, more than a little apprehensive. But that was normal, surely.

The VADs were directed to a large classroom where most of the desks had been moved to one side wall. Middle-aged ladies in Red Cross uniforms sat behind two of them, passing out pieces of paper from a box on a third desk between them.

'Wait here then go to the next free desk,' the woman at the entrance told her.

Five minutes later she did this.

'Please sit down for a moment. Miss . . . ? Sinclair, thank you.' She scanned some large envelopes. 'Here are your instructions. You'll be based in Swindon and—'

'Swindon!'

The woman looked at her over her spectacles. 'Is there

something wrong with that? You won't be able to pick and choose where you go, you know.'

Phoebe hesitated, then shook her head. She didn't want to start her new life by being awkward about where she was sent. It might give her a bad name. And surely Frank would have found himself another young woman by now, or at least given up on her?

'No. I was just surprised. It's where I come from, you see.'

'Yes, that's why we chose it, because you'll know the area. Though you won't be in Swindon itself. You're going to an auxiliary hospital nearby to complete your training. It used to be a large country house.'

Relief coursed through Phoebe. If she avoided going into Swindon, she'd be very unlikely to encounter Frank.

'There will be four girls in your group. Please go to the hall and wait underneath the letter C. Someone will collect you from there.'

She did as ordered and found herself standing with two strangers. One of them offered her hand and said in what Phoebe thought of as an upper-class accent, 'I'm Penny. This is Amy. And you are . . . ?'

'Phoebe Sinclair.'

They all turned as a fourth member joined the group. She'd been in Phoebe's class, a shy young woman who had hardly said a word. She was small and dowdy in appearance, but a hard worker who'd done anything she'd been told to without flinching.

Penny, who seemed to have appointed herself leader, introduced herself and the two others.

'I'm Jane Harper,' the newcomer said in a voice with a marked East End accent. 'I already know Phoebe.'

'Any of you done any nursing before?' Amy asked.

When no one else spoke, Phoebe said, 'I looked after my mother for two years when she was dying. And I helped lay her out after she died.' She didn't tell many people this.

'You'll know more about the practicalities, then. Actually, I'm hoping they'll assign me to driving duties. I can drive already, been practising on my brother's car. He's joined the navy, so he's had to leave it at home. It's a Model T Ford, not a big Sunbeam like Daddy's, but it gets you round nicely. My brother only bought it last year. He hated to leave it behind.'

She was obviously a car enthusiast.

A voice called, 'C Group, please!' and Amy stopped talking.

A woman in another sort of Red Cross uniform beckoned and led them out of the hall. 'Step out smartly!' she tossed over her shoulder, not even looking to check that they were keeping up with her.

They were put into a charabanc. The long vehicle had five rows of bench seats set behind the driver, each with its own door at each end. It looked as if it was ready for an excursion to the seaside – until you saw that the rear seats were loaded with medical supplies and large wooden boxes whose contents could only be imagined.

There was only just enough room for the four young women to cram on to the seat behind the elderly male driver and his younger assistant.

'Well, here we go,' said Penny, who seemed unable to keep quiet for more than two minutes. 'And they haven't even told us the name of the place we're going to.'

Jane didn't join in the conversation unless asked a direct question. She was, Phoebe always thought, like an alert little bird, her eyes darting here and there, bright with interest and intelligence. But she kept her thoughts to herself and never wasted a word on mere chat.

'Have you ever been out of London before, Jane?' Phoebe asked after a while, trying to pull her into the conversation.

'No. No one in my family has. We were all born in the East End. I'm the first for several generations to go so far away.'

'Once we arrive, I'm going to get hold of a map and find out exactly where we are,' Amy said. 'I'm from Norfolk, don't know Wiltshire at all.'

'I'd like to see it on a map, too.' Jane fell quiet again, huddling down a bit now in her inadequate coat.

Even Penny had stopped talking. After a while she unwound her scarf and passed it to Jane. 'Here. I have a fur collar. You look cold.'

'Oh. Well . . . thank you very much.'

They drove along the dusty roads at a steady pace, stopping once for refreshments and to use the conveniences behind a small pub whose owner seemed acquainted with their driver.

When they entered Swindon, Phoebe shrank down in her seat and refrained from looking round . . . just in case. She didn't relax until they left the town and headed north.

'Is something wrong?' Jane whispered.

'I used to live here. There's a fellow who wanted to marry me, only I couldn't stand him. I don't want him to see me. He got a bit violent.'

'Some men do. My cousin thumps his wife. If any man ever tries to thump me, I'll take a rolling pin to him.'

'How do you know your cousin thumps her?' Penny asked.

'You can see the bruises. She pretends she's clumsy, but

138

she ain't. It's him. We all know that. But what can you do? He's her husband.'

'Gosh. How awful!' Amy exclaimed.

'You have to be careful who you marry,' Jane went on. 'Me, I'm not going to get married at all.'

'I'd love to, but they'll be short of young men after the war, my father says.' Penny sighed. 'Just my luck.'

The other three fell silent at her words. It was as if the world was changing beneath their feet, Phoebe thought, the path different with every step they took. Things were being said and done that wouldn't have been thought of before. People were working together who'd have walked past each other in the street without even turning their heads.

What would life be like after all this turmoil?

'Soon be there now, girls,' the driver said half an hour later.

As they turned a bend, he yelled and braked hard, throwing them against one another. The charabanc came to a sudden halt because their way was blocked by a milling crowd of sheep, two of whom had to skip quickly out of the way of the vehicle, one of which got bumped aside.

It was several minutes before the road was clear and the sheep safely penned in a new field. The farmer waved at them cheerfully and went on his way.

'There's no hurrying sheep,' the driver's assistant said as they set off again. 'They scatter if you try. That was a clever dog he had. Worth their weight in gold, good sheepdogs are.'

Five minutes later, the driver said, 'Here we are, girls. This is it: Bellbourne House.'

The charabanc turned right into a long, tree-lined avenue, at the end of which stood a huge house. It looked more Elizabethan than anything, Phoebe thought, staring ahead at the big square bay windows, jutting out in four columns across the facade. She'd seen photos of places like this in books borrowed from the library.

The scene would have been idyllically beautiful, if it hadn't been spoilt by two ambulances standing to one side. From one of them, injured men were being carried into the building on stretchers, covered in grey blankets; from the other ambulance, the walking wounded were being helped to get down and move into the house. It reminded Phoebe of the scene at the railway station.

The wounded soldiers stopped moving to stare at them. One waved and gave them a cheerful grin, so she waved back.

They drove round to the rear of the house, which had two small wings, between which the driver came to a halt. 'Here we are.'

A maid stuck her head out of the door. 'They're all busy with the new patients. Sergeant Buchanan says to come inside and have a cup of tea while you wait for the orderlies to be free to help you unload the new equipment. Looks like you've got some heavy boxes there.'

'What about our cases?' Penny asked. 'We could bring those in ourselves.'

'They'll be out of the way if you leave them there for the moment. It's chaos in here.'

The four women slid along the bench seat to the car doors at each end of it, this time with no one to open it for them or help them down. Our idle days are over, Phoebe thought to herself. She followed the cheerful maid into a big room next to the kitchen, which had been set up as a mess and was crammed with tables of all shapes and sizes.

'There are always people coming and going,' their guide

said cheerfully. 'You'll soon get used to it. I'll fetch you a big pot of tea. Cups and saucers are over there, with the milk and sugar. And there are some currant buns. You'll have to help yourselves. I'm Nelly, by the way.'

'Looks like they feed you well here,' the driver said, stretching and waggling his arms in the air before settling into a chair. His assistant got him some food and a cup of tea as soon as a huge enamel teapot arrived.

It would be more like an hour before anyone could attend to the new VADs, Nelly said. 'Why don't you go out and explore the gardens? Get a breath of fresh air while it's fine. It poured down all day yesterday.'

'Won't anyone mind?'

'Why should they? They can't help you settle in yet. They're too busy with the men. And what else are gardens for but enjoying?'

Eventually an orderly came to find them and escort them back into the house to meet Matron. He left them with her in a room off the main entrance hall, then went back outside to help unload their trunks and cases.

This room must have been beautiful before it was converted into an office, Phoebe thought. The ceiling had delicate plasterwork patterns and the curtains were a rich red in colour.

'Welcome to Bellbourne House. I'm Matron Turner and this is my deputy, Sister Langham, to whom you four will answer. We're very glad to see you, because we're short-handed and still settling in here. I'm going to assign three of you to nursing and domestic duties, and one to the ambulances. Do any of you drive?'

'I do,' Amy said. 'I love driving but I've only just learnt. I'm not sure about driving a big ambulance.'

'Don't worry. Practice makes perfect. You'll be assigned to Corporal Stokes, who is our driver and general factotum, and he'll help you brush up your skills. We have to take the patients into Swindon sometimes to catch a train, or go there to pick up other patients. And we like to give the long-term patients little outings if the weather is fine. Some will have to stay here for quite a while, poor fellows, and it does cheer them up to get out and about.'

By the time Matron had finished her briefing, Phoebe's head was spinning with information.

'Now, girls, Sister Langham will take you to your quarters.'

To their surprise, the plump, grey-haired sister took them outside again, to what had been the outdoor staff's dining room, across the backyard next to the stables.

'It'll have to house eight VADs,' she announced, 'and you're the first to arrive. Here we are.'

They stopped to stare inside at some piles of bed frames and mattresses.

The sister smiled. 'Your first test of initiative. Do you need me to send you an orderly or do you think you can put the bed frames together yourselves?'

They looked at one another, then Phoebe decided to tell the truth. 'If he can show us how to do one, I'm sure we can do the others ourselves, but as it is, I wouldn't know how best to do it.'

The sister nodded. 'Right attitude. If you really don't know how to do something, find out and then give it a go. I'll see if Corporal Stokes is anywhere around. He's a handy fellow. Once the beds are up, two of you can come to me for the bedding. You'll be issued the same as the patients, all the staff will. I'll leave you to make up all eight beds.'

She vanished and they waited.

'I never thought I'd be putting furniture together,' Penny said. 'I hope mine doesn't collapse in the middle of the night. I'm a restless sleeper.'

Amy wandered across to the window at the front. 'No curtains. We'll need to change clothes in here, and we don't want to encourage peeping Toms.'

'Better make a list of the things we need.' Jane opened her big, shabby bag and took out a notebook and pencil. 'Towels, bedlinen, curtains.'

'Wash basins and ewers.'

'A screen round the washing area.'

'Find out where the conveniences are,' Amy said, grimacing. 'Not to mention toilet paper.'

'We always tore up newspapers for that,' Phoebe said.

'Ugh. Rather rough on the backside.'

'Cheap, though.'

They'd written down everything they could think of when footsteps came clumping across the yard. A huge man in uniform came into the dormitory. 'Corporal Stokes reporting for duty, ladies. I've got exactly half an hour to help you, so let's not waste a second.'

By the time he left, they had erected a second bed themselves under his guidance, and he'd said they were quick learners.

When they were on their own, Amy said thoughtfully, 'Talk about being thrown in at the deep end.'

'We're coping, though, aren't we?' Phoebe said. 'And we have it easy compared to the men who'll be sent here.'

They were all silent for a moment or two, then carried on working on the beds and arranging the furniture. At least they had a small chest of drawers each, and a half share in one of the four wardrobes.

'I'm never going to remember everything we've been told today,' Amy said as they unpacked their clothing. 'I'm no good with details, never have been.'

'We can help each other remember things,' Jane said quietly.

By the time they'd unpacked, Phoebe was exhausted and glad to sit quietly over an evening meal in the mess. Again, they had to serve themselves.

She was about to go to bed early, when they were called to help clear up the kitchen. They saw a long corridor leading out of it with a shelf along one side, where trays full of dirty dishes were standing.

Nelly took charge. 'We have to wash the dishes ready for breakfast. When it's cleaned up, that shelf is where the patients' trays are set for meals and food is served. It's been hard getting everything done, so we're all glad to see you four. It won't take long tonight with all of us piling in.'

Sister Langham came along for her evening meal as the four young women were finishing washing the dishes. She beckoned them across. 'Phoebe and Jane, you'll be on for the early-morning shift in the kitchen, setting the trays for the patients' breakfasts, washing up, preparing food, whatever's needed. You'll need to be here by five o'clock. Amy, you'll start with Corporal Stokes tomorrow morning at seven o'clock.'

She turned to the maid. 'Nelly, thank you for all your hard work. If you can bear to teach our new helpers what's needed tomorrow, you can start later for a day or two after that to give you a break.'

'Thanks, Sister.'

The nurse continued her explanations. 'The beds at the hospital are only a quarter full so far, but that still means twenty patients' trays to set out. Staff serve themselves in the dining room. Corporal Stokes is going to arrange for another line of shelves to be erected above this one, for when we've got our full quota of patients. All right?'

'Yes, Sister.'

'I should get to bed early if I were you. Oh, and you'll be answering to Cook for the moment, Phoebe and Jane. She's gone to visit her ailing mother today, but she'll be back on duty tomorrow. Nelly's in charge till then. Penny, I'll tell you each day where I need you. You're my reserve for emergencies, and don't think there won't be any, however efficient we are.'

By the time Phoebe got into bed, she was exhausted. She'd be all right here, but she wasn't going into Swindon, if she could help it. She knew too many people there, any one of whom could mention her to her relatives. And then what would Frank do?

She woke with a start from a nightmare about him grabbing her, as he had before, to find moonlight streaming in through the uncurtained windows and someone shaking her.

'You all right?' Jane whispered.

'Just had a nightmare, that's all.'

'I'll leave you to sleep, then.'

As Phoebe snuggled down in the narrow bed, she heard Jane yawning and that made her yawn too.

She'd expected to lie awake for a while, as she usually did after a nightmare, but the next thing she knew, the alarm clock Sister had given them was ringing and they had to get up.

Chapter Ten

Benedict got out of his car and studied the house more closely. Greyladies was much smaller than he'd expected and even before he went inside, that worried him. With the severely injured patients he was expecting to house here as the war progressed, a bigger establishment would be better, so that one man's death didn't leave such a big hole in the group.

He frowned, remembering a poem he'd loved, seeking to get the words exactly right in his mind:

Any man's death diminishes me
Because I am involved in mankind.

That was it. By . . . yes, John Donne: 'No Man is an Island'. He loved that poem.

How true that was of present circumstances!

The trouble was, there weren't enough larger establishments to cater for the casualties they were expecting, but this place, pretty as it was, surely couldn't be called a hospital or have the facilities to deal even with the minor corrective surgery in which he specialised. He'd place Greyladies under the category 'other' and at best call it a 'small convalescent home'.

A grey-haired woman with rather masculine features came out of the house and stood waiting for him in the doorway, arms folded, positively bristling with white starched garments. 'Dr Somers?'

'Yes. You must be the matron.' He had met her once before somewhere, he thought, but couldn't for the life of him remember her name or where it had been. Perhaps she'd attended one of his talks.

'I'm Matron Dawkins. We have met before, Dr Somers.'

'Have we? Sorry. Life's been such a whirlwind lately, I'm afraid things have passed in a blur at times.'

She scowled at him. The expression looked as if it sat regularly on her face.

'I was sorry I couldn't get here sooner to be involved in setting up the convalescent home—'

'Convalescent hospital, surely, Dr Somers?'

'Is it large enough to call a hospital?'

'A small auxiliary hospital, surely.'

The status seemed important to her, but it was the men's welfare that mattered to him. 'We'll see. As I was saying, I had some important work to finish before I could come here, including some delicate operations.'

'I was quite capable of making a start. I have, after all, been nursing for several decades now and know what is needed. Do come inside.'

He sighed at her tone as he followed her. The appointment of a matron hadn't been in his hands and he'd never have chosen a woman with such a sour expression to deal with men facing permanent disablement. He could only hope that when they got to know one another better, when they grew used to working as a team, the tension between him and Matron would ease. She had better be tactful with the men who would be coming here later. He wouldn't put up with trying to regiment badly disabled chaps.

She gestured towards a door to the left. 'I've allocated this room for your office.'

He walked inside and stopped in shock at the sight of a huge drawing room. 'This is far too big for one person! Most of my work will be on the wards or doing minor operations. And I'll still be going into Swindon to supervise training of doctors, or if there are more complex operations needed. We should try to find a smaller room elsewhere for my office, not waste this space on one man.'

'I'm afraid the authorities aren't allowing us to make any structural changes to this house, so we have to take the rooms as they are. I can't see what they're making such a fuss about. It's quite a small country house and seems nothing special to me.'

'Mr Pashley has already shared the details of Greyladies with me and even after seeing only the outside, I agree with him that this house is valuable to the country historically. We can't ruin one of Britain's architectural treasures, Matron. That would go against the very thing we're fighting for.'

A huff of air was his only answer.

'I think the first thing to do would be for you, or someone else, to show me round.'

'Wouldn't you like some refreshments first, Dr Somers?'

'No, thank you. I stopped at a friend's house on the way here.' He went back out into the entrance hall. 'Once I have a full picture of the house in my mind, I can decide where I want my office. A room as big as this would make a beautiful sitting room for our patients.'

Her expression went even more acid, if that were possible, so he changed the subject again. 'I met the owner of Greyladies on my way from the village. I thought he was one of our patients because he was limping, so I offered him a lift.'

'That man! For a cripple, he has some utterly ridiculous ideas about his own importance.'

Benedict couldn't hold the reproof back. 'Don't *ever* call someone a cripple again in that tone of voice, Matron! People with serious physical problems have enough to get used to without facing the scorn of more fortunate people with whole bodies.'

She blinked, opened her mouth, then snapped it shut like a steel trap, but the look she threw in his direction showed exactly what she was thinking.

'The tour?' he prompted.

They walked round the house, and he couldn't help exclaiming at how beautiful some parts were, especially the big stained glass window which must flood the entrance hall with rainbows of colour in fine weather.

He found a much smaller room on the ground floor which would make a perfect office for himself, and another next to it which would suit Matron, who had taken possession of the former dining room. Since he knew by now that it would be war between them, he didn't scruple to use his authority as Commandant and Medical Officer of Greyladies to ask her to move to the smaller room. Good heavens, the larger one could hold six severely injured patients.

'We must all make sacrifices for these men, who have made great sacrifices for us,' he reminded her when she glared at him. 'And there will be far worse injuries to come than those who've arrived so far.'

'Tell that to the owners of the house.' She gestured towards an ancient wooden door at the rear of the entrance hall. 'They have refused to give me the key to that door, so they can walk into the house at any time and interfere with our treatment.'

'Have they walked in without invitation?'

She hesitated. 'No. But they might do so at a crucial moment, and we can't risk that. If it were up to me, I'd burn that old door and replace it with a sound modern one. Look at it! The wood's rough and it needs painting.'

He wasn't having that! 'If anyone burnt or damaged the door, I'd personally see them prosecuted for it. It's an immensely valuable antique dating from the sixteenth century.'

'I can see that Mr Latimer has been bending your ear already, and no doubt blackening my name.'

'No. He didn't mention the door, or discuss his dealings with you in any way. It was Mr Pashley who admired the former entrance door connecting the two parts of the house.'

Even that didn't please her. 'You will find Mr Latimer too weak willed to do anything properly. He even changed his surname to his wife's when she inherited this place. What sort of man goes against the usual customs of our country like that?'

'It's family tradition for the Latimers, I gather.'

Another angry huff of sound expressed her feelings.

Benedict wondered what sin he'd committed to be given

the penance of working with this harridan, who found fault with everything and had upset him several times in the first hour. 'There's another problem that must be solved if this place is to function properly, and that's the need for a lift to take the patients up and down. There are three floors designated for use, after all.'

She stared woodenly at him.

'I'll have to discuss it with Mr and Mrs Latimer, and see if they'll agree to some minor structural changes, perhaps in the servants' area at the rear. No time like the present. I'll go and see them straight away. I should introduce myself to Mrs Latimer, anyway. We need to maintain good relations with the family, who can probably help us in dealing with the locals. Do you use the connecting door to visit them or the rear door of the old building when you want to consult them?'

'*I* do not consult them about anything. I know my job already.'

As a new young doctor, he'd been secretly terrified of a matron very much like her. As a surgeon in his late thirties, with a great deal of experience working with badly damaged human beings, he wasn't in the least bit afraid of her or anyone else. But he was angry that he had to waste his energy on the stupid, bigoted woman when there were men desperately needing his help, men who needed a calm, happy environment in which to recover.

He didn't usually judge people so quickly, but in this case, she had made her feelings and approach to the medical profession very plain: old-fashioned and authoritarian. Nineteenth-century medical practice not twentieth. She was completely the wrong person to work here. And he wasn't at all sure that Greyladies was the right place for him and his patients, either. It was too small and on too many levels. How were injured men to get up and down those staircases if they couldn't build a lift?

The War Office was doing its best, he knew, but there were bound to be some changes needed to the places allocated in such a hurry.

He had some influence with the authorities, thank goodness, and was quite prepared to use it to get the best for those in his care, and for the doctors with whom he'd share his skills.

Phyllis came bustling into the big hall where the family lived. 'The new doctor's come to see you. I put him in the servants' dining room.'

'I'll fetch him,' Joseph said at once. 'I think you'll like Dr Somers, darling. He's not at all like the Dragon.'

Harriet put down the diary she was trying to write, and waited for them to return. The doctor was a man approaching his middle years, with a face that might once have been good-looking but now looked careworn, as if he'd seen some terrible things.

He held out his hand. 'I'm pleased to meet you, Mrs Latimer.'

She shook it, pleased at this sign of respect and a modern attitude towards women. 'It's good to meet you, too, Dr Somers. Please sit down.'

He took a chair but didn't wait for her to speak. 'I should have been here at the beginning to prepare the house for patients, but I was dealing with a group of doctors I've been training *and* a group of bigwigs whose goodwill is important for my type of medicine.'

'Your type of medicine?'

'Rehabilitation surgery and the convalescent needs linked to it.'

She watched his brow wrinkle and there was a pause, as if he was unsure how to continue.

'I gather Matron Dawkins has been somewhat . . . er, aloof in her dealings with you, Mrs Latimer.'

Harriet contented herself with a nod. He was trying to be polite and professional about the Dragon, which spoke well of him, but his expression had become grim when he spoke of Matron Dawkins. That displeasure had happened quickly!

'We need to make some changes to the front part of the house, to enable our patients to get around.' He held up one hand to stop her speaking. 'If you'd just let me finish? I don't want to do anything to damage the house, which is beautiful, but some of the men need a lift to take them up and down to their various areas. They can't sit in their wards all day. And I think I know how we can fit in a small lift without damaging the fabric of the house. Would you consider it?'

Harriet looked at Joseph, and he nodded encouragingly. 'We'd certainly consider it, if it didn't damage the house. The men's welfare is important, but I'm the current custodian of Greyladies and I take that responsibility very seriously, too.'

He relaxed visibly. 'I only ask you to stay open-minded until you see what I'm thinking of. We could go and look now. I'd explain better with that part of the house in front of us.'

'Of course.' She stood up, hesitated, then decided if they were being frank, she needed to say something. 'Dr Somers . . . could you allow some of the men to visit us once they're able to walk around? They could use our garden, which is at the side and has several pleasant places to sit? It's such a waste not to use it, because there are places there which are sheltered, even during the winter.'

He looked at her in puzzlement. 'It's very kind of you to invite them. What's stopping them from coming?'

'Matron has forbidden it.' Harriet tried to soften her words. 'I think she's worried about . . . um, about their welfare. But how would it hurt for them to come here, into the house even, to borrow books and sit reading quietly? They would surely enjoy a change of scene, however minor.'

Dr Somers bit his lip as if trying to think what to say. 'Matron isn't used to the sort of hospital I shall be running. It's not necessary medically to supervise the men for every minute once they're convalescent. It can be a question of time for healing between operations and minor adjustments, and they do better if given as much freedom as possible.'

In for a penny, in for a pound, she thought. 'One of the officers, Captain Averill, is an acquaintance of my husband's family and even *he* has been forbidden to visit us.'

'I seem to have jumped straight into the deep end of a difficult situation, Mrs Latimer.'

'Yes. I'm sorry for that, but I'm not going to pretend that relations between Matron Dawkins and ourselves got off to a good start. Or that she has any goodwill about improving them.'

Joseph nodded. 'My wife is right. We've tried but we're simply not welcome to help the men. In fact, she told my wife she had enough to do, staying here and looking after our children. As for her attitude towards my . . . physical difficulties, it's not good.'

'I won't pretend either. For the patients' sake. They are more important than anything else, in my eyes. But we'll keep such thoughts in confidence and feel our way carefully. She *is* an experienced matron and has done an excellent job of setting up the wards and medical supplies.'

Heaven help the people she's in charge of, though! thought Harriet, not for the first time. She stood up. 'Then please show us your idea.'

He looked towards the old door. 'Shall we go back that way? It would . . . send a message.'

'Of course.'

When Benedict led the way through the door, Matron was walking across the hall, holding a folder of papers. She swung round at the sound of the door opening and glared as he walked through it, followed by the Latimers.

'Ah, Matron. Just the person I wanted to see.' He knew his voice was a bit too jovial, but it was the best he could manage. 'Mr and Mrs Latimer have agreed to consider giving permission for a lift, as long as it doesn't interfere with the fabric of the house, and I know just the place we might be able to put one.'

She ignored the Latimers completely. 'Surely the War Office would have had a lift installed if they'd thought it necessary, Dr Somers?'

'They've left such minor changes to my discretion. I am, after all, an expert in this sort of medicine. Let me show you all what I mean.' He led the way into the kitchen, going through it to the laundry area. 'That storage space could be used and its contents stored elsewhere, in a temporary hut, if necessary.'

He flung open the outer door. 'Let's see what the building is like here, whether I've remembered it correctly. Yes. Yes, I have.'

He waited till his three companions had come outside and studied the outbuildings.

'This part of the house seems to have been added on to the newer building almost as an afterthought. As you can see, they didn't bother to beautify the rear of it, because it's out of sight. I don't think we'd be damaging anything worth keeping if we put in a lift here.'

Joseph limped up and down, studying the building and Harriet followed him. They spoke to one another quietly, then turned back to Benedict.

'I think you're right,' Harriet said.

'And what's more,' Joseph added, 'I think you could put a glass walkway here so that the men could get into the front of the house from the lift without disturbing the kitchen staff.'

'But who would keep an eye on them? Make sure they don't stray?' Matron exclaimed in an outraged tone. 'I can't spare any staff to oversee this area.'

Benedict let out his breath slowly and threw her a sop. 'We could give official permission to those capable of it, to move about the house on their own. Others should, of course, be accompanied by a nurse or orderly – or even another patient as they improve.'

'I agree about installing a lift. It'd make the nurses' and orderlies' work easier. But I do not approve of patients wandering about on their own under any circumstances.'

'It's part of their rehabilitation, at least for those who can achieve near normality. And it's my job to help them get to that stage. Given the war, I fear we're all about to learn a lot more about what helps and does not help to rehabilitate badly damaged men. We must therefore all keep our minds open to new ways.'

She said nothing, simply scowled at the Latimers, then at him.

'I was thinking . . .' Joseph said hesitantly. 'Aren't lifts powered by electricity?'

'Yes.'

'There is none at Greyladies.'

'Oh. I see. I'd assumed that in such a big house you'd have installed electricity, even if only for the main living areas. Most people are doing it, it's so convenient to be able to light the place up without all the fuss of gas or oil lamps.'

'We don't have gas, either. There was talk about having it brought into the village, if enough people were keen, but then the war began.'

Matron's face now bore a smug smile.

'I should have checked that sort of thing before getting too enthusiastic,' Benedict said with a frown. 'But there are electrical power lines only a mile or two away. I saw them as we drove here. I'm sure we can overcome that problem, given the urgency of the situation. However, you're right about one thing. It's no use making any changes until we've got the electricity and gas supply set up.'

He turned and gestured to Harriet to precede him into the house. 'I'll walk back to the connecting door with you.'

They all looked at Matron, unsure whether to say goodbye to her.

She solved the problem by giving them a slight inclination of the head. 'I must get back to work. *I* don't have time to chat.'

What was this if not work? Benedict wondered as he escorted the Latimers to the offending door, then went to find Matron again. 'I'd like to visit the patients now, if you don't mind.'

'It would be far better to do that later on, or in the morning even. There are nursing duties to attend to, you know, and we have our routines.'

He tried to speak calmly. 'I need to see them now, so that I can review their cases tonight.'

'Kindly give me half an hour, then, to prepare.'

'Prepare what?'

She puffed up again, anger sparkling in her eyes. 'I am used to making sure doctors see a clean and tidy ward, with patients ready to be questioned, if necessary.'

He decided he'd better give in a little, in the interest of their relationship. 'Fifteen minutes, then.'

Benedict waited for ten minutes, leaving his batman to unpack and settle him in his room. Then impatience got the better of him and he set off. As he walked towards the wards, he heard raised voices and stopped to eavesdrop, in the interests of gathering real information about how things were run.

'I'm *not* going to undress and go to bed at this time of day, Matron.'

'You will do as you're told when you're in *my* hospital, Major.'

The person replying had a deep voice, an educated accent. 'Who's going to force me into my pyjamas?'

'The orderlies, if necessary.'

'I don't think they'd dare do that to a major.'

What the hell was going on? Benedict wondered. He moved quietly towards the door, stopping when he could see the speakers. Fortunately, Matron had her back to him and though the man defying her saw Benedict, he didn't say anything, but waited, his sound arm resting in his sling. He was standing next to another man, a captain by his uniform insignia. He too had his arm in a sling.

There was no reason for them to stay in bed, if that was all that was wrong. Why was Matron insisting on it?

Taking a deep breath, he entered the room.

Matron swung round and moved forward quickly to block his further progress. 'We aren't ready for you yet, I'm afraid, Dr Somers. I need to get your patients into bed first.'

He didn't want to confront her in the presence of a nurse, who was standing in the corner looking embarrassed. How the hell could he deal with this idiocy?

'It is my job to prepare patients for a doctor's round and—'

Someone yelled in the next room, a cry of sheer pain, and he turned instinctively to go and help the person.

He found a man writhing on the bed in the throes of a nightmare. The movements were giving him pain, clearly, but he hadn't woken, which was strange. 'What's wrong with him?' he asked in a low voice.

'He's lost a leg and he seems prone to nightmares.'

'Have you given him anything?'

'A sleeping draught.' She was straightening the bedcovers instinctively, not attending to the needs of the patient, but making it look tidy.

Benedict moved past her and sat down on the bed, taking the man's hand in his. After a moment the fellow opened his eyes.

'Sorry. Was I shouting again? The sleeping draughts don't help the nightmares.'

'That doesn't matter. What I want to do is help you. May I see your wound, see if we can do anything about the pain?'

Matron's mouth fell open in shock and she moved to drag the covers back abruptly, making the patient yelp in pain.

'*Don't touch him!*' Very gently, Benedict finished pulling the covers back and saw a couple of ways to help in bandaging the stump differently and putting a cage over it. 'Some people don't do well on sleeping draughts. You must be one of them. But I have some other painkillers which may help, and I'll see if we can adjust the bandages and find a cage to put over it.'

He turned to Matron. 'Could we have the equipment set up for a rebandage? I'll go and check the medical cabinet.'

She signalled to a nurse, then came out with him. 'I have the key to the medical cabinet. I keep the records for it and can supply you with what you need.'

'What I need immediately is a key of my own.'

'It'll be more efficient for one person to deal with it.'

'Do you intend to go against me on every single detail, Matron? Because I warn you, you'll lose the battle.'

Her mouth fell open.

He held out his hand. 'The key!'

Even then, she hesitated before detaching it from her key chain and dropping it into his hand.

He explored the relevant shelf quickly, giving credit where it was due. 'Well organised.' Then he took down a jar of pills and shook two out.

'Excuse me, Doctor, but we can't use these except on very major cases. They're extremely expensive. Sometimes, these

160

men just have to grit their teeth and cope with pain.'

He was disgusted by her attitude. 'He *is* a major case. And *I* make the judgements on that sort of thing.' Benedict locked the cabinet. 'Do you have any other keys? Right, then give them to me now.'

'As Matron, I need to have a key as well as you.'

'I suppose so, but kindly use it only when I'm away.'

He scribbled a note in the medicines book, locked the cabinet and went back to the patient.

He could see at a glance that the trolley was well set up, so bent his attention to rebandaging the stump, which had not been dealt with as skilfully as it should have been. The trouble was, there were doctors doing their best without the necessary training.

Matron assisted him and he let her, noting how good she was at such details.

As the pills took effect, he watched the patient relax and sigh into sleep. Then he turned to Matron. 'My compliments. You assisted me perfectly then.'

She looked more amazed at his compliment than she had at his complaints.

'We all have our strengths, Matron. You should be in charge of the surgical side of nursing in a big hospital. You'd run it well.'

'Thank you.' She gazed at him warily, but he didn't say anything else. Not then.

He returned to the major and captain, who were sitting on their beds chatting. 'Sorry, gentlemen. Had to help your neighbour.'

'He's gone quieter.'

'I think I've improved matters, with Matron's help. Now,

I'm going round meeting the patients at the moment. I can see that you two are improving nicely, so will wait till morning to examine your wounds, unless Matron thinks I should do it now.'

'And we don't need to get undressed to talk to you?' the major teased.

He grinned at them. 'You'd better stay undressed in the morning, before my round. Have breakfast in your pyjamas. But no, there's no need for bed examinations. This is a rehabilitation and convalescent home, not a hospital in the normal sense. I just want to meet everyone today. Unless someone needs help, like your neighbour.'

The major stood up. 'The place isn't full. Let me introduce you. I'm the senior officer here on the patients' side.'

Matron was very quiet as they continued their round. Her glances at Benedict seemed slightly puzzled now, as if he were an unknown and potentially dangerous phenomenon.

He was concerned about the whole situation. What to do about the amenities? What to do about *her*?

By the following morning, he'd come to one conclusion. He needed to go up to London before he did anything else.

He checked the patients quickly, then said goodbye to the Latimers as well as to Matron, telling them all that nothing should be done about making changes until he got back.

Chapter Eleven

Corin was summoned to see 'a certain gentleman' in Whitehall. The person's name was not offered to him and the message was delivered verbally by a senior officer, which intrigued him.

When he arrived, he was shown to a short corridor of offices hidden away in the depths of the building. Everything was very quiet there, with no stray people walking around and a brisk woman sitting guard at the reception desk, who showed him to a large corner office.

He recognised the man who stood up to greet him: David Brookes, whom he'd met at his aunt's house. Brookes was an anomaly, his exact role at the War Office known only to a few people and not quite explained even to them. He was considered eccentric, but was well thought of and connected.

Corin saluted smartly.

'Never mind that army stuff, Captain McMinty. You're not on parade now. Do sit down.'

He did this and waited.

'I need someone working in my group to help me deal with the damned army, someone who knows the ropes there. You seem more tactful than most, and less rigid about . . . things.'

'Sir?'

'What I'm going to tell you must be kept to yourself. No one is to know, unless *I* give you permission. Not even your commanding officer.'

Corin couldn't help hoping fervently that he would have an opportunity to refuse to share information with his arrogant fool of a commanding officer. It would be very satisfying.

When Brookes had finished explaining, Corin sat thinking it through. 'It seems . . . a prudent thing for a government to have a unit like yours.'

'So I think. Not just prudent but necessary. Do you have a strong prejudice against German or Austrian internees?'

'Not if they're simply citizens caught in this mess. I'd have a prejudice if I thought one really was a spy.'

'Exactly. But there are some who consider all people from that background to be the blackest of villains. Hysterical idiots! If I were to ask for you to be seconded to my little group, and occasionally work with internees, would you be interested?' Brookes leant back in his chair, hands steepled, waiting with no sign of impatience for a response.

Corin was surprised. The army didn't usually ask you what you wanted, or let civilians ask you, either. It just told you to do it. So he took a moment or two to think carefully before replying. 'Did someone suggest me for this role?'

'Yes. But we checked you out before contacting you. We don't take just anyone.'

'Well, to answer your question, I don't believe I'm prejudiced against individuals, whatever I think of their country's activities. But I am loyal to my own country and that comes first.'

'I have to say, it's possible there may be an occasional spy among the internees, and one of our jobs is to keep our eyes open for such annoyances as we deal with the others. We never forget that possibility.'

'I wouldn't forget to be watchful, I can promise you.'

Brookes slapped his hand down on the table. 'Ha! Watchful. That's a very good word to sum up what we do in all sorts of areas. I gather you have some skill with foreign languages.'

'I speak French with reasonable fluency, passable German and I understand some Italian, though my skill in speaking the latter isn't anything to boast of.'

'Mind if I check that?' He switched into fairly fluent French and they conversed for a few moments, then he switched suddenly into German, which he spoke far better than Corin.

When he fell silent, Corin said, 'My gift for languages is modest, compared to yours, Mr Brookes.'

'Multilingual family. I grew up all over the world. Children learn without realising it. Take your time thinking. Oh. I nearly forgot. You'll be working directly under me at this and that. I don't have a rigid view of the world. It'd be very different from the army.'

Corin took a sudden decision. After all, he had been intending to leave the army till war was declared, though only his aunt and Phoebe knew that. 'I don't need more time, but can you give me any details about what the work would entail?'

Brookes' smile faded and his eyes became chill, suddenly the sort of man to fear, for all his previous affability. 'You'd need to do anything which might help our country win the war. Anything at all.' After a pause, he added, 'Right down to murder.'

'I doubt I could kill someone in cold blood, but I'd give a good account in self-defence or in protecting someone else.'

'Good answer. I'm the same. I don't employ men who enjoy killing. Sorry to keep testing you, but it's important to get the right people into place. We get involved in some rather ticklish situations.'

'Very well. I accept your offer. It sounds a lot more interesting than what I'm doing at the moment.'

Brookes held out his hand. 'Welcome on board, then, Captain McMinty. I gather you already have somewhere to stay in London.'

'I own a flat.'

'How many bedrooms?'

'Three.'

'No one else living there?'

'No.'

'Excellent. We might need to put someone up suddenly. We all do it, if needed. Would it be all right with you for us to use your flat, just occasionally?'

'It'd be fine.' The more he was told, the more intrigued Corin was by what the job might entail.

'And you're Lady Potherington's nephew?'

'Yes.' Was Beaty the one who'd put his name forward?

'So you'll have an entrée into upper circles, should it be necessary.'

'If you can call it that. It's Beaty who has the entrée. But I've only to hint to her that something might help the war effort and she'd do what she could to help, I'm quite sure of that.'

'So am I.' He saw Corin's surprise and gave him a grin that was surprisingly boyish in a man with silver hair. 'I'm well acquainted with her. Have been for years. Knew Podge before I knew her. Shame he died so young. Sorry about your wife, too, but accidents happen. I lost a nephew in a car accident, poor lad.'

Corin didn't say anything. He'd thought at one time he'd not get over Norah's death, not because theirs had been such a great love, but because he felt so guilty. They'd quarrelled the evening of the accident and she'd flung out in a rage, saying she was going to meet her lover.

He'd not even tried to stop her driving off in her little car, even though he knew she'd been drinking and wasn't in a fit state to drive. By that time in their marriage, he hadn't cared where she went as long as it was away from him. He'd regretted his inaction bitterly. Norah hadn't deserved to die like that, her beautiful face battered and bruised. And his unborn child hadn't deserved to die, either.

Brookes too was having a thoughtful moment, then he sighed and became brisk again. 'I'll contact your regiment and get you seconded to "special duties" straight away. I think we'd better get you made up to major as well. It'll give you more power to get things done.'

'Just like that?'

'Yes. Once everything's fixed, my deputy will get in touch with you. You'll like Andy.'

Corin walked out of the building with a lighter heart, for all the seriousness of the interview. He'd not been looking forward to acting as a human bludgeon in the war that was building up across the Channel, though he'd have done what was necessary if called to the actual fighting.

But this job sounded interesting, and far more valuable to his country.

* * *

Benedict didn't return to Greyladies for three days. He sent a telegram to Matron in case she was concerned about his absence, but it was brief, giving nothing away about what he was doing in London.

When he drove back to Wiltshire, he was followed by Mr Pashley in an official car, accompanied by an officer whose role they didn't explain.

'Shall I show you gentlemen round?' Matron asked.

'Oh, we wouldn't dream of interrupting your busy day,' Mr Pashley said. 'I did the initial inspections here, so I remember the place well. Dr Somers and I can act as guides to Captain Rainham. Captain, this is Matron Dawkins.'

The officer inclined his head, but said nothing, then the three men walked away, leaving her standing scowling after them.

They went all over the house, speaking only in near whispers. It was surprising how many times they met Matron traversing the corridors or stairs, which greatly annoyed Benedict.

He stopped to speak briefly to his patient Major Humphreys, who had looked well on the way to recovery when he left, but was looking tired and wincing when he moved the injured arm unwarily.

He offered no explanation to the major of why his companions were there, only said he'd come round after he'd finished this to check on that arm.

They finished their tour at the old laundry. Captain Rainham tapped walls, and studied the building both inside and out, then walked to and fro again, before grimacing. 'Not the best place for a lift. Could have one put in, but only with a lot of trouble and expense, because you'd need to strengthen the walls. Is it worth that to you?'

Mr Pashley let out a grunt. 'I doubt it, not with the alternative we have in mind. Shall we see the owners about that alternative now? We need to check the final piece of the jigsaw, before we decide. I have permission to broach the matter with them, as you know, but I will emphasise that it's top secret.'

Benedict led the way back to the entrance hall and knocked on the connecting door to the old house. He caught the flash of a white, starched headdress on the landing above them and made a mental note to tell Matron to keep away when he was showing people round in future.

She'd find nothing out from her snooping, but it still irritated him – and it was disrespectful. But then old-fashioned matrons often were disrespectful towards the medical staff, particularly the junior doctors. Only he wasn't a junior doctor now; and he was the commandant of this establishment as well as its medical head.

Harriet opened the door to them.

'May we have a word with you and your husband, Mrs Latimer?'

'Of course. Do come in, Dr Somers. Mr Pashley, how nice to see you again.'

He waited until the door was shut and they were seated near one of the windows, before introducing Captain Rainham and explaining their difficulties about installing a lift.

'There is another way we could use the old house, though, one you might find more pleasant to live with, and which would entail no structural changes. I'll let Mr Pashley explain.'

Harriet and Joseph listened, nodding and exchanging glances from time to time.

When Mr Pashley stopped speaking, Joseph turned to her and asked openly, 'What do you think, my dear?'

'I think it'd suit Greyladies much better than the present arrangement, and it'd suit us too.'

'I agree.' Joseph turned to Mr Pashley. 'So what must we do next?'

'Leave that to me. I'll speak to a certain gentleman, who is in charge of this sort of project. He's very capable and he has the power to do something about this quite quickly.'

'Thank you for letting us know what's going on,' Joseph said. 'We appreciate the courtesy.'

'And we appreciate your co-operation.'

When they'd gone, Harriet turned to her husband. 'This could make our lives much more pleasant.'

'It could indeed. Shall you mind?'

'No. I much prefer it that way. It'd be wonderful to be rid of the Dragon, don't you think?'

Phoebe found the work of a VAD hard physically. General dogsbodies, the group of young women soon called themselves. However, a sense of camaraderie built up quickly, and that helped them to cope. It made such a difference to have friends to support you.

And there were the injured men, always the men to care about, to help in any small way they could. Some of the patients were so badly wounded, she wondered how they'd survived. Or if they'd have chosen to survive with such wrecked bodies.

The patients were brought into the hospital lying on stretchers, covered in grey blankets, some moaning or occasionally crying out in pain, others grimly silent.

170

Occasionally a man was taken out again, still lying on a stretcher, but this time covered completely by a flag, in honour of the sacrifice he'd made by giving his life in the service of his country.

Everyone stopped work and stood with bowed heads when a stretcher bearing a body was carried out to the waiting hearse.

She felt lucky in her companion VADs, because the other three were all hard workers. When four more young women joined them, there were a few problems with one of them. How anyone could complain about something as unimportant as getting her hands dirty when lives were at stake, Phoebe couldn't understand.

By the time she'd been there three weeks, Phoebe had settled in and was ready for her first day off. She'd written to Beaty two or three times, and her friend had insisted she travel up to London to have lunch and a chat. If Corin was available, they'd invite him to join them for lunch, too.

Phoebe wanted to see Beaty for reasons other than her own pleasure. She was still worried about the Steins. Their money remained sewn into her handbag lining, which seemed as safe a place as any for the flimsies, as everyone called the white, semi-transparent five-pound notes.

It made her smile sometimes that she, who had never had a five-pound note of her own, now carried so many of them around in a shabby old handbag. It was good leather and well made, passed on by the doctor's wife when Phoebe was looking after her mother. The bag would serve her for a few years yet.

She would have liked to put the money in a savings bank for them, so that it would earn interest, but it would have to go under her own name and she didn't like the thought of doing that. Besides, how would she explain having such a large sum of money?

She'd tried to write to her former employers but her letter had been returned with 'whereabouts unknown'. It had been opened and no doubt checked. She didn't mind that precaution, but she still wanted to find the Steins, so she was hoping Beaty could discover where they were. So far, however, she hadn't managed to come up with any information.

Everyone knew that males of German extraction resident in the UK had been taken away and interned, but people weren't always sure who had been taken where. The situation was even less clear with women, who were not always interned with their husbands or fathers. Mrs Stein might have gone to live with friends. Well, Phoebe hoped she had. But the poor woman must be worried sick about her husband.

Most people didn't care what happened to such enemy aliens and said good riddance, but the Steins had been kind to Phoebe and she didn't like to think of them suffering. She knew them well enough to be quite certain they weren't enemies to her country.

Early in the morning on her day off, Phoebe begged a lift to the station in Swindon from one of the hospital's suppliers. She'd take a taxi back to the hospital tonight and hang the expense. She didn't want to linger in the town centre in the cold waiting for buses, because it grew dark early at this time of year. And anyway, buses didn't run very frequently out to the village near the hospital. The final one left at eight o'clock.

What if Frank happened by and saw her? She shuddered at the mere thought of that. But she'd have to be very unlucky for it to happen.

She arrived at the station a little early and after buying her ticket, went straight to the platform to wait, finding a sheltered corner where she wasn't immediately visible and keeping her head down to hide her face under her hat brim.

At last the train arrived and she moved out of her hiding place towards the nearest compartment, one at the end of the train. That was when she saw him. Frank. Waiting at the end of the platform at the other side of the line. He had a clear view of her getting into the last compartment of the train, because she couldn't move any faster. There was a queue of people waiting to board the train.

She saw all too clearly the way Frank's mouth dropped open in shock when he noticed her. It didn't take him a minute to react. He turned and began running back along the other platform towards the bridge stairs, intending to cross over to her side of the rails.

She didn't know what to do, could only get in the compartment and sit praying that the train would leave before he reached it. If not, if he tried to grab her again, she'd yell for help. Surely someone would come to her aid or at least call the guard. They wouldn't let him drag her off the train.

Heavy doors began to slam shut.

Hurry! she begged mentally. *Please hurry.*

A whistle blew and the train started to move. 'Oh, thank heavens!' she murmured.

As it gathered speed, much too slowly for her liking, she saw Frank reach the platform. He saw her and ran alongside, trying to open the door of her carriage, because the rear part of the train had not yet left the station.

She thought for one terrible moment that he would succeed, but a porter dragged him back and the train rattled out of his reach.

He threw off the porter, then stood pressing one hand to his chest and shaking the other at her.

She began to calm down, but her heart was still beating faster than usual. Thank heavens she wasn't wearing her VAD uniform or he'd have had clues about how to find her.

The train rattled along through some beautiful countryside, but apart from an occasional glance out of the window to see where they were, Phoebe didn't pay much attention to the scenery. She was too worried about how she would get back to the hospital that evening without Frank seeing her.

He'd be waiting, she was sure, checking the trains. He'd have found out where her train was going, too. That would have been easy.

She knew him well enough to be sure he wouldn't stop looking now that he thought she was back in Swindon. He'd hunt her down till he found her and then . . . What? Why could he not leave her alone?

Chapter Twelve

Beaty's house was like an island of calm after the busy London streets. Phoebe stood still as the maid closed the door, closing her eyes and enjoying the peace and quiet.

'Phoebe, dear, I've asked you twice what's happened. Something's obviously upset you.' Beaty's voice made her open her eyes again.

'Sorry. I saw Frank at Swindon station. And he saw me. Luckily I was on a train that was just leaving. But he knows I'm back in Swindon and he'll be watching out for me from now on, I know he will. He's like a bulldog when he wants something. Why did they have to station me in Swindon?'

'Why didn't you ask to be sent somewhere else?'

'I didn't want to make a fuss.'

'Well, it's not too late to arrange a transfer, and if you have a good reason, they'll transfer you quickly.'

'Do you think so?'

'Yes, of course. They're not unreasonable.' She put an arm round her guest's shoulders. 'Now, come and sit down. What you need is a nice hot cup of tea. We want the colour back in your cheeks before Corin arrives.'

'Corin's coming?' Phoebe asked eagerly, before she could guard her words, and saw that Beaty had noticed.

'Yes. He's stationed in London at the moment, seconded to some minor government department or other. Don't ask me what he's doing here, because it's all very hush-hush. But he's free to have lunch with us today.'

Phoebe abandoned the attempt to sound indifferent. 'That'll be lovely.'

Beaty looked at her thoughtfully. 'Look dear, I'm worried about you. I'll go and speak to Rosemary Rufford about your situation straight away. Maybe she'll think of somewhere else to send you once she understands that the problem isn't of your making.'

'Would you? I'd be so grateful. I won't dare go into Swindon again after today. I only hope Frank isn't waiting for me at the station when I return tonight.'

Beaty looked shocked. 'You think he'd do that, accost you in public?'

'I'm sure of it. He had it fixed in his mind that I was going to marry him, even without asking me. I've told him I won't, but he just ignores that, as if I don't get the choice.' She wasn't so naïve that she didn't know what went on between men and women. She shuddered at the mere thought of him touching her like that. In fact, she didn't even like him to touch her hand.

'You must stay at the hospital and not go anywhere until we can get you transferred.'

'It might be a bit difficult if they want me to go somewhere with a patient.'

'Then we must get you transferred quickly. We don't want to lose a good worker.' She patted Phoebe's hand. 'I've been keeping an eye on you, since you have no family left. I've had excellent reports about your work.'

Phoebe could feel herself blushing. 'Oh. That's nice.'

The front doorbell rang just then and they heard Corin's voice in the hall.

'We're in here!' Beaty called.

He stood in the doorway of the small sitting room and when he saw Phoebe, he ignored his aunt. 'You're thinner. Aren't you well?'

'I'm very well. They work us hard, but I don't mind that.'

'Don't I get my usual kiss, nephew, dear?' Beaty demanded.

He smiled at his aunt. 'Sorry. You know how it is.'

'I think I do.' She indicated her cheek and he bent to kiss it, before sitting down. Then she noticed his change of status. 'Corin, darling! They've promoted you. Major McMinty, no less. How grand that sounds.'

'It's still the same old me.' But his eyes were on the younger woman as he said that.

'Phoebe's got a problem.'

'It doesn't matter now, Beaty,' she said hurriedly. 'I don't want to spoil the lunch.'

'It does matter, dear. You must always pay attention to your enemies.' Beaty turned back to her nephew. 'She was seen at Swindon station today by that Frank person, the brute you rescued her from the first time you met. Luckily the train was just leaving, so he couldn't get to her.'

'Did he threaten you?'

'I'd not have heard him if he did, but he shook his fist. I'm afraid he'll trace me and . . . I don't know what he'd do. Luckily, I wasn't wearing my uniform.'

'You need to ask for an *immediate* transfer.'

Beaty nodded. 'There! Didn't I tell you? And you need

some way to get back safely tonight. *Not*, I think, by train.'

'Definitely not,' Corin said firmly. 'Look, I have something to do in Wiltshire tomorrow morning. I could drive you down tonight, Phoebe, and find myself a bed somewhere.'

'Are you sure? I don't want to put you out.'

'I volunteered to help you. And I'd be glad of your company on the drive down.'

Beaty sat watching them, smiling smugly. 'I shall go and see Rosemary at once about getting Phoebe transferred. I'll have to miss our lunch, I'm afraid, because it's the best time to catch her.'

Corin smiled. 'I'll take her to lunch, then. All right with you, Phoebe?'

She nodded. More than all right, as far as she was concerned.

'I was hoping you would take over for me, Corin, since she's come all the way from Wiltshire to see us. We can't leave her wandering about town on her own, can we?' Beaty looked at the clock. 'I need to leave now, I'm afraid.'

'We'll go too. I'll bring her back after lunch.'

'Not till at least two o'clock.'

'I think we can stand each other's company until then.'

Once they were out of the house, Corin offered her his arm and they began to stroll along the street. He glanced sideways and saw a curtain twitch and guessed his aunt was watching them. He didn't care. He was happy to have Phoebe to himself.

'Do you mind?' he asked as they turned the corner.

'Mind what?'

'Beaty throwing us together. It was deliberate, I'm sure.'

Phoebe gave him one of her glorious smiles. 'I don't mind at all.'

He squeezed her hand at that response. It was reddened with hard work, the nails short and practical. Most things about her were practical, not fussy, and he preferred that.

Some of the things the women they passed were wearing these days looked so silly: skirts draped into strange, geometrical folds, and some skirts so tight at the ankles their wearers had to hobble along like old women. Some had buttons they let out to make the skirts wider, which added to the stupidity. Why not make them wider in the first place? And – one of the things that particularly irritated him for some reason – they were wearing hats with large bunches of feathers sticking out at strange angles.

Phoebe wasn't wearing a silly hat, or a too-tight skirt. She was striding along beside him as if she enjoyed walking. It was a pleasure to have her by his side.

'Here we are.'

She hesitated. 'It looks expensive.'

'They do good food, and it's convenient.' He opened the restaurant door and she had no choice but to go inside.

It touched him that she didn't want him to spend his money on her.

Phoebe saw several other officers sitting in the restaurant, but though Corin nodded to one, he didn't go across to speak to him. Once the two of them were seated at a table in a corner, she leant towards him and said, 'The officers look very smart, don't they?'

'Yes. That one's a captain and that one is—'

She laughed. 'It's all right. We VADs have learnt to recognise the various ranks.'

'I should have realised. I've had other civilians say that.'

'Well, it wouldn't do to offend someone by giving them the wrong rank. I feel a bit sorry for the other men, though. Their dark suits look so dull against the military smartness.'

He looked down at himself in surprise. 'I suppose it is quite smart.'

'Definitely. Am I allowed to ask why you're coming down to Wiltshire, Corin?'

'I can't tell you, I'm afraid.' He took the menus their waitress was offering. 'Let's order, then we can chat in peace.'

Phoebe saw the waitress give him an admiring look, and felt a sudden spurt of jealousy. She was glad when the young woman walked away. Then she looked at the menu and gasped. 'Look at the prices! Corin, you shouldn't have brought me to such an expensive place.'

'I like the food here.'

'Yes, but—'

'And I can well afford it. Please don't stint yourself. Choose something you really like.'

She looked across at him. Did he read her so easily? She'd have chosen the cheapest dishes on the menu. 'You order, then. I don't recognise the names of half these dishes. They're in French, aren't they?'

'Yes, they are. All right.' He checked that Phoebe liked a couple of items, then beckoned the waitress across and placed their order. 'Are you enjoying the VAD work?'

She shrugged. 'Not the work itself, which is very . . . rough sometimes. But I like to think I'm doing my bit to help my country.' She began to tell him about some of the more amusing things the VADs had had to face, like putting together their own beds that first day.

'Most of the others had never held a hammer before, let alone used one,' she ended.

'And you had?'

'I looked after my mother and we couldn't afford to pay for help, so I did the minor repairs round the house. There's always something going wrong in an old cottage. I wouldn't say I'm *good* at fixing things, but I manage better than most women.'

Their soup arrived just then, oxtail with lovely crusty rolls, so conversation lagged as they both did justice to it.

While they waited for the next course, Corin said, 'Tell me the details of your encounter with this Frank person.'

She shivered. 'I don't want to spoil today by talking about *him*.'

'You must. We mustn't let him think he can get away with threatening you. What does he do for a living?'

'I'm not quite sure. He always tells his parents he buys and sells things. When they ask what, he says, "This and that". But when I called on him at his house in Swindon to ask for help in moving the Steins' furniture, it wasn't a shop, and the door was opened by a woman who was . . . she looked . . . Well, not a very nice sort of person. The sort who walks the streets.'

'Hmm. Perhaps he's a petty thief. And a pimp.'

'I don't know what a pimp is.'

He didn't pretend. She was no wilting flower. 'A man who sells the use of women's bodies to other men.'

'Oh. I didn't realise . . . but it could be. Oh, how awful.'

'He could be a thief as well.'

She couldn't protest that Corin was wrong, because somehow the words both seemed to fit Frank. 'Yes. That's quite likely. He certainly doesn't have any decency or morals. I knew that already, but the way he treated me was

181

dreadful . . . as if I was just an object to pick up and take. His mother would be so upset if he was breaking the law. Janet's a very decent sort.'

'Do you know where he lives?'

'I know where he used to live. He may still be there.'

'Give me his address. I'll ask a friend who's in the police to keep an eye on him.'

'All right.' She watched him write various pieces of information down on a little notepad set in an embossed leather case, then put it back into his breast pocket.

'Let's talk about more pleasant things now, like the letters you're going to write to me.'

She couldn't resist teasing. Just a little. 'Oh. Am I?'

'Definitely. We're both going to write very regularly,' he said with mock fierceness, then his voice softened. 'If we can't be together in person, then we can be together in thoughts and spirit . . . Don't you think?'

'I'd like that very much.'

After lunch they walked slowly back to Beaty's, chatting away.

'How did it go?' Corin asked his aunt at once.

'Rosemary understood perfectly, and she'll find you somewhere within a week or two. She suggests you don't leave the hospital, or even walk in its grounds on your own.'

'I'll be careful. Thank you so much.'

When Corin went off to pack and bring his car round, Phoebe said, 'He shouldn't be wasting his valuable time driving me home. He has more important things to do.'

'Let him take care of you. He's that sort of person. You can always rely on our Corin. After all, we don't want you getting attacked on your way home, do we? Did you enjoy your luncheon?'

'Oh, yes. Corin's so easy to talk to and the food was absolutely delicious. I've never tasted anything like it.'

She knew why Beaty was asking, of course she did, but she pretended not to understand the hidden questions behind the casual questions. If Corin remained interested in her, it'd be as if all her dreams had come true. If he wrote . . . If they got to know one another . . . perhaps it might.

But Phoebe didn't dare trust in that. Dreams had a way of vanishing as quickly as a soap bubble. Well, hers did. And at the moment, with a war on, all sorts of people's lives were being turned upside down.

Hers might be too.

And Corin was a soldier. He might even be killed.

She shook her head vigorously. No. She mustn't even think of that.

To Phoebe's astonishment, Corin returned in a large car with a driver. Only, the latter wasn't in military uniform and he didn't look quite like a chauffeur, either. He had a wary, watchful expression on his face, and he looked physically strong. More like a bodyguard.

After kissing his aunt goodbye, Corin handed Phoebe into the back of the car and joined her there.

She felt a bit embarrassed to chat about personal matters with the driver sitting so close. 'Your car's . . . um, very comfortable.'

'Should be. It's a Standard Landaulette: 20 horsepower, six-cylinder.' Corin patted the side panel affectionately. 'My uncle on my father's side had only just bought it when the war started. He said if it was good enough for B-P, it was good enough for him.'

'B-P?'

'Lord Baden-Powell.'

'The man who founded the Scouts movement? Even I've heard of him.' She leant back, watching the countryside flash by. 'It's a lovely car. I don't know how your uncle could bear to part with it.'

'Oh, he has others. But he donated this to my current department when I moved there, because Mr Brookes said it would be useful to have a few motor cars – a patriotic gesture, as it were. My new boss has a way of getting things done or acquiring the items he needs. He's amazing.'

After that, Corin changed the subject firmly and the noise of the car engine seemed to give them the privacy to chat about themselves.

They stopped once for refreshments and arrived at Bellbourne House Hospital in the early evening.

Corin told the driver to stay where he was and helped Phoebe out himself. 'I shall know exactly where you are now.'

'I'm hoping to get a transfer. But if I succeed, I'll let Beaty know where they send me.'

He took hold of both her hands and pulled her to one side, where they were out of sight of the house and the driver.

He was going to kiss her, she knew he was, and she lifted her face to his without hesitation, sighing with pleasure as he pulled her into his arms. She couldn't pretend that she didn't welcome it.

His lips were warm and it was heaven to be so close to him. She didn't want the kiss to end . . . but of course it did. At least he was still holding her close. She nestled against him with a contented murmur.

'Phoebe, dear Phoebe, this damned war means I can't

even make plans to see you again, but I will manage it from time to time. You won't forget to write to me?'

'Of course not.'

'You'd better send the letters care of Beaty. And I'll get her to forward mine to you till you settle down somewhere else.'

He put one hand under her chin, and kissed her again. Then he sighed and glanced at his wristwatch, the time showing clearly by the light of the rising moon. 'I've got to go now. Don't forget me.'

'How could I?' She raised her hand to caress his cheek.

'You don't pretend, do you?'

'No. It's a waste of time.'

'I don't like pretending and playing silly word games, either. I'm afraid we won't have much time for each other, though, till this damned war is over.'

'We'll do our best.'

'Our very best,' he echoed softly.

She stood at the door leading up to the VADs' quarters until his car had turned off the drive on to the main road, then went up the rough wooden stairs to face her friends' questions.

They knew her too well, said she looked like a woman who'd been thoroughly kissed, and wanted to know who the gorgeous officer in the car was.

She laughed at their teasing, feeling on top of the world. Surely Frank wouldn't find her here. She'd taken great care to keep her destination secret from any but those close to her. He didn't know Beaty or anyone in her circle.

That was such a relief.

But Corin would know she was here. And she'd be waiting for him.

Chapter Thirteen

At Greyladies the weeks seemed to pass slowly as the Latimers waited to hear when the longed-for changes would take place.

But when news came, it wasn't anything to do with their home.

Joseph received another black-edged envelope and stared at it in dismay, reluctant to open it. Then he muttered, 'It's from my mother.'

He looked at Harriet, sitting across the breakfast table from him, waiting quietly. They both knew it could only be bad news.

He slit the envelope with slow care and pulled out the black-edged letter. After reading it quickly, he covered his eyes with one hand, shaking his head slowly from side to side, reluctant to believe what he'd read.

Harriet got up from the table. He felt her stand behind him and lay one hand on his shoulder. He reached up to grasp it, drawing strength from her silent support.

'Who is it, darling?'

'Thomas.'

'Oh, no.'

'Yes.' He gulped but didn't manage to hold back the tears. Well, if you couldn't weep at the loss of a brother, what could you weep for?

'How was he killed?'

'Shot. Died instantly. Only, I've heard the patients here talking. The officers always tell the family that the man died instantly and didn't feel any pain, but it isn't necessarily true. I pray it was true for Thomas. He was a banker, not a soldier, poor chap. I remember what a demon bowler he was when the boys played cricket. He was a good shot, too, though he didn't care for hunting. But his quick eye for a ball didn't do him any good in the fighting, did it? Oh, hell! Thomas dead!'

'Is there to be a funeral?' she asked after a while.

'No. Mother doesn't even have that comfort. They couldn't stop the offensive to retrieve the bodies, so had to bury the men where they fell. She's holding a memorial service *faute de mieux*. I'll have to attend. Harriet, darling, will you come with me?'

'Will your mother want me there?'

'Hang what she wants. *I* need you.'

'Then of course I'll come.'

Harriet was always there when he needed her. He had been so lucky to win her love. He kept hold of her hand for a few moments longer, then sighed and began to make arrangements to travel.

They left their sons in Miss Bowers' care and hired a car to drive them across country, since trains tended to be full of soldiers and not run on time these days. It was only their position as owners of Greyladies, not to mention Joseph's

187

problems in walking, that got them the car – with Dr Somers' help.

'When you come back, we may have some news for you,' he said as he saw them into the vehicle.

'I've almost given up expecting anything to happen, Dr Somers,' Harriet said with a wry smile.

'Oh, it'll happen, believe me. Quite soon now, I gather. Definitely before Christmas.' Dr Somers closed the car door and stepped back, waving goodbye.

When they arrived, Mrs Dalton, who had been staying at the big house with her eldest son to manage the memorial service arrangements, greeted them by bursting into tears and letting Joseph comfort her.

Thomas's wife stayed in her room, emerging with puffy, reddened eyes and clinging to her own mother, who had come to support her.

They were driven to the village church in two old horse-drawn carriages. Even inside them, their breath clouded the frosty air and the ground seemed like iron. They were digging graves 'in case' these days, because there were too many deaths to allow a spell of icy weather to hold up the digging.

The grieving mother led the way inside, supported by her eldest son, who was showing some sense of family loyalty, for once. Selwyn had even refrained from acid remarks about his crippled brother this visit.

He was silent throughout the whole ceremony, not joining in the hymns or the responses, but standing with shoulders hunched, a scowl on his face. Watching him, Harriet thought he might have been handsome when younger, but his face was now puffy with dissipation and his eyes were bloodshot, seeming deeply sad when he wasn't being rude to people.

'This fuss comforts Ma,' he muttered to Harriet at one stage, waving one hand towards the minister holding the service, then turning to frown at the rest of the family and their friends, who were sitting in black-clad rows at the front of the church. 'So I let her do what she wanted for today.'

She looked at him in surprise because he didn't usually bother even to speak to her.

'This fuss don't comfort me, though,' he went on in a low voice. 'I didn't get on with Thomas. We've hardly spoken a word to each other for years.' He laughed, but it was an acid spurt of sound. 'I don't get on with any of my family, come to that, never have done, as you must realise. They're a bunch of milksops. No fun at all.'

She didn't allow herself to comment on that insult to her husband. What was the point with Selwyn?

'But still . . . Thomas *was* my brother.'

'Yes. But you still have two other brothers left.'

He shrugged, his eyes on the empty bier draped with a huge flag, then pulled out his pocket watch and checked the time, sighing at what he found.

Once the ceremony was over and they were back at Dalton House, gathered in the drawing room, Selwyn took over Joseph's wheelchair. 'Excuse us, Ma. I need a word with Joseph.'

He didn't wait for her to acknowledge that remark, but began pushing his brother out of the room.

'Stop. I prefer to walk. I was merely using the chair to have a bit of a rest.'

Selwyn let go and watched Joseph get up and walk out of

the room beside him. 'Never thought you'd manage to move about this much. Just goes to show: you can't predict the future. Does it hurt to walk?'

'It gets painful if I do too much. Which is why I was resting. But it's just as painful if I do nothing, and let the muscles grow weak. So I walk as much as I can.'

'Mmm. You never give in to it, I'll grant you that.' He led the way into the library, slammed the door shut by kicking it with one foot and gestured to Joseph to sit near the blazing fire. 'I need a drink. Want one?'

'No, thank you. Alcohol doesn't agree with me.'

'You drew the short straw in our family physically, didn't you? Or perhaps you're the lucky one, given this damned war. At least one of us will survive it.' Selwyn half filled a cut-glass tumbler with whisky and swallowed it in two audible gulps, then set the glass down without refilling it, which surprised Joseph.

'I haven't told Ma and I shan't do till tomorrow, but I've volunteered, joined Thomas's old regiment, actually. I'm leaving tomorrow for training. I *was* in the officer corps at school, but that's a long time ago.'

'That'll devastate her. She's worried sick about Richard, and he isn't even at the front.'

'I know. But I *want* to go to the front. I want to kill Huns. It's the only thing I can do for Thomas now.' He looked longingly at the bottle of whisky but made no move to pick it up, going to stand at the window, swaying to and fro as he talked.

'I haven't got the brains for desk work. It bores me, anyway. But I'm strong, or I used to be. I've been cutting down on the booze for a while now, and I'm getting fitter again. Preparing to join up, d'you see?'

190

Joseph looked at him in surprise, then wondered why he was surprised. He could see Selwyn fitting into a wartime army. He listened as his brother spoke, sensing that for once Selwyn wanted to talk, to share something. Was that because of the war? Or was it because of the funeral, which had left Joseph feeling deeply sad.

'I'm going to do my bit. It'll be better than mouldering away here in the country, avoiding the debt collectors. They won't dare foreclose on the property of a serving soldier, will they?'

'I doubt it. What about your wife? Have you said anything to her about this?'

'No. We were all set to go with the divorce, then she put it off. The idea of a divorce upset her family and they got at her. She agreed to postpone the divorce until after the war. She's probably hoping I'll be killed. It'll save her a heap of money and trouble. A widow is so much more acceptable than a divorced woman, isn't she?'

Joseph was startled. 'Is she really that heartless?'

Selwyn shrugged, hesitated, then said in a burst, 'Yes. But I wasn't a good husband to her, either. Now, she's met someone else. And he won't have to fight. His family is involved in munitions.'

After another short silence, Selwyn looked at Joseph. 'Thing is, I need your help. I'm leaving tonight, but Ma won't know what I've done till tomorrow. I've written her a letter. It doesn't say what I want it to, but it's the best I can manage. I never was good with words.'

'She'll be upset.'

'Yes. Can't be helped, though. Anyway, you'll be the only son left in England, so you'll help her, won't you? She's not good with money. I've had to slip her a bit extra a couple of times now.' He let out another of his scornful snorts. 'As if I've got any to spare. But I sold a couple of those mouldy old paintings and that put a bit in the coffers.'

'I don't have any money to spare, either. And surely Mother has more than enough to manage on, if she's careful?'

Selwyn let out a crack of genuine laughter. 'I'd like to be there if you tried to tell her that and ask her to economise.' He made his voice go higher and mimicked her. *My dearest, it's our bounden duty to maintain standards at a time like this.*'

'Yes. I can hear her saying it. Look, I'll help her as much as I can from Wiltshire, but I'm not giving her money.' He'd worked too hard to amass it and provide for his sons' education and future. He still had only a modest amount by the standards of his parents but he and Harriet weren't bringing up the boys to expect everything they wanted to drop into their hands. He'd help them train in suitable professions.

Selwyn grunted. 'Don't blame you. Anyway, I've told my lawyer he can sell more paintings or silver to help her, if he has to, so that's not on your shoulders. You could move back here while I'm away, y'know. Keep an eye on the old place.'

'Why? Greyladies is my home now, with Harriet and the boys. We're still able to live in the old house.'

'Strange business, that, changing your name. Still, you got a nice house and an adequate income out of it, didn't you, even if you had to marry a servant to do it?'

'If you say one word against my wife, I'll leave this house and never speak to you again.'

Selwyn shrugged. 'Didn't mean to upset you. She's all

right, really, your Harriet. She don't look like a servant, either. Quite pretty. And got a bit of sense in her head. Don't gabble on at you, like most females do.'

If this was meant to be a conciliatory speech, it wasn't a good one. Joseph decided that his feelings towards this brother hadn't changed: he disliked Selwyn as much as ever. 'Is that all you want to talk about?'

'Not quite. If I get killed, this place will go to Richard. If he hasn't found someone to marry, you'll have to nudge him into doing it and producing an heir. Pity *you* aren't the next in line. You've already managed to father two sons who aren't cripples. But we have to do this right, follow the traditions. Next son gets his chance and all that.'

He began drumming his fingers on the small table next to him. 'Strange thing is: Richard don't even seem to notice other women since his wife died. Ma says he's grieving. What the hell for? His wife didn't seem anything special to me. Colourless. Not even pretty, like yours. Damn! I can't remember her name even.'

'Diana.'

'Yes, that's it. She must have been good in bed, I suppose, for him to miss her so much. He only married her for money, after all.'

Joseph waited, biting back angry words because it never did any good to reason with Selwyn.

'I've made a will. Left everything to Richard, as I said. *I* ain't going to marry again, that's for sure. It's horrible to see the same female across the breakfast table every day, to listen to her nagging and going on about boring women's stuff. So . . . if anything happens to me, you'll nudge Richard into marrying again. All right?'

'Yes.'

'Promise.'

'I promise.'

'Good. That's sorted out. We can go and join the others. Tonight will be my last time on duty as master of the house for a good while, and thank bloody goodness for it. What a bore living in the country is! Give me town life any day.' He stared round with loathing.

Joseph waited, but Selwyn offered no more confidences.

This was as close as he'd ever come to understanding what motivated his eldest brother. What little there was to understand. Selwyn might have a big, strong body, but he didn't have much of a brain.

Heaven help Dalton House if Selwyn survived the war. There would be nothing to leave to Richard.

That night in bed, Joseph went over his conversation with his brother so that Harriet would understand the situation.

'Selwyn wasn't here very often when I was a maid. He was nearly always in London. So I don't know much about him. But the other maids didn't seem nervous when he was around. When some people were staying, the housekeeper always reminded us to lock our bedroom doors at night.'

'It was another world, that one, and my family acted as if it existed only for our sort of people, didn't they? That's changing quickly.'

'Yes. Your mother was finding it hard to get servants even before the war. And talking of the war, I was reading a newspaper article prophesying that women will get used to working like men do, with weekly wages in hand, and every Sunday free. It said they won't want to go back into service. That'll cause a lot of letters to the editor.'

He considered this, head on one side. 'I think whoever wrote it was right.'

'There was a man's name, but it sounded more like the way a woman talks and thinks. I hope women do get better chances of education and jobs in future. I didn't at all want to go into service. I was so excited when I won a scholarship to train as a teacher, but my father wouldn't allow it.'

He reached out for her hand. 'Well, you got me instead. I hope I make up a little for your disappointment.'

She chuckled. 'Oh, yes. I got an excellent bargain.'

He rolled over to plonk a kiss on her cheek, but his mind was still on his family. 'You know, tonight Selwyn reminded me of an animal who looks tame but is wild underneath, and is fighting back against an enemy with all its might. I believe going to war will suit him far more than living here does. Do you agree?'

'Yes. It may even be the making of him.'

'I wouldn't go so far. He'll still be stupid. *You* aren't, thank goodness. Even Mother is warming to you.'

'She was looking older tonight, wasn't she? So sad about losing Thomas.'

'Yes. Ravaged. And she'll be even more upset in the morning when she finds out what Selwyn's doing. We'll have to get up early, in case she needs us.'

There was a formal family breakfast arranged for nine o'clock, which was late for Joseph and Harriet, who were usually busy well before that time. But they humoured his mother and waited, helped by a pot of tea and some biscuits brought up to their bedroom by a plump, dull-looking maid.

195

When they went down, they found Richard and Mrs Dalton about to sit down at the dining table.

There was a letter beside Mrs Dalton's plate. She picked it up, frowning. 'I didn't think the post had come yet. No, this hasn't got a stamp on it. See.'

Joseph watched her squint at it, knowing she was too vain to wear the spectacles she really needed.

'It looks like Selwyn's handwriting. I suppose he's gone off to London early. He hates it here. No matter what I do, I can't get him to take the estate in hand. He'll gamble the last of it away in the end, I know he will.'

She put the letter down unopened. 'I'll read it later.'

Harriet jerked her head slightly, a signal to Joseph to speak to his mother.

'You need to read his letter now, Ma,' he said gently.

Her voice grew suddenly sharper. 'Why?'

'Read it.'

Richard looked across at him, then glanced at the ornate ormolu clock on the mantelpiece, as if impatient to leave.

Joseph wondered why Selwyn hadn't confided in Richard. He watched his mother sigh and fumble in her embroidered velvet handbag for her pince-nez. She perched them on her nose and used her butter knife to slit open the envelope. After reading the letter, she let out a sob and read it a second time. Then she dropped the letter, fumbled for her handkerchief and began to weep, a terrible despairing sound.

'I'm going to lose him. I'm going to lose you all.'

Harriet couldn't bear to see such pain. She got up and went to put an arm round her mother-in-law's shoulders, making shushing noises as if the older woman was a child. For once, Sophie Dalton clung to her, but the weeping didn't stop.

Richard moved to sit next to Joseph. 'Do you know what's in the letter?'

'Yes. He told me last night. He's joined up.'

'Oh, hell! Couldn't he have waited till Thomas's death wasn't so raw in her?'

'It's Selwyn's way of dealing with his guilt and grief about that. He wants to hit out at the Germans for killing his brother. For all the difference one person can make.'

Silence, then, 'It's a mess out there. You're well out of it, Joseph.'

'No, I'm not.' He gestured to his twisted body. 'Don't you think I resent being like this? Not able to join in anything properly.'

Richard stared at him in surprise. 'You never seem to be fretting about your problems.'

'Because it won't do any good to mope and complain. Besides, I don't want to upset Harriet more than I have to. But I'd really like to play my part, you know. It's *my* country you others are fighting for, too.'

For once, Richard looked at him approvingly. 'Well, it's the right sentiment, but I'm still glad you're not able to go out there. It's a bloodbath. They sacrifice men, and for what? Another few yards of mud. Then they sacrifice more men to keep it, only sometimes they don't succeed and they lose the little ground they've gained, which costs still more lives.'

Joseph was startled. 'I thought you had an office job.'

'I used to have. But after Diana died, I transferred. She was my guiding star. She made a better man of me. I feel lost without her, can't stand to live in our house, been staying in a hotel.'

'You should marry again. For the family's sake.'

'I can't bring myself to do it. When I lost Diana, I lost all that mattered to me.' He blinked furiously. 'I don't even like to say her name out loud. Selwyn mocked us for our placid way of life, but we were happy . . . *right* for one another. As you and Harriet are. I shall never marry again, Joseph. And I don't even care whether I survive the war.'

'I'm sorry.'

'I'm glad you've got a good wife, and two sons. Maybe the family's going to need those lads one day.'

Joseph looked at him in shock. 'What?'

'Haven't you considered the possibility? *You* might inherit, or more likely, your sons might. I daresay Selwyn will survive the carnage, but *he* says *he* won't marry again.' He hesitated. 'Actually, I don't think he can love a woman.'

It felt to Joseph as if the ground shivered beneath his feet. '*Selwyn?* You don't mean—'

'I think – no, I know he's a fag.'

'Selwyn? He's a big, strapping fellow.'

Richard chuckled. 'What's that got to do with anything? There were one or two of 'em at school. You could always tell. Didn't you meet any? No, of course you were educated at home. Well, take my word for it, they come in all shapes and sizes.'

'Selwyn can't be like *that*.'

'I'm only guessing, because I think he's denying it to himself, but I've heard that he can't perform with a woman. I think that's why he drinks so heavily, so people will blame it on the booze.'

Joseph suddenly remembered what Harriet had said. It all made sense now that the housekeeper hadn't worried about the maids when Selwyn was home.

They heard the sound of a chair being pushed back and looked up to see Harriet guiding their mother out of the room.

'Mother's taking it badly,' Richard whispered.

'Yes. Thomas was her favourite.'

'No, you've always been her favourite.'

Joseph let out a snort. 'I don't think so.'

'It's true. You needed her so badly when you were little. I once heard Nanny say that if it wasn't for her, you'd have died. Thomas was her second favourite, I will admit. I was too independent for her, answered back too much. And of course, poor Helen made the mistake of being a girl, so she didn't get much of a look-in. Mother only cares about her sons.'

When Harriet came back, the men stood up till she'd taken her place again.

'I've left your mother with her maid. She's very upset about Selwyn.'

Richard glanced at his watch and didn't bother to sit down again. 'She'll be lying down there for hours, so I might as well get going. Say goodbye to her for me, Joseph. Tell her I had urgent regimental business. It's true enough. Don't tell her it's to do with me being posted to France. I'll write to her later about that.'

Which left his once-despised youngest brother to comfort their mother and try to find someone to manage the estate.

And to worry about Selwyn.

It was several days before Harriet and Joseph could return to Greyladies, and they were greeted by a scene of what looked at first like chaos, but resolved itself into several activities being undertaken at once. It reminded Joseph of a wasp's nest that had been disturbed.

They directed their driver to take them round the back to their own entrance, and he edged the car past an ambulance. Near it, two men were carrying a stretcher out of the house. Its occupant was staring round as if the move had taken him by surprise.

When the car drew up at the kitchen door, an orderly came hurrying out to them. 'Dr Somers saw your car turn off the road. He's in his office and he'd be grateful if you could see him straight away, if you don't mind.'

They exchanged surprised glances, then Joseph nodded. 'Fine. We'll do that.'

As they walked through the old part of the house, the boys came running out of their schoolroom followed by Miss Bowers.

'The Dragon's leaving,' Jody yelled at the top of his voice. 'Isn't that lovely?'

Mal was young enough to hold up his arms to his mother for a quick cuddle, something never denied him by either fond parent.

'Dr Somers wants to see us,' Joseph said.

Miss Bowers nodded. 'I know. Come along, boys. You've seen your parents now. You can talk to them again later.'

They pulled faces, but when Miss Bowers spoke in that quietly firm tone of voice, no one ever disobeyed her.

Harriet led the way into the new part of the house, stopping just inside the main hall, and putting out one arm to keep Joseph back till two men on crutches had limped past them.

They had to thread their way through piles of boxes and

chests of medical supplies, to get to the doctor's office, whose door was wide open.

Dr Somers looked up from his desk. 'Ah, you're back! That's good. Jervis, please keep everyone away from me for the next half-hour. And close the door.'

A young lieutenant they didn't recognise nodded, smiled at them and left quickly.

'Do sit down. You must be wondering what's going on.'

'I gather the change you mentioned is being put into effect.'

'Yes. Which is, I hope, good news for you.'

'Very good news.' Joseph chuckled. 'Even Jody said how glad he was that the Dragon was leaving.'

'She is a fierce one, isn't she? But she's a shocked dragon at the moment, because I've found her a new position to which she's really well suited, so she's having great difficulty staying angry with me.'

'Oh? What's that?'

'She's going to become the deputy to the fellow in charge of army hospital supplies for all the extra places we've set up. They're two of a kind, sticklers for details being correct. They should do an excellent job. Unless they murder one another first.'

'I'm glad she's not been put on the scrap heap,' Joseph said in his gentle way. 'I should think she only has her job to care about, which is why she's so possessive about it.'

'I suppose so, but I find it hard to be as charitable as you, because she's trampled on a lot of people during her lifelong reign of terror, and it isn't necessary to behave like that. Anyway, now we've disposed of her, it's you two I need to have a chat with.'

'Is it what was suggested?' Joseph asked eagerly.

'Yes. Please keep this to yourselves, but we're going to stop Greyladies being a convalescent home for officers, and use it instead to house some very special enemy aliens. Well, they're not enemies, at least I don't think they are, even if they're foreigners. They have knowledge and skills our side can use, and are more than willing to share them. So we'll base some of them here permanently, pretending it's still a convalescent home, and bring other aliens in and out as needed. Do you speak any foreign languages?'

Joseph grimaced. 'I speak a little appalling French.'

'I don't speak any foreign languages at all,' Harriet admitted.

'Then we'll need to bring in a woman who does, or who can learn quickly. The man who's going to be in charge of setting things up here speaks German, French and Italian, so we can rely on him to manage problems. But women usually deal better with other women, so we need a female to deal with them. Of course, most of the aliens speak reasonable English. But still, we'd like to know what they're talking about to one another.'

'These are all internees?'

Dr Somers hesitated. 'Most of them. It will seem as if they all are, but if any of them come to you for help and mention the phrase "a certain gentleman", then I hope you'll give them whatever they ask for, because it'll be an emergency.'

'We'll do anything we can, of course we will. In fact, I for one am delighted to have a better way to serve my country.'

'You'll be doing that, don't worry. I'd be grateful if you and Mrs Latimer could invite small groups to tea, befriend them, get to know individuals. We don't think there will be spies among them, but we can't guarantee that. You'll oblige us by keeping your eyes open on our behalf, as well as sharing your house.'

Joseph's eyes were sparkling with interest. 'Good heavens! How exciting.'

Harriet watched him, love squeezing her heart as it so often did. He was such a kind, patient man. His decades of being an invalid seemed to have made him wise beyond his years.

Their sons adored him, the people from the village respected him. And she loved him more with every year they were together.

Chapter Fourteen

There was an ambulance going into Swindon and just at the last minute, the VAD who was to accompany the men tripped and fell, spraining her ankle.

'Do you think you could go with them instead, Sinclair?' the head nurse on this shift asked.

She hesitated.

'I know about your little problem, but we won't ask you to be on your own at any time, so you'll be quite safe. The trouble is, what with two nurses being down with colds and a whole series of minor operations necessary for our patients, I'm a bit pushed for escorts. You'd have been transferred before now if it weren't for our staffing problem.'

'They've found a place for me?' Phoebe asked eagerly.

'Yes. But I can't tell you anything about it because I don't know. Anyway, I won't force you to do this, but I'd really appreciate it.'

She suppressed a sigh. She couldn't refuse, of course she couldn't, but she felt uneasy about going into Swindon.

At the larger hospital where further corrective surgery was to be carried out, she kept her head down and stayed close to one of the orderlies at all times.

To her relief, they didn't bump into anyone she knew and she was able to get back into the ambulance and let it whisk her out to Bellbourne again without incident.

Please let me not have to go into Swindon again, she thought as they drove back. She hated the way she feared encountering Frank, but she couldn't shake off the dread of him grabbing her, as he had before. She'd felt so utterly helpless.

Cyril stared at the VAD helping the orderlies with the new patients. He recognised her at once, with that red hair, because Frank had pointed her out in the street one day and boasted that this was the woman he was going to marry.

'Does she know it?' Cyril had asked, thinking heaven help the poor bitch who does marry you.

'I'm not in a position to wed at the moment. I'll tell her when it's time.'

Cyril had been in a rash mood after a couple of drinks, so had dared to say, 'She might turn you down, though.' He regretted it when he saw Frank glare at him. It didn't do to be on the wrong side of that one.

'I don't take no for an answer. Especially from a woman.'

'Well, she'll probably grab you with both hands. You'll be a good provider.'

The anger on his companion's face was replaced by smugness. 'You're right there.'

And now Frank was offering money to anyone who spotted her, so she must have turned him down and run away. She should have left town, the silly bitch.

Well, Cyril wasn't going to lose the chance to earn ten quid, no bloody way.

Once his shift had ended, he went round to Frank's, but the tart who lived there said he wasn't at home.

'Where is he? It's urgent.'

'How should I know? You don't think he tells me where he's going.'

She shut the door in his face.

Cyril set off down the street. He'd go to the pub and have a pint or two. Someone might have seen Frank.

He fell lucky. Frank was sitting on his own in a corner, scowling into a glass of beer. Cyril went over to join him.

'Still interested in finding that young woman, Frank, the one with red hair?'

He looked up. 'You know where she is?'

'Not exactly. But I saw her and I know where to start searching.' He looked pointedly at the half-empty glass. 'That beer looks good.'

Frank stared at him, fish-eyed, for a moment, then waved his hand to attract the attention of the barman, signalling him to bring over two more beers. 'Sit down, then, and keep your voice low.'

Cyril did that and waited, deliberately making Frank have to ask for more information.

'Well, where did you see her?'

'I want the money first.'

They locked glances and Cyril shivered inside, but he needed that money so he didn't give in.

Frank slapped a note on the table. 'Five quid for the information. The other five if I find her because of it.'

Cyril reached out for the money, but a large, meaty hand slapped down on it.

'You can look at the money, but you don't get hold of it

206

till I hear what you have to say. And it'd better be good.'

'All right. Your young woman's a VAD, so she'll be at one of the new hospitals, and it won't be far away because she was escorting some patients into Swindon Hospital when I saw her.'

'Ah. Was she now?'

The hand slackened and Cyril snatched the money, stuffing it in his inside jacket pocket.

The barman brought across the beer and the two men lifted their glasses in a silent toast.

'If this leads me to her, I'll be just as grateful to you again, another fiver.' Frank wiped a frothy moustache off his upper lip with the back of his hand. 'How did she look?'

'Thinner. She didn't stay around long, but I knew her at once.'

'Did she see you?'

'Wouldn't have made any difference if she had. She don't know me from Adam. I only knew her because you pointed her out in the street once.'

Frank smiled, not a nice smile. 'I'll have her married and out of that damned uniform within the month. I don't want *my* wife wiping the arses of injured soldiers.'

Cyril took another slurp of beer. What did you say to a remark like that? Frank was a bit strange sometimes, but he got things done, and people said he was making good money with this and that. 'I knew you'd be pleased, Frank.'

'I am. Very pleased. I'll send her out to my parents' farm as soon as we're married, then they can keep an eye on her when I'm busy.'

He went on talking, more to himself than his companion,

so in the end Cyril went across to join some other friends. No woman was worth all that fuss, as Frank would find out after he got married.

Phoebe was sent to the stores to get some more bandages. The stores were located at the rear of the hospital, in a building that had been the stables at one time.

As the orderly in charge gathered together the things Matron wanted, Phoebe loaded them on her trolley. He was a dour fellow with a badly scarred face, and never offered you more than a word or two, but he knew his job and always seemed to have what was needed.

She pushed the trolley along the corridor, and since it was a fine day, took the outside way back. It was nice to get a breath of fresh air. Some of the smells in the wards were unpleasant, however hard the nurses tried to keep things clean.

She didn't think anything of it when she saw a figure in the distance. People were always coming and going. A small box bounced off the trolley just then, and she bent to pick it up. As she put it back more securely, she glanced across the garden again, and saw the man moving towards her.

Her heart began to pound in shock. It looked like. It was . . . Frank!

She abandoned the trolley and began to run, but he got to the turn off to the stores before she did.

She stopped a few paces away and so did he. He'd chosen his place well, was blocking the nearest entrance to the hospital buildings.

'I want to talk to you,' he said.

'I don't want to talk to you.'

'You'd better. I told you I'd find you and I did. What the hell are you doing in a place like this? You could be married to me and living in comfort.'

'I haven't changed my mind and I never will. I won't marry you, Frank. Go and find someone else if you need a wife so desperately.'

'I don't want someone else. I want *you*, Phoebe, and only you.'

The way he said that made her shudder, he sounded so implacably determined.

As she was trying to work out how to get away from him, he suddenly lunged towards her. She was stronger after the hard physical work of the last few months and managed to run away from him.

But she could hear his feet pounding after her, and he was still between her and the house.

This path led only to the gardens and the further away she got from the house, the less likely she was to find help.

What was she to do? Would anyone even hear if she yelled for help?

Only one way to find out. She began shouting for help at the top of her voice.

Nothing happened and she could hear Frank panting. She glanced over her shoulder to check on him and that was her undoing. She tripped over a tree root and felt herself falling, landing with a thump.

She screamed as loudly as she could, and when he grabbed her, she managed to stop him covering her mouth for a few more seconds. Then that big hand clamped down on her and struggle as she might, he held her beneath him on the damp ground, pressing his body against hers.

'I told you you'd not get away from me. You're mine, Phoebe Sinclair, mine and no one else's.'

She bit him hard and he slackened his hold, so she screamed again at the top of her voice.

She had given up hope of finding help when she heard someone shout, 'What's that?'

Someone else yelled, 'It came from over there.'

Frank still had her mouth covered but he was cursing under his breath.

Two of the patients came into view. One realised immediately what was happening and shouted, 'Get off her, you brute!'

But Frank was already doing that. 'I'll find you again!' he told her in a low voice, then set off at a shambling run through the gardens.

Since the patients weren't able to move fast, he got away, but Phoebe was safe. For the moment.

Shuddering with relief, she began to get up. One of the men held out his hand to her and she took it gratefully, letting him steady her once she was upright.

'Thank you.'

'He . . . er, didn't manage to do anything to you, did he?'

'No. You got here just in time. Frank's very strong. I couldn't fight him off.'

'Do you know him, then?'

'Yes. He's my uncle's stepson. He wants to marry me and I won't agree. I've been hiding from him for months.'

'Sods like him should be castrated,' the smaller man said suddenly. 'Excuse my language, miss, but they should.'

'I agree.' She gave a shaky laugh. 'Shall we get back to the hospital? I shan't feel safe till I'm inside it. And I've lost the trolley of bandages and supplies.'

'Someone else will go back for it. Here. Hold my arm. You're still trembling.'

Matron gaped at her dishevelled appearance, listened to her faltered explanation and sat her down in the office with a strong cup of sweet tea. 'Shock. That'll help.'

It helped very little. This was the second time Frank had manhandled her and Phoebe still had nightmares about the first attack.

Matron called in Major Burroughs, the officer in charge, and he listened to the tale, asking a couple of questions, telling her to take care not to be alone from now on.

When she and Matron left his office, Phoebe let out a shuddering sigh. 'What am I going to do? Wherever I go, I'll be looking over my shoulder, worrying about Frank.'

'If you stay indoors, you'll be safe enough till you leave, at least.'

'I won't *feel* safe, though. He's a very determined man. And there are a lot of entrances into this hospital.' If Frank had found her once, he would probably find her again.

'Well, this will probably speed up your transfer.'

She heard the restrained impatience behind Matron's words, so went back to work with a quick, 'Thank you. I'm feeling better now.' But she didn't even sleep inside the hospital and she knew she'd continue to worry every time she crossed the yard to the dormitory.

The other VADs were full of the incident and kept asking her about it and how she'd felt when he grabbed her till she yelled at them. 'Leave me alone! I don't want to talk about it. I just want to get away from here.' Her voice broke on a sob.

Penny came to put an arm round her shoulders in a gesture meant to comfort.

Phoebe didn't want touching. She just wanted to be left alone. No, she didn't. She'd be terrified unless she was with other people.

As if reading her thoughts, Penny added, 'We've got orders to make sure you're never on your own ever. It's time for tea now. If you're ready, we'll walk across together, shall we?'

Phoebe pulled herself together and tried to look as if she was listening to what they were chatting about. Only it was going in one ear and out of the other, because she still couldn't pull her thoughts together, couldn't decide what to do.

After the evening meal there were further duties, but she asked Matron if she could make one phone call before she began.

'Whom do you wish to call?'

'Beaty. I mean Lady Potherington. I stay with her when I'm in London.'

Matron's voice grew warmer. 'Of course you can phone her. Use my office. I'll help you.'

But she stayed there after she'd got the call put through, so even then Phoebe couldn't say what she really wanted to. But she did ask Beaty for help in arranging an immediate transfer.

She had no shame in begging for such help. If she didn't get away, Frank would come after her again, she knew he would.

Beaty put the phone down, upset for Phoebe. She'd heard her young friend's voice wobble a couple of times as she was explaining what had happened. That Hapton fellow must be a lunatic, to be so obsessed by a woman who didn't want him.

She picked up the phone again. This needed more rapid action than she or her friend Rosemary could arrange, and it must be done very carefully, so that there was no easy way for him to follow poor Phoebe.

'Corin. I'm so glad I've caught you in. Listen, Phoebe's in trouble and I think you can help her better than anyone.'

He listened, asked questions, the answers to some of which she didn't know, then there was silence.

'Right. I'll see Brookes first thing in the morning, and in the meantime I'll work out a plan to get Phoebe away without being seen. We'll have her out of there by nightfall tomorrow, I promise you.'

'I knew you were the one to ask. The official wheels grind so slowly. Shall I phone and tell her?'

'No. The fewer people who know the better. I'll phone them tomorrow, once I've worked out the details.'

Corin sat next to the phone even after the conversation with his aunt had ended. Apart from being upset for Phoebe, he was conscious of a burning desire to beat Frank Hapton to a pulp. Which was a highly uncivilised thing to desire.

How could you not feel that way, though, when the woman you loved had been attacked for a second time? He smiled wryly. If he'd been uncertain how much he loved Phoebe before, he wasn't now. He wished he could drive through the night and take her away from Bellbourne, look after her, care for her.

If he was lucky and survived this hell of a war, he'd ask Phoebe to marry him – he smiled, fairly certain she'd say yes – then he'd care for her with every fibre of his being.

*   *   *

The following morning, he was in the office before anyone else, impatient to see David and get things moving.

When his boss did arrive, he was humming cheerfully, but stopped to ask, 'What's wrong? You look like a man who didn't sleep very well.'

'You're right. I didn't.'

'Worrying about Miss Sinclair, were you?'

'How did you know about Phoebe?'

'I ran into Beaty yesterday evening and she told me. We'd better get your young woman out of Bellbourne, so that you can concentrate on departmental matters. There are too many doors into and out of a hospital, anyway. It's not a good place to keep someone safe. Have you any ideas how to get her away without anyone seeing?'

'Yes. This is what I thought we could do . . . I'd welcome your advice, though.'

After incorporating a couple of additional suggestions made by his boss, Corin nodded. 'I think that'll do it. You're sure the matron and commandant will help me?'

'Oh yes. I know them both. Good sorts to have helping you in an emergency.'

After they'd finished discussing the details of how to get Phoebe away, Brookes gave Corin an assessing look. 'Your plan was impressive. The more I think about it, the more I realise you're definitely the best person to set up the new so-called *convalescent home* at Greyladies. You can spend, say, two months doing that, then we'll move you to another project. Though I may call you up to London now and then for help with the army wallahs. I like how you think. We need clever, devious chaps in our group.'

He brought in his adjutant, dictated a brief note and said to Corin, 'All right. Take it from there.'

'Don't you have any specific things *you* want doing at Greyladies?'

'It's an unusual situation. No precedent. If I think of anything else apart from my basic briefing, I'll let you know.' He grinned. 'Otherwise, use your initiative.'

Corin walked out feeling rather shocked. After several years in the regular army, he wasn't used to being set free to work as he chose.

Then he thought of Phoebe and forgot his doubts. The first thing was to rescue her and get her somewhere safe, then he'd turn his attention to those enemy aliens.

He went into his office and picked up his phone . . .

Rain was falling steadily as the delivery van turned into the drive of Bellbourne.

'Just what we need,' the driver said with satisfaction. 'Anyone keeping watch on this place will be soaked, cold and thinking more about staying dry than who's going in and out.'

'We won't even know whether Hapton is watching the hospital, let alone from where. We passed any number of houses in the lane leading to the gates, and there are sheds, too. He could be hiding in one of those.'

As the van stopped at the rear of the hospital, he tugged at his workman's overalls, which were a bit short for a man of his height but were the best he'd been able to find on the spur of the moment, then got out. Picking up the smallest box from the rear, he carried it towards the kitchen door. It was opened just before he got there by an orderly.

'Special delivery.'

'We're not expecting anything else today.'

'Well, they sent me down from London with this, so someone must be expecting it. It's supposed to go straight to Major Burroughs.'

'Well, you've got the name right, at least. Shall I take it up to him?'

'No, I've got orders to see it into his hands. Tell him it's from a certain gentleman of his acquaintance.'

'Who?'

'How the hell should I know? It's some sort of officers' joke.'

'I'll check whether he's free. I wonder what it's all about?' The orderly gave him a questioning look.

'Haven't the faintest idea, pal. I just do my job. What do I know about medical supplies?'

The orderly shrugged and walked out.

'Do you and the driver want a cup of tea?' the cook called across the kitchen. 'Nasty sort of day, isn't it?'

'That'd be lovely, but not till I've delivered this box. I'm not supposed to let it out of my hands, and there are two bigger boxes out in the van as well. The driver's keeping an eye on those. We won't bring them in till the major decides where he wants them.' He rolled his eyes. 'Such a fuss they make sometimes over medical deliveries.'

She smiled. 'Well, we all want to save lives. I'll keep the pot warm for you.'

He wondered what she'd say if she knew he was an officer on a rescue mission. He hoped his plan was good enough. No one except Burroughs and people he felt were safe must find out. They didn't want word getting back to Frank about who had turned up unexpectedly the day Phoebe dropped out of sight.

The orderly returned. 'You're to take the box up to him. This way.'

Corin winked at the cook and followed him out.

Not until the office door closed behind the orderly, did Major Burroughs gesture to a chair. 'How can I help?'

'I'm here to spirit Miss Sinclair away.'

'Good. How are you planning to do it?'

'We're delivering two larger boxes containing supplies. They're big enough for her to hide in, so we'll just carry her out in one. Can you arrange for someone reliable to empty them? They really do contain useful supplies.'

Major Burroughs smiled. 'The orderly in charge of the stores will be the perfect person to help hide her. I'd trust him with my life, and as he speaks mainly in grunts and doesn't hold with what he calls "this modern gibble-gabbling about nothing", he'll not reveal anything about the escape. I'll send Matron to fetch Phoebe. Matron's a stout old bird and we can rely on her too. What about your lass's clothes and so on?'

'If we can't get them packed quickly without anyone realising, she'll have to do without.'

He grinned. 'Matron will find a way. She doesn't believe in waste.'

Chapter Fifteen

Matron came into the area where Phoebe was setting out the trays for the patients' meals. She was followed by another VAD. 'I need your help with something, Sinclair. Amy will take over here.' She led the way out immediately without further explanation.

Phoebe followed her, puzzled.

Matron led the way to her office. 'Someone's arrived to take you away from Bellbourne. We need to pack your things immediately and sneak you out of here without anyone realising what's going on. I've got you a nurse's uniform and if you tuck your hair out of sight under the cap and keep your eyes down, no one should give you a second glance. Hurry up and change.' She gestured to a pile of clothing and turned to look out of the window.

After one surprised glance, Phoebe put on the other clothes as ordered, then Matron bundled the discarded VAD uniform into a towel as if it was dirty washing, and handed it to her to carry.

As they set out for the stables, Matron complained loudly about not putting up with untidiness, and Phoebe hung her head as if in trouble.

Once in the dormitory, Matron stopped scolding. 'There's no time to waste, so pack your things into your suitcase as quickly as you can. Leave something out to change into, so that you're no longer in uniform when you leave.'

'How am I going to leave without anyone finding out?'

'In a box.'

Phoebe paused, open-mouthed. 'You mean . . . in a coffin?'

'Sorry. I forgot some people call coffins that. No, this box is a big packing case. Supplies have just been delivered. They sometimes take the empty wooden boxes away again for reuse, but this time the box won't be empty.'

'Right.' She began piling things into her suitcase any old how, thankful she didn't have as many possessions as Penny and the other VADs from more wealthy backgrounds. She checked her drawers and wardrobe one last time. 'That's everything.'

'Right. We'll leave now. I'll carry that suitcase, you carry the bundle.'

Frank didn't go far. As soon as he was sure he wasn't being pursued, he slowed down to a walk, gasping for breath. He'd never enjoyed running, which always gave him a strange feeling, as if his knees were made of lead and he couldn't breathe properly.

He found a fallen log and sat down on it for a rest and a think. What would Phoebe do now? It seemed obvious that she'd leave the hospital and go somewhere else. Would she leave straight away? No. She'd need to find somewhere, make plans, give notice.

So he had a bit of time to catch her. He just needed somewhere to keep watch.

When he found a tumbledown barn in the field next to the end of the hospital drive, with an excellent view of the road, he punched one fist into the other and said, 'Ha!' in tones of satisfaction. It could have been put there just for him. There was only one way out of Bellbourne, so if she left, he'd see her passing by, or at least he'd see vehicles in which she might be hidden.

He needed food, though, and blankets, if he was going to keep watch. She might try to slip out at night. Luckily he was a light sleeper. You had to be in his job. Sometimes he had to go out at night to pick things up.

He'd keep watch for a couple of days – he didn't think it'd take longer than that for her to leave, because he'd given her a real fright. And he'd make a list of the vehicles which came and went, in case she got away. He knew people who'd help him follow up on anything suspicious.

When he thought about it, he realised he should have planned what he was doing today better. He usually took more care, which was why he was making such good money. He hadn't been thinking straight, because Phoebe had looked so pretty in the dappled light of the gardens, he'd simply grabbed her. He'd not make that mistake again.

He went back into Swindon to pick up some supplies, then got a lift out of the town from a fellow who owed him a favour.

He left some blankets and a bit of food at the barn and arranged to be picked up again in a couple of days, then went into the village to get himself a drink.

The pub was full up and he couldn't even find a seat, but the beer was good. He saw one of the orderlies from the hospital, and got into conversation by the simple method of pretending to trip and spilling his beer. He insisted on buying the fellow another pint in compensation, which put him in a good mood, because the glass had been nearly empty.

They had a nice little chat and he listened sympathetically as the orderly complained about the VADs, who were, he said, treated too well and didn't work half as hard as the men did.

By the time Frank left, they'd arranged to meet the following evening, because Frank had said wistfully that he got a bit lonely when travelling round. He'd bought more drinks than the orderly, which no one could object to.

It was damned cold in that barn, and Frank got a lousy night's sleep, but he didn't care. He'd wake up if any vehicle passed by. Phoebe wouldn't get away from him. At least the old barn was watertight, so when it began to rain, he didn't get wet. It was damned chilly, though.

It seemed a long time till morning, but as soon as it was light, he got up and took out the paper and pencil he'd brought to note down which vehicles passed.

He'd planned everything he could think of, now he could only wait.

Phoebe and Matron left the hospital openly then made their way to the supplies section, following a rather circuitous route that avoided most people. 'Go inside,' Matron ordered. 'I'm waiting for Scorton to arrive. I came with a nurse, and I'll be leaving with one.'

Corin stepped out from a corner, his expression brightening at the sight of Phoebe. 'That was quick.'

'I know how to organise things in my own hospital.' Matron's expression was smug. 'Change quickly into your own clothes, Sinclair. You can go behind the cupboard door to do it. I'm sure Major McMinty won't peep.'

He turned round immediately, so that his back was to them, but not before Phoebe had seen him grin. She concentrated on changing her outer clothes as quickly as possible, then handed the nurse's uniform to Matron, who bundled it up in the towel.

'Good luck, Sinclair. I'll leave you now.' She walked outside to the other nurse, handed her the bundle and they left at once.

The supplies orderly came out from the back of the building and gave Phoebe an assessing look. 'Come through to the back. We need to get you into the box.'

'We'll talk later,' Corin told her. 'You'll have to trust me for the moment.'

'I do.'

They'd put a blanket and two pillows in the box to cushion the bumping. Phoebe tried to make herself comfortable inside it, but couldn't, because she was too cramped and had to crouch down uncomfortably.

'Sorry,' Corin whispered. 'For the moment we don't want people to have the faintest idea of how you've left the hospital or where you've gone. I'm taking steps to get Hapton removed from Swindon, but it can't be done overnight. We have to catch him at something illegal first.'

Then the lid came down and they hammered in a couple of nails.

She winced at the noise, so close to her head, and winced again as they picked the box up and started carrying it outside, bumping her from side to side. She was sure she'd got a splinter in her bottom from the rough wood it was jolted against. She had trouble holding back a cry as someone stumbled and the jerky movement banged her head against the side of the box, which seemed to be getting smaller by the minute.

They stopped moving and she felt them hoist the box into the back of the truck.

Silence followed and seemed to go on for ages. She wondered what was happening. Although there were slight chinks where the wood didn't fit perfectly, they were too narrow to do anything but let in a little light and air.

Another bump next to her must be the second box with her suitcase in it, followed by metallic clunks and what sounded like bolts sliding into place. A couple of minutes later someone started up the engine, cursing as the starting handle hit his hand hard. At last the motor started, the truck door banged shut and it set off.

As they jolted along, she braced herself, hoping she wouldn't be shut up for much longer. Surely they'd stop soon.

But they didn't.

She'd always hated being shut in. She began counting her breaths, trying not to let panic overwhelm her. But it was hard to keep calm.

The following evening, after a tedious day spent watching the road and seeing only delivery vans and ambulances, Frank was beginning to think this wasn't the best idea. But since he'd started he carried on, noting down every vehicle that passed, because he couldn't think of anything better to do.

The main trouble was, he couldn't see who was inside the back of the ambulances.

He'd carry on checking vehicles, especially ones from

somewhere else, just in case, but he reckoned the orderly might be his best way of finding out whether she went out in an ambulance.

He couldn't bear to leave anyone else to do this. If you wanted a thing done properly, you did it yourself. By the time he introduced Phoebe to his acquaintances, he'd have tamed her good and proper. He'd enjoy doing that.

When evening came, he went to the pub and sat down to wait for his new friend.

The orderly sauntered into the pub with another fellow and they joined Frank, who promptly bought the pair of them a drink, claiming a lucky bet had put him in the money and he wanted to celebrate with someone.

When the new fellow asked what he was doing in the area, he said he was looking for somewhere for his parents to retire to, a nice cottage with a bit of garden, but he hadn't liked what he'd seen and maybe they'd be better staying in Swindon, after all.

The drink certainly loosened the other men's tongues and he had a bit of luck. Without him even needing to do any prompting, they got on to the topic of the pretty, red-haired VAD who had vanished mysteriously earlier today, without farewells and without anyone seeing her go. *And* her bed had been allocated to a new woman who'd just turned up, so the redhead clearly wasn't coming back.

From their talk, the new fellow had fancied Phoebe and she'd told him to leave her alone. Frank pretended to sympathise with him, though in actual fact, he felt like punching the idiot in the guts and teaching him to leave other people's women alone.

He felt a sourness in his stomach, because it was obvious

that for all his care, his bird had flown the cage. 'How could this woman have got away from the hospital without anyone seeing her?' he asked innocently.

'That's what everyone wants to know. She took all her clothes, too, so she had time to pack. But I was on gate duty and I saw every vehicle that went in and out, and believe me, she wasn't in the ambulances.'

'Perhaps she was crouching on the floor.'

'It was a quiet day. Only a couple of ambulances went out and I asked the drivers if they'd seen her. They said they were fed up of being asked and *they* hadn't driven her anywhere. The only vehicles I didn't know were the delivery vans, one from down Devizes way and one from London. They both had open backs to put stuff on, and there was only room for two people to squeeze into the cab, so I'd have seen her if she'd been in one of them. Believe me, I know a lot about motor vehicles. I'm going to go for a job as a chauffeur once this damned war is over.'

'Strange, that.' Frank hid his anger by taking a sip of beer. 'Your young woman must have had help, then.'

'Who the hell from? There was no one to get her away, I tell you. I'd have seen them. There were just ordinary fellows delivering supplies.'

'What about the two who weren't local? You said one from Devizes. Where exactly was the other from? London's a big place.'

'How should I know? I've only ever passed through it. They'd come down to bring drugs, which happens every now and then. I noticed the labels on the boxes they delivered, same as usual. These two were just ordinary fellows, not even in uniform.'

Frank left the pub an hour later, abandoned his blankets and set off walking into Swindon. He'd missed her going. Definitely. So he was going to sleep in his own damned bed and get a decent night's sleep.

He was lucky. A car stopped after he'd walked about half a mile and the driver gave him a lift nearly into Old Town. The fellow didn't want to talk, so Frank sat quietly as if tired and thanked him for the lift.

What a sod of a week!

Phoebe was relieved when the truck stopped and a cracking sound above her was followed by the lid being wrenched off.

Corin held out one hand and she grasped it, letting him pull her up and lift her out of the box.

The other man nodded at her and set about securing the lid again.

'Do you mind sitting on my knee with my greatcoat covering most of you?' Corin asked. 'There isn't a lot of room in the cab, but we want you out of sight as much as possible.'

She shivered. 'I'll be glad to be warm again.'

When the truck set off, she nestled against him, feeling safe and getting warmer by the minute. He kissed her forehead and whispered, 'I was upset when I heard about your incident. That brute didn't hurt you, did he?'

'No. Two patients came along and he ran away.'

'If I ever catch him, I'll make sure he *limps* away.'

'I hope I never even see him again. Where are we going?'

'To a place called Greyladies, a convalescent home. It's only about an hour and a half's drive from here, to the south-west of Swindon, near a village called Challerton. I'll brief you properly once we get there.'

'Nice name.' She closed her eyes and didn't wake until the truck stopped and the engine was switched off.

Corin shook her gently. 'You all right?'

She blinked up at him in the light shining from the windows of a big house. 'Yes. I'm fine. Fancy falling asleep on you like that. Only I didn't sleep very well last night for worrying about what Frank might do next.'

He glanced sideways but the driver had got out. 'I enjoyed holding you in my arms, Phoebe.'

She wasn't going to lie about something so important. 'I liked being held close by you.'

The truck door was opened and a voice said, 'Shall I help you out, miss?'

'Thank you.' She wriggled carefully down and turned to look at the house.

It was as if everything suddenly started to move more slowly, as if every little detail of the scene was taking time to impress itself on her.

It was a beautiful old house. She'd never seen anywhere as lovely in her whole life. Grey stone walls, grey stone tiles on the steep roof and gables. Above the front door was a stained glass window. Though she couldn't make out the scene depicted in the window very clearly, she loved the way the window seemed to be casting subdued jewelled tones over the puddles lying on the path.

She took a step forward, then another, not waiting for Corin, unable to resist the sudden compulsion to go inside.

Chapter Sixteen

Harriet suddenly broke off mid sentence, frowned and stood up from the table. 'I have to go to the front door.'

She didn't know why, just knew she had to do this. She didn't even wait for Joseph's reply or finish answering a question from Jody, but walked through the old oak door and into the entrance hall of the new part of the house.

She was vaguely aware of other people moving about the hall, but her attention was focused on the front door. She didn't stop to greet anyone, just walked straight towards it.

Before she even reached the door, it swung open and she stopped in surprise. There was no one near enough to open it and the person standing outside was too far away to have done so. She gasped, reminded of the time she'd first come to Greyladies. The door had swung open to her then without human help.

Was this . . . could it be something Anne Latimer's ghost was doing? Was another lady about to take over here? She'd felt for a while that her own days at Greyladies were numbered, but not known how the changes would happen. It had made her sad, but seemed inevitable, given Joseph's family situation.

She stayed where she was, about three paces away from the entrance, waiting for she knew not what. It had stopped raining and the figure standing outside was haloed by sunlight, which glinted off the puddles. It was hard to make out any details except that it was a woman. Well, of course it was. Another lady to care for the old house.

Phoebe began walking towards the grey-stone house, drawn by something, she couldn't have said what. She only knew that she *had to* go inside it and must do so on her own. She wasn't in the least afraid. How could you be in such a beautiful place?

She felt as if she knew this house, even though she'd never been here before. It was like coming home, reaching not only a place of safety, but somewhere filled with warmth and happiness, finding a family even. Which was a wonderful feeling for someone who no longer had any close relatives to care about her, and who missed her mother dreadfully.

Still feeling as if everything was happening slowly, she walked up the shallow stone steps. The door swung open before she reached it, and she paused, but though a woman was standing staring at her, she didn't move to greet her.

That didn't matter. Something was urging her on, so Phoebe walked inside. She stopped for a moment to look round the huge entrance hall, marvelling at how lovely it was, with its panelled walls and the elegant staircase at the rear.

Before she moved on she looked to the left and saw that the woman was still standing watching her, smiling now as if glad to see her.

How she knew this person had come to greet her, she

couldn't have said. It was all part of the strangeness of this moment. She wanted very much to speak to the woman, but she had to do something else first. It was important, seemed to be the most important thing she'd ever done in her life.

A movement near the top of the stairs caught her attention and she looked up to see a faint light shining there. It grew brighter by the minute until she could see the outline of another woman. This person had come to welcome her to Greyladies, she knew that instinctively.

As she crossed the hall, people fell back before her. She sensed that vaguely but couldn't speak a word of thanks. Happiness began to well up inside her as she mounted the stairs, not hurrying, no need for that. There was all the time in the world and this must be done properly, with measured steps and a loving heart.

Once she reached the landing she stopped, puzzled. The lady waiting for her was wearing strange, old-fashioned clothing, all grey and white.

It was a costume from the Tudor age, Phoebe decided. She remembered seeing one like it in a book at school. The long grey skirt was topped by a grey bodice, which ended in a point in front below the waist. The low, square neckline was filled by a white lawn and lace insert. Full sleeves opened out over softly ballooning white undersleeves, the latter gathered at the wrist, with a frill edged in lace.

The lady's hair was parted in the middle and drawn back under a headdress like a stiffened half-moon of grey velvet. From the back of this crescent, silky grey material hung down past her shoulders. She was holding up the folds of her skirt with one slender, graceful hand and her toe, in a pointed shoe, peeped from beneath the heavy floor-length folds, as if she was about to dance.

As Phoebe stared, entranced by this delightful vision, the lady stared solemnly back, then smiled and gave a slight curtsey which seemed to be a way of greeting her. Phoebe inclined her head in return.

Words whispered across to her, blurred by an echo. 'Welcome to Greyladies, my dear Phoebe. May you be very happy here.'

'Thank you.' The lady looked wise, not old but not young either. She was beautiful, but in a gentle, rather than a showy way. No, it wasn't her face that was beautiful, Phoebe decided – it was her expression and the soul that lit those glorious eyes. She looked as if she loved everyone and wanted to help them.

The light began to shimmer and fade. The lady became transparent against the oak panelling.

'Don't go!' Phoebe called.

'I'll visit you again.'

The vision shimmered into a drift of sparks, then nothing, and Phoebe was left standing alone, feeling bereft. She caught her breath. It hadn't been her imagination; she'd been speaking to a ghost. And she hadn't been in the least afraid, nor had she doubted that this was real.

As she turned, dizziness swept through her, but she felt an arm go round her shoulders and someone led her across to an old wooden settle on the landing. The person helped her to sit down and after a few seconds her head began to steady.

But the wonder stayed with her, and the sense of welcome. She had come home.

* * *

Harriet caught her breath as she watched the young woman walk slowly across the hall. People turned to watch, then turned away again, as if nothing of interest was happening. Some moved out of the way, but no one tried to stop the stranger, thank goodness.

A man came through the front door and looked round, searching for someone. When he saw the newcomer, he stood watching her, with a worried expression.

Harriet went up to him. 'It's all right. Let your friend do this. It's important.'

He frowned and opened his mouth, but she held up one hand. 'I know exactly what's happening. It happened to me once. Please leave me to deal with it. She'll be quite all right, I promise you.'

She crossed the hall in her turn, to stand at the foot of the stairs, watching Anne Latimer curtsey to the newcomer. She didn't know the young woman's name, but she *knew* her, oh, she did.

Sensing that now was the time to join them, she too began to walk up towards the landing.

She arrived in time to see the vision start to fade and as Anne Latimer left them, Harriet moved quickly forward to support the stranger, who was swaying dizzily. 'Come and sit down for a moment. You'll be feeling a trifle disoriented.'

She'd worried how to find the right person to look after the house, because she'd understood since the beginning of the war that her time here was nearly over. It was all so obvious. And here was her successor, the next chatelaine of Greyladies, come to join them.

The stranger had richly auburn hair and a face that bore a distinct resemblance to Harriet's own. To Anne Latimer's as well. She was undoubtedly a family member.

'Welcome to Greyladies,' Harriet said, once she was sure the newcomer had recovered.

'That's what *she* said.'

'Of course she did. We've been waiting for you.'

'How could you be? I only found out today that I was coming here.'

'You realise that you were seeing a ghost?'

'Yes.'

'She's called Anne Latimer and she built the original house, the one behind this new part. You and I are her descendants.'

'But you don't even know who I am.'

'I can tell that you're one of the family.'

'I'm Phoebe Sinclair. My mother's maiden name was Latimer, though.' She looked round with an expression of wonder. 'This house is beautiful.'

'Yes. Anne founded it and still seems to guard it. I'm Harriet Latimer, by the way.'

'You look a bit like my mother. She had the same colour of hair. Mine's darker.'

There were footsteps on the stairs and they looked round to see Corin hesitating near the top.

'Are you all right, Phoebe?'

She smiled at him radiantly. 'Oh, yes. I don't think I've felt as right as this for years. Did you see her?'

'Who?'

'The ghost.'

He pursed his lips for a moment, then admitted, 'I saw a light that didn't seem to come from anywhere specific, if that's what you mean. Then it faded.'

The two women exchanged glances, already drawn together by what they'd seen.

'Not many even see a light,' Harriet murmured. 'Your friend must be a good man.'

She stood up and held out her hand to pull Phoebe to her feet. 'Welcome to Greyladies, both of you. Why don't you both come down and have a cup of tea with me and my husband.'

She laughed, breaking the tension. 'We always seem to offer tea when someone needs bracing, don't we?'

'It's very comforting.'

A strident voice interrupted them. 'What are *you* doing up here, Mrs Latimer? You should return to your own quarters and not get in the way of people who have important *work* to do. I don't think the new occupants will want you wandering about at will, getting under their feet.'

An older woman dressed in a matron's uniform came towards them. She was wearing a tall, winged headdress, which exaggerated the jerky movements of her head. Her face bore a sour, pinched expression.

'And workmen are *not* allowed to come in by the front entrance,' she said sharply to Corin. 'Who let *you* into the house?'

He stiffened and said in his impeccable upper-class accent, 'Actually, madam, I'm not a workman. I'm Major McMinty, come to take over here.'

The woman had opened her mouth to say something else, no doubt equally disagreeable, but this remark stopped her dead. Mouth still open, she gaped at him. '*You're* Major McMinty?'

'Yes. And this is Miss Sinclair, who will also be working here.'

She turned to stare doubtfully at Phoebe. 'Are you a nurse?'

Corin answered for her. 'Her position is nothing that need concern you.' He turned to Harriet. 'We'd be delighted to accept your offer of a cup of tea, Mrs Latimer. We don't want to get in the way of Matron's preparations for departure, do we?'

'I'm not leaving till tomorrow morning, Major.'

A voice called, 'Corin, old fellow, what on earth are you doing in those clothes?' Dr Somers joined them on the landing, looking from one to the other, assessing the situation. 'I'll deal with this, Matron. You have your own packing to finish.'

'But I—'

His voice grew chill. 'Matron, your responsibilities here have ended. It's for others to manage what happens from now on.'

She glared at them, swung on her heels and walked away.

Once she'd gone, he smiled at them. 'I apologise for letting her get to you before I did. What a poor welcome! She's a dreadful woman. They call her the Dragon, for obvious reasons. But she'll be gone tomorrow morning early. Don't let her order you around in the meantime. Her jurisdiction here ends when the last patient leaves, which will be within the hour.'

'I've been offering our new friends a cup of tea,' Harriet said. 'Will you join us, Dr Somers?'

'Delighted to.'

Phoebe still felt as if she could only move slowly. She stared down into the hall as she started down the stairs.

'Are you all right?' Corin asked.

'I feel strange, and yet happy.'

'I only saw a light. What did you see?'

'A woman in Tudor costume. Harriet said she was Anne Latimer, the founder of Greyladies. Isn't it strange? My mother was a Latimer and I seem to have come to my family's original home quite by accident.'

She was frowning as she went across the hall and stopped by the door to the old part, muttering, 'Or was it by accident? Perhaps I was meant to come here. Oh, sorry, Corin. I'm holding you up, aren't I?'

But she had to stop to stroke the ancient wooden door between the two halves of the building. It was such a wonderful old thing. She felt someone's eyes on her and looked up to the landing, seeing Matron glaring down at them. Poor woman. So full of hatred even a stranger could sense it.

'Oh, my goodness! This is wonderful!' Phoebe stopped again just inside the old part of the building to marvel at the former medieval hall.

Two children ran across to join them, hugging their mother, and a man followed them, a man with a striking, intelligent face who limped very badly. By the way Harriet's face lit up at the sight of him and the children, these people were her family. Phoebe envied her that. She stole a quick glance at Corin. Perhaps one day . . .

They sat down to tea and small cakes brought by a smiling maid, who took the children away with her to help bake some more cakes. Phoebe heard Harriet murmur to Joseph, 'This is my successor.'

He looked startled, then took hold of her hand, as if to comfort her, while he studied Phoebe more closely. 'She could be your sister.'

As they continued to chat, Phoebe noticed that Dr Somers

seemed quite at home here. He seemed a very pleasant man, and she was sorry that he was leaving the following day.

'When are your people coming, McMinty?' Joseph Latimer asked.

'My new adjutant arrives tomorrow. I've not met him yet. Apparently, he's very capable. The convalescent patients won't come until he thinks everything is ready for them.'

'All we've been told is that they'll be people considered to be enemy aliens, who are not in fact enemies of our country,' Joseph said.

'Yes. People with skills and knowledge useful to the War Office and government. It'll be my job to settle them in, then someone else will take over at Greyladies.' He looked across at Harriet and Joseph. 'We're hoping you'll help the people in the village to understand that these people aren't enemies, so that they can go for walks and generally live as normal a life as possible, though of course they must stay in the district.'

'We'll do our best. Miss Bowers will be a great help in that, if we're allowed to tell her the true situation. She used to be the headmistress of the village school and now she's our sons' governess. She's a very capable woman and is greatly respected in the district.'

'My department will be happy to accept help from anyone who has skills to share. It's not as hidebound as the army proper.'

'Could we ask what your department is?'

'Oh, it's just a side shoot of the main operation. It tidies things up and does little jobs that don't fit elsewhere, like setting up this not-so-convalescent home.'

Joseph didn't press the point. Clearly there was to be no clearer explanation offered.

After they'd finished their meal, Corin asked Harriet and Benedict to show him round both the old and the new parts of the house, and invited Phoebe to join them.

She was looking forward to seeing the rest of the house, but she felt sorry for Joseph. She looked round from the door and saw him sigh. It must be galling to face life with such limitations on your movements when there was nothing whatsoever wrong with your brain.

Then she forgot everything as she enjoyed her tour. They started at the attics, because people were still carrying things out from the ground floor, though the piles of boxes and bundles in the hall had decreased considerably.

As Benedict walked round with the others, commenting on changes made to accommodate the hospital, he felt sad at the thought of leaving this lovely house. He hadn't been here for long, but there was something special about Greyladies. He'd felt immediately at home here, which wasn't something that normally happened to him. He was sorry it wasn't suitable for his purpose.

He led the way down from the attics and saw Matron moving rapidly away from the foot of the narrow stairs. The woman had clearly been eavesdropping again.

'Wait there while I deal with this,' he told the others and ran down the last few stairs, calling, 'Matron!'

She gave him one of her frosty looks. 'Yes, Dr Somers?'

'I know what you're doing. Please mind your own business from now on and confine your activities to the ground floor and your office while Mrs Latimer is showing the major round upstairs.'

'I beg your pardon?'

He abandoned the attempt to be tactful. 'I don't appreciate the way you're trying to eavesdrop on the rest of us.'

'How dare you accuse me of such a thing! I was going about my normal business.'

'No, you weren't.' He held up one hand. 'Don't argue. Just go down to the ground floor, if you please, and don't come back up here till we've finished our tour.'

Her face went so dark red, he wondered if she was going to have a seizure, but she tossed her head and stormed off. Drat the woman! She had been the thorn in his flesh all the time he'd been here. He hoped he'd never have to work with her again.

He was glad the arrangements for moving his patients had gone through so quickly and smoothly. It was partly a result, he suspected, of McMinty's department intervening.

Then his sense of fairness compelled him to admit that it was also thanks to Matron's excellent administrative skills. He smiled at that thought. Wouldn't she be surprised to know what he thought?

As the tour continued, Corin said quietly to Phoebe, 'You bear a close resemblance to Mrs Latimer.'

She beamed at him. 'My mother was a Latimer, so we're some sort of distant cousins. Isn't that a happy coincidence?'

'Wonderful for you.'

Benedict overheard and wondered about that. This was such a strange house, you could almost believe it wasn't just a coincidence.

When the tour was over, he excused himself and went to tackle his bedroom, not wanting an orderly fiddling with his clothes and personal possessions. He had the way he packed his things down to a system now, because he'd moved several times since the beginning of the war.

Since all the patients had left, he worked solidly through the rest of the afternoon and soon had the things in the bedroom packed, after which, he went to tackle his office.

But it took him most of the evening to deal with that. He really must find himself an adjutant for the next hospital. He'd thought he could manage without, but as he gained more responsibilities, he couldn't, even with clerical help.

He closed the lid of the last box and sat down at the desk, feeling utterly weary after the frenetic activity of the past few days.

He woke with a start some time later to find that the lamp had gone out. It'd probably run out of oil. The hospital he was going to had brand-new electric lighting, which would be wonderful for operations.

There was enough moonlight coming in through the windows for him to find his electric hand torch and he was just about to switch it on before finding his way through the boxes when he heard a sound in the hall.

He went out of his office, moving as quietly as he could, not switching the torch on. Who was wandering round the house at this hour of the night? Could it be a burglar? Some people were taking advantage of the war to steal and sell small pieces of hospital equipment when they could, he knew. If that was so, he'd teach them a lesson they wouldn't forget.

The white figure stood out clearly in the moonlit darkness. A woman. Not the family ghost. He smiled grimly as he recognised her. Matron was far too solidly built for a ghost. What the hell was she doing wandering around in the middle of the night?

Then he frowned, seeing something in her hand. It looked like some sort of small hand tool. She moved and the moonlight showed him a chisel. What on earth did she want with that?

She was standing by the door into the old house and he suddenly realised what she was about to do. To his horror, she raised the chisel to the ancient door, ready to gouge the wood. He'd seen her glare at that door many a time. Had she run mad? She must have.

And he wasn't close enough to stop her damaging the dark old wood.

But someone else was. Before he could yell at Matron to stop, light flared suddenly around the door.

Matron uttered one shrill yelp of shock and froze. She still had the chisel raised, ready to cause damage. Why wasn't she moving? Had a ghost really been able to stop her? He could see the figure of Anne Latimer clearly now. He'd seen her a couple of times before, though he'd not told anyone. Who'd believe him if he did?

The founder of Greyladies looked stern tonight, not at all like the usual smiling, kindly figure.

Matron began panting and whimpering in her throat, seeming unable to speak or move.

'*You will not – harm – my family's house.*'

Suddenly Matron moaned and said, 'Let me go! You *can't* exist. You're a toy of the devil.'

He didn't attempt to intervene. The house had its own guardian. He had never been quite sure whether ghosts could exist till he came here, still believed most tales about them

241

were figments of people's imaginations. But in this house, he believed that Anne Latimer was indeed still here, protecting it.

Well, it was more than a mere house; it was a legacy that had lasted through several centuries to help women in trouble. Even during his short stay, Harriet had quietly given help to the wife of one of his patients, doing things beyond his remit, using Latimer money.

He'd had a couple of chats with Miss Bowers about ghosts and even that practical woman had seen Anne Latimer, it seemed. She'd smiled at him and said confidently, 'You've seen her, too.'

He hadn't denied it.

He was startled by the chisel falling suddenly from Matron's hand, to clatter on the wooden floor. She remained standing perfectly motionless, though, eyes staring, alive with hatred.

Then slowly, her face began to change. Something was calming her down. He'd seen that expression on patients' faces many a time, at the moment when their pain medication started to take effect.

Slowly Matron's raised hand fell. Her body relaxed visibly, then she began to sway.

At last he was able to move and crossed the last few paces between them in time to catch her before she hit the floor.

Kneeling down holding her unconscious body, he looked up at Anne Latimer, waiting for her to speak to him, quite sure she would have something to say.

'*We shall meet again, Benedict Somers.*'

'I shall look forward to it, ma'am.'

And just like that, he was alone, crouching awkwardly on

the floor, with a plump woman he detested lying unconscious in his arms.

He got up. He couldn't carry her on his own, so he used the rug to drag Matron across to a sofa and arrange her decorously on it. He put the rug back and hid the chisel.

What should he do about the incident? Ought he to report it? Did one moment of madness mean a person must be locked away, or sacked from their career?

He hoped not. He'd study Matron carefully when she regained consciousness. It might not be necessary to do anything. After all she was going to a job dealing with equipment not patients.

It took longer than he'd expected for her to come fully back to her senses and by that time he'd found and lit a lamp. He waited where she could see him but not too close.

When she sat up with a start, he said quietly, 'I think you must have been sleepwalking, Matron.'

She gasped and peered across the dimly lit space. 'Dr Somers?'

'Yes.'

She frowned and stared round. 'I can't remember how I got here.'

'I believe that's normal when people sleepwalk.'

'I used to wander round in my sleep when I was a child. I don't know why I'd start doing it again, though.'

'I think you must have been overtired, Matron. You've worked extremely hard to wind things up here.'

'Yes. Of course that must be it.' She shivered and stood up. 'I shall be glad to leave, I must admit. I don't like this house. I think I'll go up to my room now.'

'Do you want me to accompany you?'

'No, of course not.'

Without a glance in the direction of the door, she walked up the stairs, not moving as briskly as usual. She'd spoken in a calmer tone, too.

He let out his breath in a long, slow burst of relief. She didn't remember. She'd probably be all right in charge of supplies. He'd have a word with her boss, tell him she'd been overdoing it and to keep a close eye on her at first.

Benedict looked round for the chisel and went across to pick it up, taking it through the unusually quiet kitchen to the back door. The key wasn't in the lock, so he put the chisel on the floor and left it. Let them wonder how it had got there. He was too tired to hunt for the key and even if he got outside, he didn't know where the chisel came from.

It was only as he was snuggling down in bed that he remembered what the ghost had said.

'*We shall meet again, Benedict Somers.*'

He'd like that. One day, when this dreadful war was over and he didn't face the heart-rending and often impossible task of trying to mend badly damaged bodies, he'd take a quiet drive through the countryside and call in at Greyladies. He was sure he'd find a welcome here.

Chapter Seventeen

Major McMinty proved to be very efficient, and also showed respect for the old house. Joseph watched in approval as the new commandant set about preparing the place for its unusual occupants and purpose.

The adjutant arrived the day after the major, a round-faced youngish man, whose amiable expression belied his extreme efficiency and shrewdness.

He arranged for the first group of aliens to arrive in mid December. They were older men, who looked nervous, as if they expected someone to shout at them, or worse. Corin's uniform seemed to intimidate them, because in his presence they spoke only when they had to.

They'd come from several different camps and only the three from the internment camp on the Isle of Man had met each other before, and they even seemed wary of the internees they didn't know.

They were extremely courteous towards Harriet, and warmed visibly to Phoebe when she tried out her rusty German phrases on them. But she couldn't persuade them that it would be all right to bring their wives here and no one wanted to force that.

They seemed less nervous with Joseph than any of the other men and he did his best to make them feel comfortable, inviting them into his home in trios for tea and small cakes.

It was his sons who had the most success in breaking the barrier between the internees and the men running Greyladies. The two boys treated the newcomers as friends, stopping to chat to them in the gardens, asking questions, persuading them to throw and catch balls. By association with her charges, Miss Bowers too became less frightening.

Soon Jody and Mal were sprinkling their conversation with German words and phrases, and teaching them to anyone who would listen.

Christmas was very quiet. People had stopped expecting the war to be over quickly and had begun to feel the pain of losses.

The first young man from the village had died in France, a cousin of Jody's friend Tim Peacock. Only twenty years old.

On a cold day in the middle of January, Joseph was in the new house, enjoying a quiet chat with two of the men about Vienna, which he'd read about and longed to visit, when Harriet came to find him, looking solemn.

'Do you have a moment, Joseph?'

'Of course.' To his surprise she led the way back to the old house, taking him into their bedroom, which was on the ground floor next to the living area.

'It's bad news, I'm afraid, darling.' She held out a black-edged envelope.

He didn't take it from her straight away, didn't even want to touch it. 'Dear God, who can it be this time? Please, Harriet, will you open it? I don't think I can bear to.'

She did so, reading it rapidly, then turned to him, her eyes filled with tears. 'It's Richard. Your mother says she was told he died in an attack on the farmhouse where he and several of his men were billeted.'

Joseph didn't move. He closed his eyes and stood fighting for control. But he didn't find it. With an inarticulate cry, he turned to his wife and let her take him in her arms as he began to sob. It was a long time before he calmed down.

She could think of nothing to say or do to comfort him. Two brothers dead. Two! And both in the first year of the war. The months felt to be passing slowly, but the deaths were mounting up quickly – and the injuries people had to cope with, too. So many families destroyed already by the deaths from this war, so many young men's lives as permanently damaged as their bodies, even though they were the 'lucky' ones, still alive.

'I must go to Mother,' he said eventually. 'Will you come with me?'

'Of course. I'll go and ask Miss Bowers if she can look after the boys.'

He stood for a moment, head bowed, then said quietly, 'No. I think they should come.'

She stared at him in shock, immediately understanding his reason. 'Because Jody may inherit it one day? Yes, of course. I hadn't thought ahead to how Selwyn's . . . preferences might affect us.'

He had told Harriet about the likely reason for Selwyn's dislike of women, so didn't need to elaborate. 'That probably makes me the eventual heir – or if I die before Selwyn, young Jody.'

'Perhaps Selwyn will make an effort to provide an heir once the war is over.'

Joseph took her hand. 'I think he expects to die in the fighting and I don't think he cares. He's not been happy for a long time, not since he started growing into manhood. At least *I* never thought he was happy. I did a lot of watching people while I was confined to a wheelchair and I always thought he only pretended to be in high spirits. Sometimes he looked downright puzzled, as if he couldn't understand life.'

'Surely, if he doesn't have children, he'll leave Dalton House to you? You *are* his brother, after all.' That was why, she realised suddenly. Why she was being prepared to leave Greyladies quite quickly. Because Joseph was going to inherit. She didn't say anything about her presentiment because he was still struggling with his grief for Richard.

But she knew. Oh, she knew with a certainty that surprised her that they would have to leave Greyladies, and before too long.

That was why Phoebe was here already, in order to take over.

Harriet didn't want to leave Greyladies. She didn't. But what choice did she have? Much of life was decided by chance, she always felt. Chance had brought her here and chance was going to take her away again. Chance and a terrible war.

She looked round, feeling anguish sear through her. She loved every stone of the old place.

'Are you all right?' Joseph asked suddenly.

She pulled her wandering thoughts together. It was no effort to smile at him. Chance had also given her Joseph, who was a wonderful husband, and two sons to be proud of. She had no right to complain if she didn't get everything she wanted from life. At least she'd had Greyladies for a decade.

'Yes. I'm fine, my darling. Just thinking.' She wouldn't tell him yet. Sufficient unto the day . . .

She forced herself to speak briskly. 'We'd better see if we can hire that motor car again, and get the boys' things packed. We should set off as soon as it can be arranged. Your mother will be on her own. She'll need us.'

'Let's tell the boys first. They'll be excited more than sad, I should think. They didn't really know Richard, so we can't expect them to grieve.'

Before they left for Dalton House, Harriet went to look for Phoebe. It was time to tell her. She went to find the new matron first, a very different person from the old one, unobtrusive and kind to people. Permission was given for Phoebe to go for a walk in the gardens with her 'on urgent family business'.

'Have you realised why you're here, Phoebe?'

'I thought . . . maybe to help you with what you do for other women. Because I'm a Latimer. It's such wonderful, worthwhile work.'

'You will be helping, but you're here mainly because quite soon you'll become the next owner of Greyladies.'

Phoebe stopped walking to gape at her. '*Me?* But you're the owner. You're not . . . ill, are you?'

'No. But this house is a trust and doesn't really belong

to anyone, not even the Latimers who nominally inherit it. Some chatelaines stay here their whole lives; others just for a few years.'

'I didn't realise that.'

'I knew I'd be leaving when the War Office took over the house. I lay awake one night, knowing somehow that I'd never go back to live in the front part, that I had other things to do with my life. Important things. It's now my turn to help a new Latimer lady settle in.'

It was a moment before Phoebe replied. 'Why did you choose me?'

'I didn't. I don't understand how it works, but Anne Latimer seems to appear at crucial times and . . . well, the new ladies turn up in one way or another. It's part of the strangeness of Greyladies.'

Phoebe was looking startled.

'Amazing, isn't it?'

'Shall *I* be staying here permanently, or will my stay be only temporary?'

'I don't know. You'll sense it if you're going to leave. I don't know when exactly Joseph and I will be going. Not quite yet. It'll be good to have time to show you the house's secrets.'

Another thought slid into her mind, another one which upset her. 'Miss Bowers will be staying here too, I think. She won't want to leave the village. She's so much a part of Challerton and Greyladies that she wouldn't be happy elsewhere. She'll be able to help you once I've gone.'

Phoebe's hand was gentle on her arm. 'That's very sad for you.'

'In some ways. But there isn't only me to consider. It will

be wonderful for Joseph to have his own purpose in life. He's followed my path for long enough. Now he can follow his own.'

'He's such a wise person.'

'Yes. He is. I think he'll make a good employer and landowner.' She waited but there were no more questions at present, though she was sure Phoebe would have plenty of things to ask after it all sank in. 'I'd better go now. Our motor car will be arriving soon. The boys are very excited at the thought of seeing their father's old home.'

Phoebe's expression softened. 'They're fine lads.'

Harriet wondered suddenly what Corin would think of Phoebe's new role. She had seen the way he looked at her, the way she looked at him. Would he give up his own life to marry someone tied to Greyladies as Joseph had? She'd heard him talk about his home in Lancashire very fondly, and as he was an only child, he would expect to inherit it and take over the reins.

If he survived the war. That was a phrase people were beginning to toss into conversations now.

She sighed. Life pushed people into some difficult decisions at times. She couldn't do any more than help her successor settle in here. Phoebe and Corin would have to sort out their own lives.

When Joseph and his family arrived, they found Dalton House and its staff decked in black, with black crêpe bows on the doors. Curtains were half drawn and they were shown into a dim hall, which made the boys shrink closer to their parents.

'Mrs Dalton is in the drawing room, Mr Joseph,' the

elderly maid whispered. 'She's hardly eaten a thing since we heard. I'm so glad you've come.'

'And I'm glad you were here to help her, Enid.'

'Where else would I be, sir? *I'm* not a flibbertigibbet as wants to dash off to London.' She looked towards Harriet as if unsure how to greet someone who had once been a maid here herself.

'I think you met my wife some time ago, didn't you?'

The maid spoke stiffly. 'Yes, sir. Pleased to see you again, Mrs Dalton.'

'She's Mrs Latimer,' Joseph corrected gently, 'and I'm either Mr Joseph or Mr Latimer. That's not going to change.'

Harriet was grateful for his instant support of her difficult role here. 'I'm pleased to see you again, Enid. These two terrors are Jody – short for Joseph like his father – and Mal, short for Malcolm.

Both boys murmured, 'How do you do?'

The maid gave them a more genuine smile. 'Eh, they've got their father's eyes and hair, haven't they?' Then she recalled her place. 'I'll tell madam you've arrived.'

But Mrs Dalton had heard the car and appeared in the hall in person. 'Joseph! Oh, my dear boy, I'm so relieved you've come. And Harriet, too.' Then she noticed the two lads and dabbed at her eyes. 'At least the next generation is secure, as secure as anything can be in this vale of sorrow.'

Joseph went across and put his arm round her shoulders to lead her back into the drawing room.

'Is there a vale of sorrow here?' Jody asked in what he considered a whisper, but which was loud enough to echo round the entrance hall.

'No, dear. Your grandmother means the sorrow she feels

because your Uncle Richard was killed in the war. Remember, we talked about that?'

'Yes, Mother. I won't forget to be kind to her, even if she kisses me.'

'Good boy. We'd better go and join them now.'

But Mrs Dalton was weeping in her son's arms, so Harriet brought the boys back into the hall and took them through into the kitchen instead.

When she opened the door, the two women there turned to stare at her in a rather hostile manner.

'Your mistress is upset and I didn't think it right for the boys to be present while we try to comfort her. Do you think these two terrors could sit quietly in the kitchen and perhaps have something to eat? I spent a lot of happy hours in here as a young maid, and it still smells as good.'

Cook thawed slightly at this remark. 'Of course they can stay. I daresay you two boys like biscuits, don't you?'

'Yes, please,' they chorused, brightening up at once.

Harriet caught Cook's gaze. 'Thank you.' She went to join Joseph and his mother, quite sure the boys would charm the two middle-aged women. They always did.

Selwyn was in France and couldn't get back for the funeral, so Joseph was the only family member there to support his mother.

Thomas's widow had sent her apologies. She was nursing a heavy cold and didn't think it prudent to travel.

'I think she can't face another funeral here,' Mrs Dalton told Harriet. 'And who can blame her? I'm grateful that you came and brought the boys. Their cheerfulness makes me feel better, as if life is continuing, with better times ahead.'

So it was a small group of family members who attended the church, and an equally small group of neighbours who joined them, mostly people of Mrs Dalton's age, who counted her among their friends and were there to support her. Richard certainly hadn't been popular.

'What shall you do now, Mother?' Joseph asked when the visitors had gone. 'Does Selwyn want you to look after the house for him?'

'No. He wants me to close it down, says he can't afford to pay the servants.'

He was startled. 'Are things that bad with him?'

'He said he'd stopped gambling, but I gather there are still old debts to pay. I shall go back to my flat in London.'

'What about the servants?'

'I can't take them.'

He looked at Harriet. 'What if I paid them board wages and we let them stay on here?'

'I think that's a good idea. And what if we sent one or two of the women in need to join them here while they're recovering? Especially ones with children. That would mean Cook and Enid are contributing to the war effort.'

He hesitated.

'The Latimer Trust would pay the expenses of the women staying here. It would have to pay for them one way or another, and it'll probably be cheaper to send them here . . . as long as you didn't charge us rent.'

Mrs Dalton looked from one to the other in puzzlement. 'What do you mean?'

'Part of my inheritance was a trust fund to look after women in trouble. People who know about this, like clergymen or ladies running missions in the slums, send them to me. And there's a new sort of woman in need, one who's lost her man in the war but wasn't married to him, so can't receive a widow's pension.'

She waited, half expecting her mother-in-law to make some disapproving remark, but Mrs Dalton surprised her.

'I have a friend who runs a mission. I thought it was for fallen women, but she insists it's to stop women having to take to the streets.' She flushed a little. 'I have in the past been guilty of thinking very unkind thoughts about such women, but Mary has made me see that they can't always help it: it's that or starving – or worse still, letting their children starve.'

Joseph gave her a cracking hug. 'Mother, you are wonderful.'

'No, I'm not. But since your father died, I'm starting to care more for the people around me. He was . . . rather arrogant and very old-fashioned. I loved him, but sometimes I grew angry with him.' She looked at Harriet. 'He treated you badly when you inherited Greyladies, and I didn't even try to stop him. I'm sorry about that.'

Joseph waited a minute, then asked, 'Shall we speak to Enid and Cook and see what they think, then?'

'And write to Selwyn. We'll need his permission to use the house.'

'He won't care,' Mrs Dalton said sadly. 'He doesn't seem to care about anything these days, except killing our enemies.'

Cook and Enid were relieved that they were not to lose their jobs, but Cook seemed a bit doubtful about the women who might come to stay.

Mrs Dalton drew herself up. 'The Bible says, "Though I speak with the tongues of men and of angels, and have not charity, I am become *as* sounding brass, or a tinkling cymbal." *Corinthians*, I believe.' She fixed the two servants with a firm gaze. 'I have learnt that these are women, just as we are, but less fortunate. If *I* am willing to help them and associate with them, so should you be.'

'Sorry, ma'am.'

Mrs Dalton unbent for a moment to add, 'It's the children of such unfortunate women who upset me most, so hungry their poor little legs and arms are like sticks. Some have rickets, too.'

Enid gulped. 'I can't abide to see children going hungry. We'll help all we can, ma'am. Won't we?' She nudged Cook with her elbow and got a nod out of her.

'Thank you,' Harriet said.

As they went outside to the car, Joseph gave his mother another hug. 'You're a wonderful woman.'

'Sadly, I've frittered my life away. But I'm learning to be more helpful. It's my friend Mary who is wonderful. Very inspiring.' Mrs Dalton stared into space for a moment or two, then added, 'It gives me something to do, to feel good about. I was a bit lost without your father and my former life, when I first went up to London.'

As they sat in the back of the car, Joseph said to his wife, 'Isn't my mother wonderful?'

'She is. And so are you,' Harriet said quietly. 'You're very like her in some ways.'

He looked at her in surprise. 'Am I?'

'Yes.' She chuckled. 'Well, you certainly don't take after your father, and you're not at all like Selwyn.'

They were silent then, remembering the other two brothers.

'I don't know how your mother bears it,' Harriet said. 'If I lose our two . . .'

'You won't. The war will be over long before they grow to manhood.'

'There seems to be a war for each generation. Why, there was more than one Boer War. I wish men didn't try to settle things by fighting.'

'It's all some men know.' He reached for her hand and held it most of the way home.

Chapter Eighteen

Frank slipped out of his house just after midnight to meet a man with goods to sell. He'd not dealt with this fellow before, but he'd been recommended by an acquaintance. The list of goods on offer was enough to tempt an angel.

If they agreed on a price, Frank would take most of the goods out to his parents' farm, keeping back some of the items that were selling well.

The man was waiting for him behind the church, as agreed, jacket collar turned up, though it was quite a mild night for the time of year.

'I'm Frank.'

'I'm not interested in names. You want to buy some goods. Have you brought the cash? I don't give credit.'

'Of course I have. Let's see what you've got.'

'I've brought samples. The rest of my stuff is in a safe place.'

'I'd want to check everything out.'

'They all do,' the man said in a bored tone. 'Don't worry. I'd not last long if I cheated people. Here. These are some samples.' He led the way to one of the gravestones, where goods were laid out, and switched on an electric torch.

Frank checked everything and they agreed on a price.

'Come on, then.' The man led him to a back lane and into a garden. 'Here they are, but you don't take them till I've got your payment.'

Smiling with pleasure at the thought of the money he'd make, Frank handed over the cash.

At once another torch flashed in his face and a hand grasped his arm. 'Frank Hapton, you're under arrest for black market dealing.'

He tried to lunge away, hoping to take the policeman by surprise, but another man grabbed him, and though he struggled, they were too much for him.

'*And* you'll be charged with resisting arrest,' one of them said.

He was marched through the dark, empty streets to the police station, feeling sick with dismay. All his plans, ruined. Wait till he caught the fellow who'd helped set this trap for him. How long did they give you in prison for such a crime?

At the police station, he was taken into a small room at the side, where a man in army uniform was waiting.

'This is him,' the policeman said. He was a big man and shook Frank's arm hard as he said, 'Pay attention, you. We can charge you and you'll go to prison. No doubt about that. But the government in its kindness is offering you an alternative. You can volunteer for the army instead. Which is it to be?'

Frank thought rapidly. He didn't know which was worse, prison or fighting in a damned war. Then he thought of being locked up, perhaps for years, and that made his mind up. He couldn't abide being penned in. 'Army.' The uniformed man was a sergeant, by his stripes, and was smiling smugly now.

'They usually choose that,' he said with a laugh. 'Fetch my men in, will you? We'll go through the formalities before we leave. And if you have any more of that nice strong tea, I'd welcome another cup.'

Frank gave his details and signed the piece of paper as directed, then was handed over to two burly soldiers.

'Take him back to the barracks, lads.'

Frank tried to get them talking as they walked, but one said brusquely, 'You shut your mouth. I hate black marketeers. We're fighting a war, lads are losing their lives and rats like you make money from it. That stinks.'

At the barracks, Frank was locked in a room till the doctor could see him.

'The medical is only a formality,' one of the soldiers said. 'You look a nice strong fellow to me, a bit flabby around the middle, though.'

He punched Frank suddenly in that very place and he doubled up, gasping for breath.

The soldier grinned at his mate, then turned back to their prisoner. 'I shall enjoy helping you get fit, training you to kill . . . or be killed.'

There was a bench along each side of the room and a man was lying on one of them, snoring.

'He's another like you,' the chatty soldier went on. 'Two rats caught in one night is nice going, don't you think? You'll make good cannon fodder and I personally hope you stop a bullet! Scum, that's what you are. Scum.'

The two men were left there till morning, then another soldier came for them.

'You're not going to give me any trouble, are you?' he asked affably, studying one clenched fist and slamming it into the palm of his other hand.

'No,' Frank said.

'No, Corporal,' the man corrected, slapping him on the back of the head to emphasise the point.

'No, Corporal,' the other prisoner said hastily.

Frank wasn't going to buy trouble, so repeated meekly, 'No, Corporal.'

'This way, men. The doctor's waiting to stamp your cards. You'll soon be in the army and you won't know what's hit you.'

The doctor gave the smaller man a cursory examination, listening to his heart and chest, and ordering him to drop his trousers before subjecting him to a bored check of his manhood. 'You'll do.' He looked at the corporal. 'Take him away. Next.'

Frank stepped forward, feeling sick at how easy it was to pass a medical.

The doctor took his wrist and felt his pulse, then frowned. 'Take your shirt and vest off.'

Wondering what the hell was going on and hoping they weren't going to beat him up, Frank did as he was told.

The doctor held a very chilly brass stethoscope to his chest, frowned again, and said, 'Turn round.'

He looked across at the sergeant. 'A word.'

The two men left the room.

Frank reached for his shirt, feeling chilly.

'Leave it off. He may want to check your chest again.'

There was the sound of voices, then the doctor returned and listened to Frank's chest again.

'How do you feel when you run?'

'I don't like running, so I don't do it.'

'I'm not surprised. You've got a heart murmur that can be heard a mile off. We can't have that in the army. You'd probably drop dead during the training.' He stepped back and picked up a rubber stamp. 'Rejected.' He slammed it down on the piece of paper. 'Pity, but there you are.'

'This way, you!' the sergeant roared.

Frank hated the sod already, but did as he was told. His heart sank. That must mean he'd be charged and sent to prison.

'Wait in there.'

He scowled round at the cell. What now?

It was a full half-hour before they came to get him, by which time he was so hungry and thirsty, he'd have eaten anything put before him.

But they didn't put anything to eat before him; they took him in to see a magistrate, who glared at him.

'Damn you and all like you!' he said by way of greeting.

'You are charged with black market crimes.' He took a deep breath and tapped an envelope. 'This is the money that was taken off you last night. Two hundred pounds.'

Frank brightened. At least he'd get his money back.

'The doctor tells me it's no use sending you to prison, not with your tricky heart. You'd be more trouble than you're worth. So I'm going to fine you instead. Two hundred pounds. Pay it or you will go to prison.'

He gave Frank a smile that was more like a snarl. 'Well?'

'I'll pay it, Your Worship.' He indicated the money in the magistrate's hand. 'With that.'

The man roared with laughter. 'This isn't your money

any longer. It was confiscated. You'll need to come up with another two hundred pounds.'

'*What?*' Frank caught his eye and bit off further angry words. They'd got him coming and going. 'I'll have to fetch the money sir, get it out of the savings bank.'

'I'll send my clerk with you, and a police officer.' He consulted his watch. 'The bank doesn't open for another half-hour. Give the fellow a cup of tea and something to eat. We don't want him fainting on the way there, do we? The government needs the money to fight the war.'

Frank was given a cup of lukewarm tea and a piece of dry bread. He was hungry enough to eat the damned thing, but had to dunk it in the tea to soften it.

They left him sitting there for what seemed a long time.

He could hear the loud voice of the sergeant in charge of the police station and realised the man was talking on the telephone. No one else was around, so he listened carefully. You never knew when you might learn something useful.

'Yes, sir. Hapton fell into the trap meek as a mouse, just like you said. Trouble is, he failed the medical.'

Silence, then, 'I'm really sorry, sir. The doctor was adamant. He doubted the man would last through training. Might look big and strong, but he was flabby under it, and no wonder. If he did anything physical, his heart would have played up.'

Another silence, then, 'I hope you find another way to keep him in check. I don't like fellows who beat up women. They're as bad as black marketeers in my books.'

Frank couldn't help but realise they were talking about him. He didn't care what they said about his heart. He'd not had any trouble with it, except for a few episodes of

263

fluttering, because he knew what to avoid doing. Damned doctors. They couldn't even save themselves when they fell ill. Still, it had got him off both prison and the army.

But it was clear that he'd been set up by someone, lured into a trap, and he cared very much about that. Who could have borne him a grudge?

The sergeant had been talking to a superior officer by the tone of his voice, and the way he put 'sir' on the end of every other sentence. Frank grinned. *He* wouldn't have to do that now.

He stopped grinning. They'd been talking about him beating up a woman. It suddenly clicked in his mind: the fellow who'd rescued Phoebe must have been an officer. Could this be in payback for that? Why would a complete stranger do that? Only one reason that Frank could think of. Phoebe must have been giving the officer what she'd refused him.

Rage filled him, but he didn't let it boil over. Rage upset his heart. *Watch me deal with this, Mr Stupid Doctor!* When something upset him, he could control his anger and get his own back later. *That* didn't upset his heart. Well, it only caused a bit of fluttering, which was nothing. Hadn't done him any harm so far, had it? He was a big strong fellow with one small problem.

And it'd got him out of the army! What a bit of luck!

When the time came to go to the bank, he walked along meekly with his escort, took out the money, and was marched back to pay his fine officially. It hurt him to see his hard-earned savings swallowed up by that damned magistrate, but at least the money had set him free *and* made sure he'd never be killed in the mud.

They let him go eventually, after fiddling round with bits of paper and signatures.

He had to trudge back to the damned bank, because they'd taken every penny of his money so he couldn't even catch a bus.

After he'd drawn out a few pounds, he went to a cafe and got himself a decent meal, sitting over it thoughtfully.

He'd have to find out where Phoebe was and teach her a lesson. He'd not let anything put him off this time. Someone must know where she was. He'd find out, oh, he would.

No one had ever got away scot-free with upsetting him, man or woman. And no one was going to do it this time.

Set traps for him, would they?

Take more than half his money, would they?

She and her fancy man were going to regret that. Oh, yes.

Phoebe settled down, enjoying life at Greyladies. It was set up so that the men detained there lived a reasonably comfortable life and earned their places by translating documents, teaching certain visiting officers to speak some simple German and doing anything else considered useful.

Corin made sure the atmosphere was peaceful.

Miss Bowers made sure that the villagers accepted the 'enemy aliens' by insisting that they were working for the British, though she couldn't reveal how.

It was a five-day wonder to have such exotic people nearby, but if Miss Bowers said the men were all right, they must be. No one could fool her.

She started taking groups of three or four men into the village, where they could do a bit of shopping at the village store or simply enjoy a change of scene. Phoebe accompanied them, not wearing her VAD uniform now, but her everyday clothes, though Harriet and Miss Bowers made sure she had enough new clothes to look smart.

And Corin was still at the house, to brighten her days by stopping for a chat in passing, and sometimes to take her for long walks on fine evenings. They grew closer, very much closer, but still he didn't do anything about his feelings, not even ask her to walk out with him officially.

She couldn't be mistaken in the looks he gave her, just couldn't. And she had grown to love him dearly. If he proposed, she'd accept him in a flash. What was holding him back?

Corin went up to London at least once a week, sometimes more. She thought he was reporting to his boss, but he never said what he was doing, though sometimes he brought her a note from Beaty, or a little gift.

The shops were not as full of items for sale as they had been, Beaty said in one of her notes, and food was limited in some ways. In the country, they had produce from their own gardens, and the cooks at Greyladies planned to follow the locals' example and bottle as much as they could for the winter.

So life was still comfortable. She hadn't been as happy as this since she was a child.

A few weeks later, Corin brought Phoebe a letter from Beaty and she cried for joy when she read it. Beaty had found Mr Stein. He was rather frail, but had proved a suitable candidate for helping the government at Greyladies, so she'd arranged for him to be transferred. He should arrive very soon.

One of the nurses was passing by and stopped to ask, 'Are you all right?'

'I'm very all right, thank you.'

The nurse lingered. 'Why were you crying then? Is there anything I can do to help?'

Phoebe deliberately made use of her friend's title, wanting to give poor Mr Stein the best possible reception here. 'Lady Potherington has arranged to have my old employer transferred here. He's Austrian and he's an absolute dear. His name is Stein.'

'That's good to know. I wondered when I first came here what these people would be like, but they're no trouble at all, are they?'

'No. They're on our side in this war, because most of them want to stay in England.'

'Your German is coming on well. You must have an ear for languages. I have such trouble with the endings of words.'

Phoebe was enjoying the language lessons the adjutant had set up for them. This job was so much more interesting than her last one. 'I had a head start. The Steins taught me some German phrases, and I could understand more than I could speak, from working with them. I liked being able to speak a bit of another language. I never thought it'd come in useful like this, though.'

The nurse lingered to chat for a little longer before moving on. Phoebe sighed with relief and started reading the rest of the letter. Mr Stein was reluctant to have his wife sent to Greyladies, but Beaty was sure Phoebe would persuade him to do that.

There were women who needed language practice as well as men, and they seemed to do better when taught by other women. Anyway, the internees would surely be happier with their families there.

Unfortunately, people in the know said it wasn't likely that the war was going to end quickly.

On a sunny day in March, Mr Stein arrived at Greyladies. Phoebe heard the sound of a charabanc driving up to the front of the house and went to peep out of the window. She let out a cry of joy when she saw him sitting in the back row of the long vehicle. But oh, he looked so much older.

'The friend I told you about has just arrived. May I go and help settle the newcomers, Matron?'

'Go on. Judging from the way you've been looking forward to seeing him, I'll get no more work out of you till you've made sure he's all right.'

'Thank you.' She raced off to the charabanc.

Mr Stein was just being helped down and to her dismay, the orderly was signalling for a wheelchair. She slowed down, not wanting to shock him if he was so frail.

But she needn't have worried. When he saw her, he beamed and she rushed to give him a big hug.

'I've been so worried about you, Herr Stein!'

'You needn't have, my dear. They've treated me, treated us all as decently as they could. It wasn't the fault of those running the camps that the places were so crowded. And I prefer to be called *Mr* Stein now.'

'And how is dear Mrs Stein?'

'I don't know. I told her not to write to me. I don't want her put into a camp.'

'But you know where she is?'

He looked round to make sure no one could overhear

him before replying, 'We will discuss this later, my dear.'

The wheelchair arrived just then and he was helped into it.

'Friend of yours, is he?' the orderly asked her.

It seemed an innocuous question but she'd noticed before that this man had a very shrewd expression, and the questions he asked were usually to elicit information, rather than merely chatting. 'He was my employer – well, he and his wife together. Mrs Stein was training me to make curtains, while Mr Stein ran the shop and did the accounts. They treated me very kindly after my mother died, letting me rent the attic at the shop to live in.'

She looked the man straight in the eyes. 'Anything else you want to know, George?'

He grinned, holding out his arms, palms towards her in a gesture of surrender. 'I'll ask if I do.' Then his smile faded. 'Most of these men are genuine refugees, Miss Sinclair, but one or two may be spies. We have to be aware of that possibility at all times.'

'Well, Mr Stein isn't a spy, I promise you.'

'I'll bear your opinion in mind.'

'You're not really an orderly, are you?'

'*Shh!*'

'It's all right. I won't tell anyone. But I can't help noticing how carefully you watch people, and what sort of questions you ask. I'm not stupid.'

'No. That's obvious. Major McMinty wouldn't be so fond of you if you were.'

She could feel the telltale blush creeping over her face and whisked back into the house to see where they were putting Mr Stein.

* * *

269

That evening Corin invited her to stroll round the gardens. 'George tells me you're on to him.'

'If you mean I guessed that he's keeping an eye on things, yes. It's all right, though. I won't tell anyone.'

'You might keep an eye on things, too. You seem very attached to this old house. You might see things he doesn't.'

'I'll do anything I can.' She hesitated, then decided to tell Corin about her new, if still secret status.

When she'd finished, he was frowning.

'What's wrong?'

'That would mean you staying here after the war ends.'

'Yes.' She looked at him, praying he'd speak out now about their future.

'You've been frank with me, so I'll be equally frank with you, Phoebe. I was hoping, after the war, if I survive—'

'Don't even say that!'

'We both need to face facts. At the moment I have a relatively safe job, and it might stay that way. Or I may be sent to the front. That's why I've been waiting to put things between us on a more formal footing.'

'Shouldn't it be the other way round, Corin? Shouldn't we seize the moment?'

'It's hard to know what's best. I thought I knew the right way to go, but every time I see you, I'm tempted, I must admit. And . . . there's something you need to know about me, as well.'

'Oh?'

'I've been married before.'

She was shocked by this. She hadn't guessed. He didn't behave like a married man, not in any way. In fact, he gave the impression of being a confirmed bachelor. 'What happened?'

'She died. She had a motor car, a "Prince Henry" Vauxhall. Her father had bought it for her on her twenty-first birthday, but I was worried because she drove it too fast. We quarrelled about that. We quarrelled if she joined me at the barracks, and we quarrelled when I went home.

'One day she flung out of the house after a particularly furious quarrel, and drove off, deliberately going fast to annoy me, even though it was raining. She didn't get far, came off the road at a corner and crashed into a tree.'

Phoebe grasped his hand to offer comfort.

He paused, swallowing hard. 'It was . . . ghastly. I felt, still do feel guilty.'

'I'm so sorry. You must miss her.'

'That's what makes it worse. I don't. We weren't well suited and things were getting worse between us. She had been talking about asking Daddy to pay for a divorce. No one in my family has ever been divorced and the idea of it shocked me. Then Norah found she was carrying my child and she was furious about that, talking of . . . doing something drastic to get rid of it.'

Phoebe didn't say anything, just waited for him to continue, but she noticed that his eyes were bright with tears.

'It'd have been a boy,' he said abruptly.

'Oh, how awful for you.'

'Anyway, after all the fuss was over, I found it a relief to live more peacefully, mostly staying at the barracks. And I swore I'd never marry again.'

He smiled and raised one of her hands to his lips. 'Then I met you, played Sir Galahad and fell in love like the naïvest of young men. I was reluctant to get involved, with a war on, but the more I got to know you, the more I loved you.'

'I fell in love with you, too, Corin.' She waited and saw him frowning. 'There's something else, isn't there?'

'Yes. My family. I'm the only child. I'll inherit the family estate when my father dies. It's not a big place like Greyladies, but I love it. I've never wanted to live anywhere else but near the moors. Only, from what you've told me today, you'll be tied to Greyladies. And I'm not sure I could give up Meredene.'

'Oh.'

'That's enough confidences for tonight, I think. We both have a lot to think about. I was going to ask you to show me the crypt. How about we do that another evening? You said you could get the key.'

'I've never visited it, but Harriet says I must, and Miss Bowers has told me about it. Tomorrow, perhaps?'

'I'd like that. I love old buildings. Imagine a crypt dating from the sixteenth century.'

They didn't discuss anything personal as they walked back to the house, and he only gave her a chaste kiss on the cheek in farewell. His expression was as troubled as she felt.

When she got up to the room she shared with one of the younger nurses, Milly said at once, 'You look down in the dumps. Did you quarrel with him?'

'What? Oh, no. Of course not. We've been having a serious talk, that's all. There are things to decide.'

'Has he told you yet that he was married?'

'Yes. His wife was killed in an accident. How did you know about that?'

'One of the orderlies let it out. George. The one who keeps an eye on things.' She yawned. 'I'm tired, so I'm going straight to sleep.'

'I'm tired too. I don't want to read in bed tonight.' She pretended to yawn.

Milly was asleep within a couple of minutes, as usual. But Phoebe lay awake till the hall clock struck one, worrying about their dilemma.

There was no obvious way of solving it.

She had been chosen to look after Greyladies. How could she refuse to do that? She'd been shown by Harriet how much good the chatelaines did for women in distress, and wanted to do the same sort of thing. And she'd fallen in love with the old house at first sight.

But she'd fallen in love with Corin at first sight, too.

How could she choose between them?

Chapter Nineteen

Phoebe thought it was about time she told the kindly old man that she had his money safe, but as soon as she uttered the word 'money', Mr Stein shushed her till they got outside. Even then he continued to whisper and kept checking that no one was close enough to overhear what they were saying.

His English grew more heavily accented in his agitation. 'I knew we could trust you, Phoebe. Once the war is over, you can give the money back to us. Not now. The government is looking after me, so I don't need it. My Trudi is safe with some very good friends. She will be relieved that we will have some money afterwards. Maybe we're not too old to start again, in a small way.'

She felt so sorry for him, knowing how frail he was, and admired his bravery in trying to think positively about his future. This man was no enemy of their country, she was quite sure of that.

She managed, with Corin's approval, to persuade Mr Stein that it was safe to send for his wife, who was allowed to join him at this special internment centre.

Corin went further and arranged for a car to pick up Mrs Stein.

Mr Stein spent the late morning staring longingly out of the window, even though there was no chance of his wife getting there so quickly. He refused lunch, accepting only a cup of tea.

Phoebe kept an eye on him and got permission to join him after lunch, because Matron was worried about him getting too excited for his own good.

When she sat down next to him and started chatting, he smiled at her. 'You are a kind girl. Very kind.'

'And you were kind to me when I was looking for work.'

Just then she thought she heard the sound of a car coming down the drive and put one finger to her lips to stop him talking.

He looked at her with hope in his eyes. 'Is it . . . ?'

The car came into sight. 'This is the one. Let's go out to meet her.'

She opened the front door, then stood back to let him lead the way, keeping an eye on him that he didn't trip and fall in his excitement.

He walked slowly down the steps, reaching the bottom just as the driver got out and opened the passenger door of the car.

'Ach, my Trudi!' he murmured softly.

Mrs Stein had lost weight, but her smile was still as brilliant with love. She walked across to her husband, moving as stiffly as he did after sitting in the car. They didn't speak, just walked into each other's arms, tears pouring down their wrinkled faces.

Phoebe stood back, exchanging glances with the driver,

and feeling her own eyes welling with happy tears for her old employers.

When the Steins separated, he offered Trudi his arm, with courtly, old-fashioned grace, and led her up the steps. 'Look who is here.'

'Phoebe. Dearest child, how lovely to see you! You look well.'

She didn't comment on the fact that both of them had aged greatly, she just went to clasp Mrs Stein's hand in hers and say, 'Welcome. You'll both be safe here, I promise.'

Corin joined them at the top of the stairs. 'I was right. It was Mrs Stein.'

More introductions, then Mr Stein said, 'I will show you our bedroom, *Liebchen*, then introduce you to some of our friends. Is that all right, Major McMinty?'

'It's fine. We'd like to check Mrs Stein's health later – tomorrow, perhaps. Just in case there's anything she needs. Apart from that, you'll show her around, I'm sure, and help her settle in here.' When the Steins had gone slowly up the stairs, Phoebe took out her handkerchief and blew her nose hard. 'That was lovely to see.'

Corin smiled at her. 'You're a soft-hearted woman.'

'Is that wrong?'

'No. It's very right.'

His eyes were so warm on her face she could feel herself flushing.

As the days passed and Mrs Stein's vitality improved, Mr Stein was so grateful, he threw himself into his work with more energy than he'd shown for the whole of the time he'd been interned so far.

'He's a shrewd old fellow, your former employer,' Corin said one day. 'He's filling in some gaps about German towns and transport systems that are most helpful. He must have enjoyed travelling.'

'He did. He and Mrs Stein used to tell me about their holidays.'

'And the doctor says his health is continuing to improve. Mrs Stein was just fretting, he thinks, and not eating properly. I like to think we look after people in our charge,' Corin added with satisfaction.

'You can see it. He's so much better since his wife arrived, as well. They're such a devoted couple.'

Corin's eyes lingered on her warmly. 'We should all find a spouse to love like that.'

She didn't know what to say and the next minute he was back using his business tone of voice, studying a list and suggesting she get on with her work.

But she carried the warmth of his words with her all day.

Surely they'd find a solution to their problem about Greyladies?

A few days later Mrs Stein cornered Phoebe and insisted on showing her the wear and tear to the curtains in various bedrooms. 'It can be stopped now if someone will get me some sewing materials, then the curtains will last another few years. I would be happy to have something to do with my time. Tell the commandant that.'

'Tell him yourself.'

'He vill listen to you. I've seen the way he looks at you.'

Phoebe took the request to Corin. 'Mrs Stein would love to do the job. I know how much she misses being busy.'

'It's a good idea. We have to keep our charges happy. What exactly will she need?'

'In the first place, help from the orderlies to take the curtains down and beat the dust out of them.'

'That's easy enough. And?'

'Sewing materials, of course. But not ordinary dressmaking equipment. The right things will be for sale in a town as big as Swindon.'

'You must take her there and buy what she needs. I'll give you an official chit to pay for that.'

She shook her head. 'I'd rather not go into Swindon. What if Frank sees me?' She was surprised to think that Corin could have forgotten that.

'Look, I didn't tell you, but I had people keeping an eye on him after the last incident and they caught him selling black market items, as we suspected. The plan was to force him to enlist in the army rather than go to prison, but unfortunately he proved to have a serious heart murmur, so he wasn't considered fit enough. The doctor didn't even want to put him in jail, said he could drop dead at any moment.'

'*Frank?*'

'Yes. Did you never suspect?'

She frowned, thinking back. 'Well, he wasn't a very *active* person, didn't like kicking a ball around, even as a young fellow, but he looked so big and strong . . . No, I never suspected a thing. If I thought anything, it was that he was lazy – and that his mother spoilt him. Do you know where he is now? Is that why you think it'll be safe?'

'No. After the police released him, he vanished and hasn't been seen since.'

'He'll be hiding at the farm.'

'We've checked the farm a couple of times and asked around, but none of the neighbours have seen him. Everyone he used to deal with in town thinks he went elsewhere. The police are still keeping their eyes open, though.'

'I still think he'll be at the farm.' Ironically, so would the very things they needed, the stuff he'd looted from the Steins' shop. But she wouldn't go near the farm, not for anything.

'Well, if he is, you should be safe going into Swindon, especially if you don't wear your VAD uniform. We will, of course, send an orderly with you, and we'll tell him not to wear his uniform, either. Mrs Stein trusts you, and you understand her needs after working with her, so you'd be the best person by far to accompany her.'

He smiled at her. 'I'd not suggest this if I didn't think you'd be perfectly safe.'

Phoebe didn't feel she could refuse for another reason. One day it would be her responsibility to look after the house and that included curtains and furniture. But the idea of going into town still worried her. She decided in the end to ask Corin to send Harriet instead of her, and her friend agreed to take her place.

But before she could tell him about the exchange, fate intervened.

Joseph's face turned white when the post was brought in and he found another black-edged envelope set before him.

Harriet moved across to stand beside him in unspoken sympathy and support.

He tore open the envelope with hands which shook, scanning the letter inside quickly, before passing it to her. 'Selwyn.'

'Oh, no! Three sons killed. Your poor mother! How will she bear that?' She waited, ready to comfort him in any way she could, but Joseph didn't weep this time, probably because he had never been close to Selwyn.

But he looked deeply sad as he echoed his wife's words. 'Poor Mother, indeed. She'll need me.'

'Are we taking the boys with us again?'

'We must.'

He didn't say it, waiting for her to say it for him.

'So it's time for me to leave Greyladies.'

'I'm afraid so.' He cupped her face in his hands. 'No man could have a better wife than you. I don't know what I did to deserve you, but you're the light of my life, Harriet. You know that, don't you?'

'I feel the same way about you.'

They stood holding one another close for a few moments, then he sighed and moved away. 'Once I've confirmed that I am indeed the heir, we'll start making arrangements to move to Dalton House.'

'I'll go and tell Phoebe. I'd hoped to spend longer with her, but she'll have Miss Bowers to guide her, at least.'

'And Anne Latimer,' he added quietly.

'Do you suppose ghosts can guide people?'

'They can frighten the villains off, that's for sure.'

'Anne has never frightened me . . . or Phoebe. Still, even after we're settled at Dalton House, Phoebe can write to me if she needs help or advice.'

'Or you can come here for visits.' He looked at her, drew her closer again, his turn to offer comfort. 'I'm only too aware how much leaving Greyladies will upset you. Thank you for helping my family like this.'

'I know it's the right thing to do. There are other people to care for Greyladies, but there's only you left now to look after Dalton House.'

Phoebe stared at Harriet in shock. 'Oh, poor Joseph!' Then the implications dawned on her. 'Does that mean you'll be leaving here permanently?'

'Within a week or so, probably. After the funeral, we'll be coming back to pack up. It'll take a while to sort through our things, and we don't know what state Dalton House will be in. They've got three young women and their children staying there now, so it shouldn't be too bad. I can't turn them out, but there's plenty of room. It's a big house.'

'That means you can continue to help people.'

'I hope so. It's the financial situation of the Dalton family that worries me. Selwyn was a gambler. If the house has to be sold to pay his debts, we shall be staying on here.' But that sounded wrong even as she was uttering the words.

Phoebe studied her thoughtfully for a moment or two. 'I don't think you'd have been prepared to leave Greyladies if you weren't going to rescue Dalton House for your husband and children.'

It was Harriet's turn to feel surprised. 'No. Of course not. You're right. I've known for a while that I'd leave. That won't change. I'm not thinking as clearly as usual, I'm afraid. I keep worrying about poor Mrs Dalton. I'd better go and round up the boys now.'

She stopped at the door to add, 'I nearly forgot. I'm afraid this means I won't be able to take your place to do the shopping in Swindon. But I'm sure you'll be all right if neither the police nor his former associates have seen a sign of Frank.'

'Yes, of course I'll be all right.'

But Phoebe intended to keep a careful look out for him, and she'd wear a hat that pulled down as well as bulky clothing that made her look a different shape.

She'd be very relieved to get back to Greyladies after her outing.

Although she tried to share Mrs Stein's pleasure at the thought of the shopping trip, she couldn't. Apprehension skittered across her skin whenever she thought about going into Swindon.

Harriet and Joseph got out of the car at Dalton House and stood staring at their future home.

'It looks different,' she said.

'The windows are clean, for a start. It's as if the old place has started coming to life again.'

This time Mrs Dalton didn't come to greet them and a young woman they didn't recognise opened the door. She was heavily pregnant.

'I'm Joseph Dalton,' he told her.

'Yes, sir. Your mother showed me your photo. I'm Mavis.' She gestured. 'She's in the drawing room. Do you want me to look after the boys? She's in a terrible state. We've done our best to comfort her, but she's crushed by this latest death. And who can blame her?' She looked down at the full curve of her stomach. 'There are a lot of men who won't be coming back.'

Mrs Dalton wasn't weeping; she was sitting utterly still, as if frozen by her grief. She looked a shadow of her normal self. In a tight voice she thanked them for coming, then sat still again, as if waiting for Joseph to take charge.

Harriet had never admired him more. He managed to make his mother relax a little, and got her permission to finalise the arrangements for a memorial service, because once again, there was no body to bury.

'You must call our lawyer as well, Joseph dear,' Mrs Dalton said. 'He'll know how things have been left.'

'I'll do that.'

She lapsed into silence, then stood up suddenly. 'I need a rest. I couldn't sleep last night. It's been . . . a very upsetting time. I feel so much better now you've come.'

'Shall I come up with you?' Harriet offered.

Looking as if she hadn't heard this offer, Mrs Dalton walked slowly out of the room and Harriet decided not to intrude on her grief. Their relationship was still awkward, and she was finding the transition from maid to mistress of the house very difficult to get used to.

In the middle of the night, Joseph woke because the grinding pain in his hip was bad, as occasionally happened when he overdid things.

He decided to go down and fill a hot-water bottle, which sometimes helped.

There was a light in the library and his mother was in there, feverishly pulling out papers from the drawers of the desk and tossing them aside when she couldn't find what she wanted.

'Are you all right, Mother?'

She jumped and let out a squeak of shock, then sank down on an armchair. 'No. I'm not all right. I suddenly wondered whether Selwyn had made a new will in your favour. He said he was going to do it. Mr Gerrington sent it to him, but he never received the signed copy back as arranged.'

'It'll be somewhere,' he said soothingly. 'Selwyn will have signed it and forgotten to put it in the post. Look, come upstairs again and—'

She threw off the arm he'd put round her shoulders. 'You don't understand. He didn't leave the property to you in the old will, said a cripple couldn't manage it. It went to a distant cousin.'

'Then I'll go back to live at Greyladies.'

She grabbed his arm and gave it a hard shake. 'No, you won't! We need you here. And I *won't* have the house going to a nasty old cousin when I still have one son left to inherit. I'll do whatever it takes to prevent that.'

Tears were streaming down her cheeks and she was in such an agitated state, he didn't try to reason with her. 'Let me help you look, then.'

But though they searched every single drawer in the library, no will was discovered.

At length she realised he was looking pale and rubbing his hip, found out why and insisted on filling a hot-water bottle for him.

As they walked up the stairs, she said quietly, 'I mean it. I won't let them take this house away from you. I'll think of something, if I have to forge Selwyn's signature.'

Joseph was too tired and in too much pain to care about that at the moment. Relieved that Harriet hadn't woken, he slipped into bed, found a slightly easier position with the warmth of the earthenware bottle in its flannel cover soothing his aching hip, and managed to get to sleep.

When they discussed it in the morning, Harriet remained serenely certain that he would inherit. It was one of the rare occasions when they disagreed, and her certainty rather annoyed him, though he tried to hide that.

He couldn't work out what could possibly happen to change things if there wasn't a will in his favour. It made him feel very sad to think he wouldn't be coming back to live in the place he had never stopped thinking of as 'home'.

Sadder than he'd expected.

The shopping trip into Swindon went very well, and to Phoebe's relief, there was no sign of Frank. After they got back, Mrs Stein was bubbling over with pleasure at having something to do with her time and couldn't wait to get started.

Mr Stein was delighted to have his beloved Trudi by his side and to see her working happily.

Only Phoebe kept worrying. She felt as if a cloud was hanging over her, a dark and threatening cloud, and as the days passed, she jerked awake from a nightmare several times.

She and Corin avoided talking about their situation, because they couldn't see any easy solution. They made the most of every moment they could spend together, always comfortable with one another, in spite of the decision that hovered between them.

Then he was called up to London and came back accompanied by the man who had been appointed to take over the management of Greyladies. The captain had lost a leg early in the war but was still considered fit to serve in an administrative capacity.

Phoebe had known Corin would have to leave, but she hadn't thought it would happen until the two of them had resolved their problems. Surely they could find a way to marry? There had to be a way to compromise.

Now the wartime needs of the country had to take precedence over the needs of an individual and Corin was busy handing over the reins to the captain. Soon he'd be gone.

On their last evening together, they planned to go for a walk, but it rained heavily, and the only sheltered place they could find to be alone was the crypt.

She unlocked the metal grille that closed off the entrance and held the lamp high. 'Harriet brought me here once, but we didn't have time to explore it properly. What a pity it's dark.'

'I think there are some other lamps on this shelf. Shall we light one?'

Even with the increased light, the place was full of shadows that tricked the eye and seemed to move. But Phoebe forgot them as they found a stone shelf to sit on and Corin took hold of her hand.

'If I haven't said anything, it's because I can't seem to decide what to do about our situation,' he said abruptly. 'I feel as if I need to see my home first and . . . get this war over. Will you wait for me?'

'Of course.' She was disappointed, though she tried not to show it.

He kissed her, but it wasn't a lingering kiss and with a sigh, he rubbed his eyes. 'I'm not good company tonight, I'm afraid. I'm very weary.'

'I can see that. I hope you'll have a day or two to recover before you start your next assignment.'

'I doubt it. I have to report to David Brookes tomorrow

afternoon. For the time being, you'd better write to me care of my aunt. You will write, won't you?'

'Of course I will.'

That meant she wouldn't know where he was, couldn't even seek his help if her worst fears were realised and Frank turned up.

She was still having nightmares about him, still feeling as if a threat was hanging over her.

In the end, Corin yawned and said, 'I'll have to get some sleep, darling.'

She thought she saw a glow in one corner as they left the crypt, but she must have been mistaken, because when she paused to look more carefully, she saw nothing unusual, only a dark space. But it comforted her to think Anne Latimer might be keeping an eye on her.

Out at his parents' farm, Frank was fretting. He had never enjoyed life in the countryside. It was too full of noisy animals and birds that seemed to wake at a ridiculously early hour, not to mention insects that stung you. Because he was in hiding, he had to spend most of his time shut up in the house, with no one to talk to because his mother and stepfather were outside working.

His mother had wormed the tale of what had happened out of him and fussed over him so much, worrying about his heart, that he kept going out to the storage barn which supposedly belonged to his boss, to keep out of her way.

Even that was frustrating, because at the moment he didn't dare try to sell anything. They'd have made him a neat little fortune, these goods would. He'd never felt as frustrated in his whole life.

Inevitably, he spent a lot of time thinking about Phoebe. He knew she didn't want him, but he wanted her, and it wasn't for women to choose who they married anyway; that was the man's choice. Anyway, once she was with him, she'd come round, of course she would. Especially when she found out how much money he'd have.

After all, the other fellow hadn't married her, had he?

He checked the post every day. The woman who ran his little sideline in Swindon was keeping watch for him. She wrote twice to say the police had come nosing round, but she'd sworn blind she didn't know where he was and they'd gone away again.

They'd asked other people if they'd seen Frank, too.

Worst of all, there hadn't been any sign of Phoebe in Swindon, and he had people watching out for her. He'd promised twenty pounds if anyone found out where she was, and he knew how eager these folk were to earn that much money.

He pulled out his pocket watch and stared at it. Time seemed to be passing even more slowly than usual today. It was a relief when his mother came back at noon to make dinner and called out a greeting.

He didn't feel optimistic as he popped his head through the kitchen door. 'Any letters for me, Ma?'

'Yes, love. I put it on the mantelpiece an hour ago. The post came early today. You were out at the barn, I think.'

Then why the hell hadn't she called him in? She knew he was waiting to hear about something.

He snatched the envelope and took it outside to read.

The memorial service for Selwyn was more thinly attended than the ones for Joseph's two brothers had been.

288

Mrs Dalton wept intermittently and when the lawyer called them together for the reading of the will, she berated him for not getting her eldest son to make a new will in favour of his youngest brother, brushing aside his protests that he had drawn one up, but could hardly have forced Selwyn to sign it.

Joseph tried to put an arm round her but she shook it off and shouted at him to let her go. 'Don't you realise what will happen? The estate will go to a stranger who will no doubt throw me and those poor women out on the streets. Selwyn has done both you and the family wrong, not leaving the estate to you. You're his *brother*!'

One of Selwyn's friends, who'd barely arrived in time for the funeral, stopped dead in the doorway as she said this, looking at her in shock.

The lawyer called across to him, 'This is for the reading of the will, sir, family only.'

'I know about the will. That's why I came.'

'I don't understand. Who are you, sir?'

'I'm Charles Parker, representing Selwyn's regiment, and . . .' He fumbled in his pocket. 'I've brought your son's last will and testament, Mrs Dalton. He wasn't killed instantly, actually, and had time to sign the will and have the chaplain and myself witness it before he died.'

'Is it the one I drew up?' the lawyer asked.

'I can't tell, but I doubt Selwyn wrote this.' He walked forward and handed a battered envelope to the lawyer. 'He was on his deathbed when he signed. The chaplain said it would serve its purpose, even though his handwriting was shaky.'

The lawyer opened the crumpled envelope and scanned

289

the will, shuddering at a brown smear in one corner that looked suspiciously like dried blood. 'It's his handwriting, Mrs Dalton, and it's the will I drew up. Selwyn has left everything he possessed to his youngest brother Joseph Dalton, now known as Joseph Latimer.'

She moaned and swayed as if about to faint, so Harriet quickly helped her to sit down on the nearest chair.

Everyone stood silently watching, not sure what to do next.

Mrs Dalton took a few deep, sobbing breaths and said simply, 'I'm all right now. I'm so very glad, not only that you've inherited Dalton House, Joseph dear, but also that Selwyn did the right thing by the family. I shall think better of him for that.'

Joseph turned to the officer. 'Thank you for bringing the will.'

He nodded.

'Can we offer you a room for the night?'

'No, thank you. I have a staff car waiting to take me back. I'm sorry I was late. We had a flat tyre.' He inclined his head to everyone and left the room.

'I think I'd like to lie down now,' Mrs Dalton announced. 'I didn't sleep a wink last night and I'm exhausted.'

Harriet helped her up. 'I'll see you to your room, shall I?'

'Thank you, dear.' This time she didn't spurn her daughter-in-law's offer of help.

The lawyer waited till they were out of earshot then turned to Joseph. 'You've inherited a poisoned chalice, I'm afraid, and—'

The officer ran back into the room. 'Sorry. I nearly forgot. This is from Algernon Smythe-Pawcett. They were playing cards the night before your son was killed, and Selwyn won some money from Algie, who says he'll honour the debt as soon as he gets back to Blighty on leave.'

He slapped a piece of crumpled paper into the lawyer's hand, and raced out again, muttering, 'Got to go. Running late.'

The lawyer looked down at it and gasped. 'This is for ten thousand pounds!'

Joseph felt angry. 'Selwyn risked ten thousand pounds at cards! Risked losing the estate. He must have been mad.'

'There are other debts, as well,' the lawyer said.

'How much?'

'About four thousand pounds, as far as I can make out.'

'From gambling?' Joseph spat the words out.

'Not all of it. There are tailors' bills, and so on.'

'I have some money of my own. If you'll find out exactly how much Selwyn owed, we'll discuss how to pay off the debts later.' He looked firmly at the lawyer. 'You will not find me as careless an owner as my brother was. And by the time my sons inherit, the estate will be worth inheriting. I swear that.'

Harriet came back just then. 'What do you swear, darling?'

He explained.

'Don't look so grim. We'll be all right.'

'I'm risking our boys' inheritance. The money owed will be a large percentage of what I've made by careful management of my money. And if this gambler chap doesn't pay the larger amount, I don't know what I'll do.'

'What *we* will do. I haven't had time to tell you, but in the same post as you heard about Selwyn, I received news from the trust lawyer that I will be given a generous sum of money when I leave Greyladies. So we'll still have something to fall back on.'

He closed his eyes and let out a low groan of relief.

She watched him sympathetically. 'You're no gambler, are you, Joseph?'

'No. Never. I couldn't live like that.' He turned to the lawyer. 'Thank you for your help.'

'I'll be in touch, Mr Dalton. There's nothing else to settle at the moment, not till I have more information.'

'Mr Latimer,' Joseph corrected, looking at his wife. 'I think this family needs a new start. Anyway, I've changed my name officially now. I'm not changing back.'

The lawyer paused in collecting his papers. 'Are you sure?'

'Very sure.'

Harriet had to ask, 'Won't that upset your mother?'

'It might. But it's you I'm concerned about. What would you really like to be called?'

'Latimer,' she admitted.

'So would I. It's an honourable name. You're giving everything else up, so you should keep your name.'

Chapter Twenty

Frank slipped out of the house and ripped open the letter, reading it quickly, then reading it again with a smile.

His mother came to the kitchen door. 'Everything all right, dear?'

'Everything's fine, Mum. I'll have to go into Swindon, though not till after dark. It's all right. I won't overdo things. I'll be staying with a friend, who'll run me round in his car.'

'I thought you wanted to keep out of the way of the police.'

'I do. I shall. But there's someone I have to see.'

He would have pushed past her into the house, but she grabbed his arm. 'You're not going after Phoebe again, are you?'

'No, of course not. And even if I were, it'd be none of your business.'

'You *are* going after her. Oh, Frank, let her be. There are other girls who'd make much better wives for a man like you.'

'Mind your own business, Ma.'

It was fully dark by the time the bus drew into Swindon.

Frank had developed an occasional tickle of a cough in the past few weeks, which made a good excuse for wrapping a scarf round his neck and mouth. He hurried away from the bus and set off through the streets, avoiding the well-lit areas.

Sid was waiting for him, eager to talk.

'Give me a minute to catch my breath,' Frank said irritably. He was feeling tired today, the excitement, probably. He had to calm down. That'd stop his heart fluttering.

'Come and sit down, love,' Sid's wife said. 'I'll get you a nice cup of tea.'

Sid joined him.

'Tell me how you're so sure about her.'

'I *saw her*. She'd got her hat pulled down, so I nearly walked past her, then I realised who it was, so I followed them.'

'Them? Was she with that damned officer again?'

'No. She was with an old woman and a middle-aged man.' Sid sniggered. 'I know him. He used to live in the next street to us. *And* I know where he works.'

'He may be her new fellow,' Frank said grumpily.

'No. He's a lot older than her and married. And anyway, he was very respectful towards her.'

'So where does he work?'

'At that old house in Challerton. Greyladies it's called. They've took it over for a convalescent hospital an' he's an orderly there.'

'Is she nursing there?'

'She wasn't wearing a nurse's uniform.'

Frank leant back, accepted a cup of tea and sipped it happily. He'd found Phoebe and she'd not escape this time.

He looked across at Sid. 'You can take me there and hang around in case she needs persuading to see sense. I've been ill, not got my strength back yet.'

Sid looked uneasy.

'I'm not going to hurt her,' Frank said irritably. 'I want to *marry* her. But I may need to persuade her a bit.'

'Oh. All right, then. As long as you pay me for the information.'

'I will if we find her. Tomorrow, we'll drive out to have a look round.'

When Phoebe woke, her first thought was how sad it was that Corin had gone away. She'd miss him dreadfully. Still, no use moping. It'd change nothing.

She got up and started her shift. Some of the internees were frail and needed help getting dressed or getting breakfast. And of course there were the meals to prepare for: endless trays to set and carry round.

The internees took the evening meal in the dining room. That meant setting the table and clearing it afterwards. At least they were tidy eaters, with good table manners, so they didn't make too much mess for her to clear up.

When she'd finished setting the table, Matron told her to take a break and go for a stroll outside.

'I'll just put my feet up in my room for a few minutes.'

'No. You're looking peaky and need some fresh air. Half an hour at least.' She patted the younger woman's arm. 'You're missing him already, I can tell.'

Phoebe could feel herself flushing. Did everyone know how she felt about Corin? Was it so obvious?

When she got outside, it was still light and she was glad

Matron had insisted on this stroll. She took a sudden fancy to explore the crypt properly. There was time to make a start if she hurried. She and Corin had caught some glimpses of carved stonework and goods from the house were stored there. She was sure Harriet wouldn't mind her looking round.

Then she realised that it'd be up to her, not Harriet, in future, to deal with the household details. All the more reason for getting to know every single part of her inheritance, what was stored where. One day it'd all need to be put back in place.

She nipped into the kitchen of the old house, telling Cook, 'I just need a key.' The huge old iron key was hanging in its usual place. It was too heavy to put in her pocket, so she carried it, smiling at the thought of how many chatelaines had used this key.

It turned easily in the lock of the crypt and she pushed the door open with a feeling of eager anticipation, leaving the key in the lock.

She felt a sense of welcome and a light began to glow in one corner. She took a step in that direction, but suddenly there was the sound of the metal grille slamming shut behind her. She spun round. There was no wind, so how could the door have closed?

Then she heard the key turning in the lock. It was just out of sight at the end of the short entrance passage. Had someone deliberately shut her in? Why? She moved cautiously sideways till she could see the door and when she did, her heart began to pound with fear.

Frank was standing at the other end of the corridor, just inside the crypt, leaning against the grille. His arms were folded and he was smiling like a cat about to torment a mouse.

He turned to talk to someone outside, then began moving forward. 'I know you're there, Phoebe,' he called.

She didn't answer.

'There's nowhere to hide. Took me a while to find you, but I never give up when I want something. Never. And you can't get out of here till I unlock the door.'

She looked round but couldn't see anything she could use to defend herself with, and there was certainly nowhere to hide properly, though she could and did duck down behind some of the packing cases.

He began to walk towards her. 'You may as well give in. After all, I'm going to marry you, aren't I? And I'll keep you in comfort. So it won't be a bad life.'

She called, 'I won't marry you, Frank, whatever you do.' She immediately regretted that and moved across to another position, in case he could trace where her voice had come from.

He glowered in her direction. 'Why won't you? You always told Ma you wanted children, and for that, a decent woman like you needs a husband.'

Perhaps if she told him about Corin? 'And I've found one.'

'*You're married?*'

'No. But I'm going to be.'

'If you value his life, you won't do it.'

'He won't need me to defend him. He's a trained soldier.'

'That lanky idiot who interfered in Swindon?'

She didn't answer that.

'It is him, isn't it? I knew it. Where is he now, then? Gone off to London. *He* won't be able to save you tonight, will he?'

She stared in surprise. Was there nothing Frank hadn't found out? 'He'll be back.'

'He may come back, but he won't find you in the same state as he left you, and believe me, a gentleman like him won't want soiled goods. Why, if we're lucky, you'll be carrying my child by then.'

'I still wouldn't marry you.'

She'd been moving here and there, to keep out of sight, but he lunged in her direction. She dodged back out of reach, then found herself penned between two stone tombs.

He lunged again, nearly close enough to grab her. This time when she jerked backwards, she bumped into the wall.

He had her trapped in the corner. There was no way of escaping him now. But she'd fight him every inch of the way.

And she would never, ever marry him, whatever he did to her.

Matron looked at her fob watch. Phoebe was late getting back from her break, which wasn't like her. Poor girl. She'd fallen hard for Major McMinty and he seemed equally taken by her.

What was keeping them apart? In times like these you had to seize the moment, and as far as Matron could tell, the major wasn't short of money, so could easily have got married.

As the minutes passed, she began to feel irritated. Drat the girl! Where was she? She was needed here. Footsteps came towards the door of her office. Ah! That'd be her.

But the footsteps went past and vanished into the distance.

She'd give Phoebe another ten minutes then she'd go looking for her. She'd seen which way the girl went after she left the old part of the house carrying a key so large you couldn't miss it.

There was only one place that path led to, only one place down there that needed unlocking.

That morning, Harriet began to feel uneasy and to worry about Phoebe. She couldn't work out what had caused this, but she had a strong urge to get back to Greyladies.

She went to find Joseph. 'Could we set off earlier than planned, love? I think there's trouble at Greyladies.'

He nodded. He knew she wouldn't ask him unless it was urgent. 'I'll send for the boys and we'll set off as soon as everything is packed.'

'Thank you. I'll be fifteen minutes at most.' She finished packing their things any old how, without bothering to fold her clothes, let alone put tissue paper between the layers. After that, she went into the boys' room and flung everything into their suitcase.

When she went downstairs, Joseph was speaking to his mother, who looked up at Harriet, head on one side.

She answered the unspoken question. 'I don't know what's wrong, Mrs Dalton. I just know something *is* wrong.'

'But you'll come back soon?'

'Yes, of course we will. And it'll be to stay.'

She gave her daughter-in-law a surprised look. 'Who'd have thought *you* would become Mistress of Dalton House?'

Harriet stiffened, expecting criticism and offers to guide her in her new role. She'd listen to advice, of course she would, but she had her own ideas of how she wanted to run the big house and make use of it for more than mere show. Neither she nor Joseph had ambitions to take their place in county society.

But her mother-in-law surprised her. 'You'll fill your new role well, Harriet. You've the modern understanding. And I, too, thank you for giving up Greyladies.'

Harriet walked across to give her a genuine hug, feeling better accepted now, relieved about that. The last thing she wanted was to be at odds with Joseph's mother, especially in such a tragic time. 'I shall need to ask your advice, I'm sure.'

'No. Don't. Well, only about details. I'm the past and you're the future. I shall go back to live in my flat in London. I've made a life there, with nothing to remind me of . . . times past and people lost.'

She gave Harriet a little push. 'Well, hurry up. Get away with you. Something must be very wrong at Greyladies to make you look like that.'

Corin was called into David Brookes' office for a second time since his arrival in London. He found an elderly gentleman sitting there with David, wrinkled hands resting on an elaborately carved walking stick.

'This is Herr Schreiber, who has kindly shared some important information with us. He's very tired of moving from one place to another, so I've promised him you'll take him down to Greyladies and settle him in there.'

Corin opened his mouth to protest that he'd only just left the place, but closed it again. If David felt this gentleman deserved an escort and a place in the special internment centre, then he would take the old man there.

'Herr Schreiber's wife and daughter will be joining him as

300

soon as you can arrange it. He'll give you their address and we'd like you to fetch them.'

'Very well.'

'I've arranged a car and driver for you.'

'When do you want us to set off?'

'The sooner the better,' the old gentleman said in near faultless English. 'I'm weary of moving from one place to another, and am looking forward to spending time in peaceful surroundings in the country, as Mr Brookes has kindly promised.'

'Greyladies is certainly peaceful,' Corin agreed. 'I'll just go and pack a few things.'

David cleared his throat. 'I don't think that's necessary, Major. I know it's quite late already, but I'd be grateful if you'd come straight back. We have a few little matters about to come to the boil here.'

Corin didn't allow himself even one sigh, but decided he was going to have a word with Phoebe while he was there, however late it was. He needed to tell her that he loved her, wanted to marry her, didn't care where they lived. He'd been stupid not to do it before he left. 'Very well, sir. If you'll come this way, Herr Schreiber?'

Chapter Twenty-One

Frank didn't lunge forward, as Phoebe had expected, but stood eyeing her as if she had no clothes on. She shivered involuntarily, but as she watched him, she quickly realised how much he was enjoying tormenting her. He was also panting slightly, as if finding it hard to breathe.

'No one will hear you when you scream,' he told her. 'No one but me. I'll enjoy making you scream. You deserve it, you bitch, leading me on all these years.'

'I've never led you on, Frank.'

'Oh, but you have. We both knew you'd be mine in the end, only you had to play hard to get.'

She couldn't believe he thought that. She despised women who played with men and would never do it. But most of all, she despised Frank, who was a bully and a brute.

She could have leapt over the nearest packing case, but where would she go? He had the key in his pocket, so she still couldn't get out of here.

A light appeared right next to her, shining softly on her face.

'How the hell did you do that?' Frank demanded.

'Do what?'

'Make that light. Is it a reflection? There's no one else in here. I saw you myself unlocking the gate to get in. I've brought someone with me to keep watch, but *he* didn't come inside and he won't interfere. So where did that light come from?'

The light moved sideways in the direction she had been intending to jump, if only to postpone Frank's attack for a minute or two. *Was it urging her to move that way?* she wondered.

He continued to stare at it. 'You must see that light. It's getting brighter all the time.'

She pretended ignorance. 'See what light?'

'If this is a trick, I'll make you pay dearly for it.'

'I'm doing nothing to cause a light.'

It grew bright enough to dazzle and he held one arm over his eyes.

The light moved to a piece of carved stone, bounced twice on a carved rose, and moved back towards Phoebe.

She saw Anne Latimer's grey robes begin to show, faint and transparent at first, growing more opaque, looking as if she was real.

'Stop it!' Frank yelled suddenly. 'I know this picture of a woman is a trick. A projection, like in the cinema. It won't do you any good. Stop it *now*.'

He was staring at the light, so Phoebe scrambled over the packing case and reached for the rose.

He roared with fury.

But before he could follow her, the light became so bright it hurt his eyes, coruscating around them, beating at Frank in particular.

Phoebe heard a faint grating sound nearby, saw a dark hole open up behind the stone and ran towards it, bending to get inside. Immediately the carved stone began to close again.

The last thing she heard was Frank yelling, 'Get away from me! Get away!'

Once the panel shut, she was alone in the darkness.

How long would she have to stay here? Would anyone hear her if she couldn't get out again and shouted for help?

Corin arrived at Greyladies to find people gathered in small groups, talking anxiously about something.

Captain Turner came out to the car. 'Sorry to greet you with this. Do come inside.'

'What's wrong?'

'One of the VADs seems to have vanished and Matron's just organising a search of the grounds. Phoebe's nowhere in the house, that's for sure.'

'Is it Phoebe who's missing?' Corin asked sharply.

'Yes. I forgot you two were . . . close.'

Matron came across the hall to join them. 'Hello, Major. Sorry to greet you like this. We're looking for Phoebe. I saw her heading towards the crypt earlier, so we're about to see if she's still there.'

'I know where it is. I'll go. Oh, this is Herr Schreiber. I believe you're expecting him. Perhaps someone can attend to him?'

Herr Stein came forward. 'I will show him the room that has been prepared and keep him company till you've found our dear Phoebe.'

'Thank you.' Corin left the house again, followed by Captain Turner and Matron.

'I hope she hasn't fallen and hurt herself,' Matron worried as they strode along the garden path towards the little gate at the side, which led to the ruins of the old abbey.

Corin stopped. 'Shh. Just a minute. There's someone standing near the crypt. When I give you the signal, call out to him.' He moved to one side, out of the man's line of sight, and crept closer and closer, glad of the soft green grass to muffle his footsteps. When he was within reach, he waved one hand.

'Hoy, you!' called the captain, obedient to his wishes.

The man swung round, panic and guilt equally present on his face. Then he turned to flee and ran straight into Corin, who grabbed him.

The man struggled but was smaller than Corin and much less fit. By the time the others joined them, he had stopped struggling.

'Who are you? What are you doing here?' Corin demanded. 'Answer me.'

'I come here with Frank. I ain't done nothing wrong.'

'Frank Hapton?'

The man nodded.

'What's he doing here?'

'Looking for that woman of his. They went into that old cellar.'

'You take care of this one, Turner. I'll go after Phoebe.'

Before Corin could move away, their captive said, 'It ain't no use. Frank's inside and he's got the key. Locked the door after himself, he did, so she couldn't get out.'

Corin's blood ran cold at the thought of Phoebe trapped in the crypt by that brutal chap. He ran across to the crypt entrance.

But the grille was indeed locked and though he could hear someone speaking, the sound was muffled. Just then a light began to shine inside the crypt, visible from the entrance, growing brighter by the minute.

'Phoebe!' Corin yelled. 'Phoebe, are you in there?'

No one answered, but they heard a man yell, then scream as if terrified. It was unnerving to hear a man make a sound like that. What the hell was happening in there?

Corin shook the grille hard, but it was firmly fixed. No one could have opened it by force, not without tools, and even then, it'd take time to cut through the thick iron bars. 'How the hell can we get inside? Is there another key?'

'I don't know anything about keys to this place,' Matron said. 'It wasn't our responsibility. The keys were all kept in the old house.'

Their captive wriggled. 'Um . . . Major.'

'Shut up, you.'

'But I can help you.'

'What do you mean?'

'Well, I'm not involved. *I* haven't broken in anywhere but—'

'Get to the point.'

'I could pick that lock easy. They're simple, those old-fashioned locks. Then I could slip away and I'd never come back here again, I promise you.'

'You can pick the lock and it'll be taken into account when we find Phoebe,' Corin said crisply. 'That's as far as I'm prepared to go.'

For a minute their eyes locked, then the smaller man sighed. 'All right, sir.' He reached into his pocket and pulled out some small pieces of metal.

'Pick locks,' Captain Turner said. 'Fellow's a thief.'

'Never mind that. We have to get to Phoebe.' Corin gave Sid a shove. 'Do it.'

The lock came open in a minute.

'There you are. You can't say I haven't been helpful.'

'Keep an eye on him.' Corin was already on his way inside.

The bright light had faded, but he had a flashlight with him that he'd snatched from the car. He shone it ahead, seeing no one at first. But when he rounded a corner, he saw a man lying on the ground – Frank.

He knelt down beside him, but was shocked when he realised that the fellow was dead. There was no mark on him, but there was a look of pain on his face and one hand was lying on his chest, as if it had been pressed against it.

'Matron!' Corin yelled.

She joined them and didn't need telling to examine the body. 'Looks like a heart attack, Major.'

'He was rejected for the army because he had a weak heart.' He looked round, surprised Phoebe hadn't come out from wherever she was hiding. 'Phoebe! Where are you? It's safe to come out now.'

But only silence met these words and when they searched the crypt, they could find no sign of her.

In the darkness, Phoebe wasn't sure where she was, but it must be a passage of some sort because she could touch rough stone walls on either side, quite close to her, but could find nothing ahead of her. She waited, hoping for some guidance from Anne Latimer, but nothing happened.

Feeling in front of her with one foot, she made sure

there was somewhere to tread before she moved forward. The ground beneath her feet seemed to be paved with flagstones. She continued to check ahead before each step, taking nothing for granted, and it saved her a fall when her extended foot found only empty space where she would have stepped next.

She spread one hand on the wall to steady herself and continued to move her foot around, deciding it could be a flight of stairs. It seemed safer to sit down and when she did, she could feel another step below the top one, and another below that.

It might have been cowardly, but she shuffled down those steps on her bottom, counting them. Five, there were, then level ground again.

She shuffled along, feeling as if she'd been going for ages. But at least there were no footsteps or shouts behind her, and if there was a passage, built with such care, it must lead somewhere, surely?

She was desperate to get out.

She didn't let herself panic, though the darkness seemed to be pressing in on her more heavily by the minute.

What was happening back in the crypt? She wished she knew. But she wasn't going back to face Frank.

Where did this lead? She couldn't tell the direction she was walking in, even.

And then the passage ended in another wall, this time made of wood. She felt across it with her hands, looking for a latch. Surely it must be a door? The passage must lead somewhere.

But she could find nothing, no way of getting out, and there was no sign of Anne Latimer, coming to guide her.

Should she go back or should she stay here? It was the thought of fumbling her way through the darkness and finding Frank waiting for her that decided her to stay.

She leant against the wall, fighting tears.

Matron went out and found someone to fetch the doctor and bring a stretcher.

'I think the doctor should see the body before we move it,' she said when she got back.

'You deal with that, please. Perhaps the rest of us should spread out and search every inch of this place again,' Corin suggested.

They did that, but still there was no sign of Phoebe.

'You're sure she went inside?' he asked Sid.

'Certain, sir. I saw her, then Frank followed her and locked the door.'

'There has to be some other way out, then. But if so, it's well hidden.'

They searched every inch of the walls for something to press, or twist, something that might open a panel, but found nothing.

Then they heard a voice outside calling for Major McMinty.

He ran to the door, hoping someone had found Phoebe, but it was Joseph and Harriet.

'They told us what had happened,' Joseph said. 'Have you found her?'

'No. There's no sign, and she definitely went inside the crypt, and didn't come out again. Frank had locked the outer door and this fellow had to pick the lock to let us inside.'

'I haven't found any sign of a passage from here to the

house, though there is rumoured to be one,' Harriet said. 'The early owners built all sorts of secret rooms and passages, to hide in during troubled times.'

'If there is a passage,' Joseph said thoughtfully, 'it'll probably come out in the cellars of the old house, don't you think, McMinty?'

'Could be. Let's go and look. I'll leave a couple of men here, in case she turns up. As for you—' He turned to Sid, but in the confusion the fellow had managed to slip away. 'Aw, let him go. He did help us, after all, and we can only charge him with trespassing, which is not worth the bother.'

Harriet and Joseph led the way into the old house, leaving the boys with Cook. The two youngsters didn't need persuading, because they were hungry and she was already pulling out some cake for them.

'This way.' Joseph drew back at the top of the cellar stairs. 'Let me light the lamp. There. You go first, Harriet. I can't get down such steep stairs as quickly as the rest of you. I think there are some wall lamps down there. You'd better light them too.' He passed her a box of vestas.

Harriet led Corin down the stairs and Matron followed. Joseph started to move slowly down behind them.

'I'll stay here, in case you need a liaison,' the captain said. 'I'm not good with steep stairs, either, with this damned tin leg, and I shan't know where I'm going once I'm down there. You will.'

The cellars were quite extensive, with stone pillars holding up the roof.

'Where do we start?' Corin wondered aloud.

Harriet considered, then pointed. 'The crypt lies in that direction. Maybe the cellar walls on that side have some sort of entrance to a passage. Or could it come up through the floor?' She looked down doubtfully, because the whole cellar was paved with large stone slabs.

'I'll dig it all up if I have to,' he said in a harsh voice.

She smiled. 'You love her.'

'Of course I do. Only I haven't said anything definite, haven't made plans to marry or even get engaged. How could I have been such a fool?' He began walking along the wall, tapping it, looking for some sign of an entrance.

'You have a lot of responsibility for other things.'

'Nothing that matters more than Phoebe. Nothing. It isn't even the war. I've been letting my family house stand between us, even though it's not much of an ancestral home. My grandparents bought it.'

'But you love it.'

He stopped, smiling ruefully. 'I do.'

'I haven't had to give my whole life to Greyladies and maybe Phoebe won't need to, either. Have you thought of that?'

'I don't care. I'm going to marry her as fast as we can get a special licence.'

'I'm sure you'll ask her opinion first.'

He smiled confidently. 'She'll say yes.' He began tapping the wall again. 'Does this sound hollow to you?'

She picked up a jar of preserves from a nearby shelf and used it to tap on the wood. 'Could be.'

They searched again, and it did sound hollow, but they could find no sign of a way to open the panel.

Suddenly they heard a sound, a faint tapping, coming from behind the wooden panel and a voice called out.

'It's her!' Corin exclaimed and yelled, 'We're here, Phoebe! Open the door.'

'I don't know how.'

Joseph had stayed behind them, watching, studying the wall. Something caught his eye, not next to the panel, where the others were looking, but further along one of the shelves. It was a small lump in the wood, showing now that Harriet had taken away the jar. Had she done that by chance or had she been guided to choose that particular jar?

'Wait!' he called. 'What's that?'

Corin followed the direction of his pointing finger and moved sideways to touch the unevenness, then press it and twist it. But it didn't move, or cause a door to open.

'Stupid thing!' In frustration, he hammered on the sturdy shelf below the small lump of wood.

There was a grating sound and the whole shelf shook.

'That's it!' Joseph called. 'Stand back, let it move.'

With agonising slowness the wall began to swing backwards. Dust swirled out of the opening.

Then the door stopped moving, still only partly open. They could see Phoebe's arm and part of her face.

'Damnation!' Corin threw himself against the door, which gave way suddenly, catapulting him through it.

He grabbed Phoebe to stop her falling as he bumped into her. 'Thank goodness! Oh, thank goodness!' Pulling her towards him, he kissed her roughly and quickly, then simply held her close. 'If anything had happened to you, I don't know what I'd have done!' he murmured against her hair.

'It didn't. Anne showed me how to get out of the crypt. Did you catch Frank or did he get away again?'

'Ah. He's dead, I'm afraid. They think it was a heart attack.'

'Oh. I should be sorry, but I'm not. I'm relieved.'

'Why should you be sorry?'

'Well. Death is so final, isn't it? Frank was . . . a strange man, and not a nice one. But he died young and poor Janet will be upset. She loved her son.'

'Do you think you two could get out of the passage and let us have a look at it?' Harriet teased from behind Corin.

He smiled, feeling tension slip away. 'Yes. Sorry. I was just so glad to see her.'

While Joseph and Harriet examined the entrance to the passage and worked out how to close and open it, Corin took Phoebe to one side. 'I couldn't bear the thought of Frank touching you.'

'He didn't. I'm fine, really I am.' She smiled at him and reached up to caress his cheek, saying more with that gesture and the love in her eyes than she could ever have put into words.

'I should have spoken to you before I left, my darling, asked you to marry me. I realised it as I drove away, but it was too late to do anything then. I was planning to come back as soon as I could wangle a few hours off and propose to you. You will marry me, won't you, Phoebe?'

'Of course I will.'

He kissed her again and caught sight of Harriet and Joseph smiling fondly at them. He gave them a rueful smile. 'Sorry. But I needed to propose to her.'

'Not the most romantic of proposals,' said Joseph with a grin. 'But she doesn't seem to mind, so I think it'll do the trick.'

'And you'll both live here,' Harriet said. 'For a while, anyway.'

'My whole life long if necessary. Wherever she is, I'll be too.'

* * *

313

Phoebe surprised herself by bursting into tears at those words. She wasn't sure whether she was weeping for relief at being free of Frank, or out of joy at Corin's proposal. Perhaps it was both.

She didn't weep for long and borrowed Corin's handkerchief to wipe her eyes. 'Sorry. It all caught up with me suddenly.'

He hugged her close. 'Cry as much as you like.'

'No, don't cry. I think this calls for a celebration,' Joseph said. 'There are a few bottles of wine down here. Let's open one and drink to your health. We ought to do something to mark the occasion.'

He limped across to the section of the cellar where some wine was stored and called out in triumph, 'There's some champagne!'

'I've never had champagne,' Phoebe said.

'I have, but this will taste better than any other I've had,' Corin said. 'How quickly can we get married? Do you want a big, fussy wedding, or can we get a special licence? I'll do whatever you wish, but I must admit, I want to make you my wife as quickly as possible.'

'I've never been one for fuss. But I'd like Beaty, Harriet and Joseph to be there.'

Harriet put an arm round them both. 'You couldn't keep us away.'

When they went up to the big sitting room in the old house, Joseph got glasses from Cook and told her the happy news, which made her mop her eyes as she wished the happy couple well.

Corin attended to the bottle, prising the cork out of it carefully, waiting for the glasses before he made the final push of the cork.

The pale golden liquid foamed prettily as he poured it into the glasses, shining in a light that had begun to gleam above them. The light didn't resolve itself into Anne Latimer's figure, but it hovered there till Joseph had said, 'Congratulations and we wish you a happy life together.'

As they clinked glasses together and sipped, the light grew briefly brighter then faded.

'I think she was giving us her blessing,' Phoebe said softly.

'Look at the time. Can you stay for a meal?' Harriet asked Corin.

He glanced at his wristwatch. 'I'm afraid not. I was supposed to go straight back and I've stayed here for three hours. Phoebe darling, I have to leave now. Will you walk me to the car?'

She took his hand. 'One day we won't always be leaving one another.'

'One day we'll live together, have children, I hope, and grow old together.'

'Oh, yes.'

When they got to the car, he pulled her close again for a final kiss and the driver carefully looked the other way.

Corin sighed as he moved away from her. 'I'll get Beaty working on a wedding. It might not happen as quickly as I want, because I'll need time off and there's a lot happening where I'm working, so it's not easy to get leave. Can we get married in London?'

'Anywhere. I'll come as soon as you send for me. I'm sure Matron will understand. And then I'll return and we can meet whenever or wherever you can get away. I love you, Corin.'

'I love you with all my heart, my dearest girl.'

She watched him leave then went inside the house, smiling, to rejoin her friends. There was a little champagne left in her glass and she raised it to Harriet and Joseph. 'To Greyladies!'

Light shone around her for a minute, then faded.

Joy was bubbling inside her as fizzy as the champagne had been. She didn't know whether she'd live here for only a few years, like Harriet, or whether she'd be here for the rest of her life, but it wouldn't matter where she was if Corin was with her.

Like Harriet, like a dozen women before her, she loved the old house, felt as if she belonged to it, rather than the other way round.

She smiled as she watched Joseph and Harriet holding hands without realising they were doing it. She hoped she'd love her husband as much as they loved one another. That thought made her raise her glass in a silent toast to the man she loved and drink the last mouthful of champagne.

Epilogue

The registry office was drab and people were queuing to get married, many of the men in uniform. But Phoebe didn't notice the others. What she did notice was how Corin's eyes lingered on her when she arrived with Beaty, who had driven them here in her car.

Phoebe and Corin had been separated for most of the past four weeks, as he took up his new post 'somewhere' in the north. Even she wasn't allowed to know where.

'You look beautiful!' he breathed as he reached her side and took her hand. 'I must be the luckiest man in the world today to have such a beautiful bride. And how on earth did you find a wedding dress so elegant?'

She smiled and smoothed the lustrous ivory silk with one hand. 'Mrs Stein found an old dress in the attic, one with a lot of material in the skirt, and altered it. She said a bride should have something very special to wear when she marries the man she loves, war or no war. She made the wreath of artificial flowers for my hair and the veil, too.'

'And all I have is my uniform.'

'You always look very elegant in it.'

She turned to greet Harriet and Joseph, who had come up to London from their new home to be their witnesses. Then Phoebe waited in a glow of happiness for their wedding to start.

The ceremony was much shorter than a traditional church ceremony, and at the end of it, the registrar said, 'You are now man and wife, and you're just as married as if you'd done this in church.'

'What a tactless thing to say to a wartime bride!' Corin muttered in Phoebe's ear.

'I don't care what anyone says. All I care about is that we're married. I love you, Corin.'

'And I love you, Mrs McMinty. More each day. What will we be like when we're old if that love continues to increase?'

'We'll be blissfully happy.'

Her words seemed to echo and she wondered for a moment whether this was the same effect as at Greyladies. When something was said there which forecast the future, it always echoed.

'We'll change our names to Latimer as soon as we can,' he added. 'I do understand the need to keep up that tradition. But I didn't want to delay marrying you.'

'Neither did I.'

They went on to a wonderful meal at Beaty's, who made a short but witty speech. Phoebe couldn't take the words in, had eyes only for her wonderful husband.

In the end Beaty stopped talking and clapped her hands to get everyone's attention. 'Listen, people, our bride and groom only have tonight, so I think we'll do no more speechifying. We'll just have one proper toast.' She raised her glass, waiting till everyone else had stood up and raised glasses.

'Long life and happiness to Phoebe and Corin.'

The words echoed again, they really did, Phoebe thought. She raised her eyes to meet Corin's, then clinked her glass against his. 'Happiness,' she echoed.

'I think we can go now, Mrs McMinty,' he whispered. He looked across at Beaty and mouthed, 'Thank you'.

Phoebe felt as if she floated from the room. She had never expected to be so happy. No matter how long this dreadful war continued, she was sure that Corin would return to her, and in the meantime, well, she'd be mistress of Greyladies. How wonderful it all was.